Praise for Gail Gallant's *Apparition*

SHORTLISTED FOR AN ARTHUR ELLIS AWARD,
BEST JUVENILE/YA MYSTERY

"Quick-paced and satisfyingly creepy, Gail Gallant's first young adult novel, *Apparition*, delivers up a tightly plotted mystery within a page-turning ghost story. . . . Just scary enough to entertain, its macabre love story will delight those who like their romance spiced with a hint of the afterlife."
—www.nationalreadingcampaign.ca

"This YA paranormal mystery/romance is a page-turner all the way."
—www.thechildrensbookreview.com

"Gallant's novel is a tightly plotted, entertaining read. . . . With a sequel already in the works, readers have much more to look forward to from this promising author." —*Quill and Quire*

"This was a real page-turner; full of mystery, suspense, drama, and romance. The plot is well developed, the characters are likeable and relate-able, and the writing style flows nicely. . . . Any fan of the supernatural should take a chance on this engaging little book." —www.edwardsbookclub.ca

"*Apparition* by Gail Gallant was one of those books that is hard to put down [with] spine-tingling creepiness, mystery and plenty of romantic tension to keep me turning pages. . . . I'm looking forward to continuing Amelia's journey in *Absolution*." —www.asimpleloveofreading.com

"*Apparition* . . . mixed mystery with a touch of romance, setting up Amelia as a strong female character/paranormal sleuth and placing her in a position where she had to choose between loyalty to the dead and love for the living." —*Canadian Children's Book News*

"Compellingly eerie and well-told, *Apparition* will draw readers in as they try to sort out the mystery of the haunted barn, its ghosts, and how they are all connected. . . . The mystery of the old barn and its ghosts carries the story along and will keep readers guessing . . . Recommended." —*CM Magazine*

"I was hooked on this story almost instantly, and found myself reluctant to put it down. . . . Gallant weaves together an intense and thrilling mystery, with a dash of first romance and the joys of self-discovery in a compellingly readable way."
—Raves & Faves, The Mabel's Fable's Blog for Big Readers

ALSO BY GAIL GALLANT

Apparition

Absolution

GAIL GALLANT

Abso

lution

DOUBLEDAY CANADA

Doubleday Canada and colophon are registered trademarks of Random House of Canada Limited

Library and Archives Canada Cataloguing in Publication

Gallant, Gail, author
        Absolution / Gail Gallant.

Sequel to: Apparition.

Issued in print and electronic formats.
ISBN 978-0-385-67964-0
eBook ISBN 978-0-385-67965-7

        I. Title.

PS8613.A459376A62 2014   jC813'.6   C2014-903127-0
                                                  C2014-903128-9

Cover images: (*boy*) © Jeff Cleveland/dreamstime.com;
(*girl*) © Martin Novak/dreamstime.com; (*sky*) © vvoevale/dreamstime.com;
(*deer*) © Tom Reichner/Shutterstock

Printed and bound in the USA

Published in Canada by Doubleday Canada,
a division of Random House of Canada Limited
a Penguin Random House company

www.randomhouse.ca

10 9 8 7 6 5 4 3 2 1

Penguin
Random House
DOUBLEDAY CANADA

In loving memory of my dear father,
Lawrence Joseph Gallant

*S*eeing isn't always believing. I've known that forever. Because for as long as I can remember, I've sometimes seen ghosts. And ghosts, well, they aren't real, are they?

At least that's what I thought. Then my mother died when I was thirteen and I started seeing her ghost all the time, gardening in the backyard. My grandmother, Joyce, who has custody of me and my two brothers, didn't think much of that at all. Instead, she thought I was crazy. Probably still does.

I don't know if I would even have survived it if it weren't for one person, Matthew. His friendship saved my life. I was secretly in love with him.

What happened next still seems unreal: Matthew's gruesome death in the old Telford barn, my brother Jack's creepy fall that broke his back, and a stranger named Morris Dyson with a secret obsession with ghosts, and a sneaking suspicion that the barn was haunted. He said I was just the person to help him prove it.

I discovered that Matthew was still in the barn, Matthew's *ghost* that is. There were actually about a half dozen ghosts hanging out in there, and one of them was pretty much evil, taking possession of teenage boys and making them kill themselves in horrible ways. The barn held their ghosts like prisoners.

In the end, the barn burnt to the ground and all of the ghosts were free to leave, to cross over to wherever ghosts go. But not before a sweet old lady gave her life to end the tragic deaths, and not before my younger brother Ethan got possessed and nearly died himself. Not to mention the close call for Kip Dyson and me. (Kip is Morris Dyson's son. *He's* a whole other story.)

I was heartbroken when Matthew left the burning barn with the other ghosts to cross over to the afterworld, thinking he was now gone forever. But the very last thing I saw that night, through the smoke and dying embers? Well, like I said, seeing isn't always believing.

(For the whole story of Amelia's previous adventure, read Apparition.)

1

I walk up the driveway of the abandoned Telford farm, my legs feeling wobbly like rubber. Beyond the farm-house, there's a heap of black remains where the barn used to be. Like the world's largest barbecue pit, in a field of snow. The fire was five days ago, and the ruins are still circled by yellow police tape. I guess they don't want anyone messing around in them. Poor Mrs. Ross died in the fire, after all. It's awful how many people have died in that barn over the years, including Matthew. He's been dead for almost four months, but he's still hanging around here. Even after everything that happened. This is the first time since the fire that I've been able to sneak back.

So where is he? Not near the tree where I last saw him standing. Not near the barn ruins. I look around and my eyes start to sting, from the smoky stench that's still in the air. Where *is* he? Maybe he's not here after all.

"Matthew?"

Maybe after we left that night, he decided to take off after the other ghosts. Maybe he caught up with them. They were heading west, over the far field, as if they were on a pilgrimage. All the dead souls from the barn, including Mrs. Ross, heading for some world beyond this one.

I rub my eyes and try harder to focus, squinting over what's left of the barn. I don't want to get too close to the charcoal beams and ash. The smell of smoke, an awful stink, is taking my breath away. It's hard to make out much in the wreckage. There are bits sticking out that look like metal, old farm equipment mixed in with the charred barnboards that came crashing down.

"Matthew?" Silence. Nothing.

I feel dizzy. I need to sit down. Walking over to the empty farmhouse, I see a small porch at the side door. I flop down on the lowest step, pull my knees up and rest my eye sockets on them, and wrap my arms around my head to block out the sunlight. I feel cold and empty and exhausted.

Then I sense a presence and lift my head. He's about twenty feet away, white face, black hair, four dark red holes across his abdomen dripping blood, blood trickling from his nose and smiling mouth. I jump up and scream so loudly that he disappears.

I bend over the porch railing, gasping, trying to catch my breath. When I finally manage to look up, I can see him again. He's standing farther away, without the pitchfork wounds and blood. A smile creeps across his face, as if everything's fine. A flood of emotions overwhelms me. I want to run to him, kiss and hug him, I'm so thankful he's still here. *Matthew! Thank God, Matthew!*

But you can't embrace a ghost, and now I feel my anger rising. The truth is, I don't know how much more of him my heart can take. And that makes me feel terrible, because I do still love him.

I always will. Besides, his friendship practically saved my life. It's not his fault that he couldn't save his own. But what am I supposed to do now? "I can't believe it!" I blurt, finally finding my voice.

"What can't you believe?" Matthew moves a little closer, cautiously.

"I can't believe you are still here!"

"Why not? You make it sound like a bad thing."

"Well, what do you expect me to do? You're here but you're not here. You're gone, you're back, you're gone, you're back—like a yo-yo. Do you know how painful that is?" My eyes are blurring with tears, and I'm fighting a flat-out crying fit. I take a deep breath. "And what's with the pitchfork holes, anyway?"

He looks down at his shirt like he's a little embarrassed.

I sit down on the porch again, holding my head, elbows on knees. A few sobs escape before I calm down.

"I'm not sure," he says. "Sometimes the blood and everything—it just happens. I think I have flashbacks—it really freaked me out at first. But why are you so angry? It's like you hate me or something. Was that . . . not a good idea? Staying behind?" He pauses, waiting for me to answer. "It seemed like a brilliant idea at the time."

I'm not sure why I am so upset. Maybe it's because right after the fire, when I thought I'd lost him for real, forever, and was devastated, I also felt a bit of relief. Like I had to accept the inevitable. The pain would soon start to get better, and someday I'd be able to get on with my life.

"Well, it's . . . just complicated," I finally say.

"Complicated by what?" he asks. "By Kip?" I hear jealousy in his voice.

"No, not by Kip. Kip's not . . . Kip's not in the picture."

"Not in the picture?"

"I just said that, didn't I? What are you? Deaf?" Now I'm angry, because I'm lying and I know it. I feel so horribly guilty about falling for Kip, and so hurt that I had to let him go. Then I see Matthew's wounded expression. I would never have talked to him like this when he was alive. "Kip's . . . Kip's got his own life to live," I say, trying to calm down again. He looks at me, kind of perplexed. "He's gone back to Chicago." Now I'm really depressed. "Matthew, I'm sorry. I don't hate you. I love you. I would probably be dead myself if it weren't for you. I just don't know how much more of this I can take, that's all. You being a ghost—it's not easy."

"Like it's easy for *me*?" he shouts. "Like this is *easy* . . . ?" His voice trails off and he looks away as if he's forgotten something, or lost something, and I realize he's fading. I can see through him.

"Matthew, don't go! Don't disappear. Please? Look, I'm sorry. I'm just not used to this new situation yet. But . . . ," I nod as I start to see him better, "but I'm getting more used to it all the time. I am. Just . . . let's think for a minute. I mean, the barn is gone. You can't hang out in a field all day and night, can you? What are your options?" I look around. "Do you even know? Do you have a preference, at least? Would you rather have a roof over your head? Would you rather have . . . I don't know . . . privacy?"

"I don't know what I want," he says sadly. "Nothing feels quite . . . right. Everything feels strange. Sometimes I feel like I got a bad hit on the head. Like half my brain got stolen or something. Sometimes I wish whoever stole it had taken the whole thing."

I think for a few moments. "Okay, here's an idea. Let's you and me break into this house and check it out. No one else is using it, so maybe you can hang out inside for a while. That's better than wandering around out here, don't you think? That way, maybe I can keep track of you, find you more easily. If I get this door open, do you think you could go inside?" I've noticed before that as a ghost Matthew seems limited in what he can do and where he can go. He was trapped in the barn until it burned down. He seems stuck on the Telford property. Kip's father, Morris, studies ghosts, and he has theories about their geography. He thinks some places, even some pathways, are more ghost-friendly than others.

"Do you think you could do that? Just . . . hang out in there? You know—haunt the place? Like a proper ghost. Maybe learn some ghost tricks."

"You don't think I'm a proper ghost?" He almost sounds hurt.

"I'm just saying . . . who knows what you're capable of in your new state? You haven't really tested your . . . ghost powers, have you? I mean, we know what you're *not* capable of." I have a brief flashback to Kip's arms tightening around me the night the barn burned down, a memory of leaning against his warm chest. I look at Matthew's ghostly figure, which I'll never be able to touch. He's thinning out again, almost see-through. "I'm sorry. I shouldn't have said that."

I examine the door, trying the doorknob. Locked, of course, but a little wobbly, like there's a loose screw. "Maybe we can take the knob off. A screwdriver would be good. Or maybe I should just break the window and reach inside and unlock the door, like they would on TV. What do you think?"

I look over my shoulder at Matthew but he's not there. I turn back to the door just as the curtain behind the glass flies up. His white face appears on the other side of the window, mouthing "BOO!"—making me jump. The doorknob turns and the door opens.

"You nearly gave me a heart attack!" I'm almost yelling now.

"You said I needed to learn some tricks."

"Not tricks on *me*!"

My heart's still pounding. I don't even feel like going in, but I take a deep breath and pull myself together. I take off my boots—I don't want some real estate agent to see footprints and think the house has been burgled. I step inside, then shoot an angry look at him. "I'm not hanging out with you if you're going to pull that kind of thing."

Standing in the middle of the kitchen, in my socks, I realize that this floor is freezing. I look around.

"Will this do? Could you make yourself at home here, at least for a while?" A sudden thought makes me uneasy. "You don't think it's already occupied, do you? By another ghost, I mean? Can you tell?" I couldn't take another ghost right now—especially a psycho like Jimmy, the killer ghost who did such horrible things in the barn.

He looks around and shrugs. "I don't think anyone's here."

"Okay. It feels empty to me too. So you can party. You can be a poltergeist. I'll try to sneak away to visit you as often as I can." How tricky is this going to be? How risky? "But I meant what I said. What you do on your own time is your business, but just . . . try not to be scary when you're with me. Understood?" He turns away from me, but not before I notice that he's smiling. "I'm serious, Matthew. My nerves are shot," I say, trying to sound tough like Joyce.

I head back to the kitchen and pull on my boots. "I'll slip back in a few days. In the meantime, please be careful and lie low." Hoping to sound reassuring, I add, "Everything's going to be okay." But he's not listening. He's looking around the kitchen like he's suddenly curious about his new digs. I step out the door and close it behind me.

Who am I kidding? This could be a disaster.

———

The night after the barn burned down, I lay awake for hours in some kind of shock. I couldn't stop thinking about the horrible images of Jimmy, of Mrs. Ross in flames and, when it was all over, ghostly Matthew standing alone against a tree, smiling at me, his finger to his lips. I couldn't sleep at all. And then I remembered something I hadn't thought about in ages. A plastic bottle with my mother's name printed on it, filled with sixty small white pills. I hadn't thought about it because I hadn't wanted to.

The next day, I dug the bottle out of the bottom of a box in the back of my closet and stared at it. As if, somehow, that long-empty bottle was the key to everything. As if, if I stared long enough at the unpronounceable drug name on the pharmacy label, I'd unlock the secret to my soul.

That was when the doorbell rang. I ignored it, but then I heard Morris's voice in the hallway. I was a mess. I got up and looked around for something to throw on over my ratty T-shirt. A big old sweater. It turned out that Joyce had decided to call a meeting. With absolutely no warning.

I opened my door a crack and, looking down from there, I could see legs in the front entrance. Joyce said something in a low voice as Morris stepped into the hall, and then his son, Kip, came in behind him. My heart began to bang in my chest. I stood frozen at the top of the stairs as they walked down the hall toward the kitchen, Joyce rapping on Jack's bedroom door as she passed it, and then leaning into the living room, telling my younger brother, Ethan, with a jerk of her head to come along too. Then she called up to me. I honestly didn't think I'd be able to move.

Kip stopped at the kitchen doorway. I couldn't see his face, only his thick, dark blond hair. Then he looked up at me. He had a few fresh scars high on his cheekbone and on his forehead, souvenirs from his fight with Ethan. Ethan, now back to his annoyingly exuberant self, went bounding past him as if nothing had happened between them, racing into the kitchen to claim a seat like it was a game of musical chairs. Jack, hopping on crutches, wasn't far behind. But Kip just stood there, his blue eyes so intense and questioning that I had to look away.

Sometimes, when you hold back the truth from the people you care about most, you feel like you've told a big lie. By saying nothing at all. That's how I feel. I haven't told anyone that Matthew's ghost stayed behind the other night. Not Kip, not Morris, not Joyce or my brothers. At first, I think, it was because I was in too much shock. Also, Matthew was motioning for me to keep quiet about it. But since then, I've been so worried about what to do about him that I can't think of anything else. Except Kip, of course.

Anyway, with the rest of them already in the kitchen, I forced myself down the stairs, thinking how, on top of everything else, I hadn't washed my hair in four days. I stood at the kitchen entrance as they sat around the table. Joyce and Ethan on my left, Morris and Jack on my right, and Kip at the far end, watching me. They were all waiting. Finally, Joyce insisted I take a seat. She's been the head of the family since Mom died three years ago, and she's a take-charge type. You don't want to interfere with Joyce's plans when she's in her take-charge mood.

"I'm calling this meeting because I think we need to get a few things on the table, about what happened on Sunday night, and the sooner the better. Starting with the fact that, apparently, Amelia can see ghosts."

Wow! I didn't dare react, but I gasped inside. I never thought I'd live to hear my grandmother come out and admit it like that, in front of witnesses, even. She always refused to accept that my mother saw ghosts, and she made me start seeing a psychiatrist after my mother died, when I was thirteen, just because I told her I could see Mom's ghost in our garden. She seemed to think it was something I could be talked out of, just some dumb idea I had. I assumed I'd have to keep this big dark secret to myself for the rest of my life. But then Matthew died. And Morris showed up—he's an obsessive ghost-tracking expert with his own private reasons for feeling haunted.

Joyce paused, looking mostly at Jack and Ethan and not so much at me. She didn't seem happy. But Jack and Ethan did. They love having a sister who can see ghosts.

"This has to be kept a secret between us. It can't go beyond the six people in this kitchen. Ethan, do you understand how important this is?" Ethan blinked and grinned, which is something he does when he's nervous or excited. It's a facial tic. It started when Mom died, and now he's fourteen and still doing it. He nodded his head like mad, saying, "Uh-huh."

"Jack?"

Jack is eighteen, and very mature for his age. Probably because he's the oldest, and our father died when we were really young, so he's always been the protective type. "Yes. Understood. Totally," he said. You can always depend on Jack. Even Joyce knows that.

Then Joyce talked a little about what had happened to Ethan in the barn that night. She blamed the fact that he doesn't remember anything about how he got there, or why he had a fight with Kip, on "temporary amnesia." A knock on the head he doesn't remember getting. Nothing about the truth, which is that Ethan was possessed by a vicious ghost who tried to get him to kill himself, and to take out anyone else he could while he was at it. The same ghost had possessed Jack and Matthew. With Matthew he had totally succeeded. Jack survived but with a broken vertebra in his lower back. He's treating it like another of his battle scars from playing sports, like the broken nose he got in a hockey game.

"We have to put the whole melodrama behind us now," Joyce said. "It's over. It doesn't matter if we never understand it."

Easy for her to say.

I was starting to feel something like relief, like I'd gotten off easy, when she turned to Morris and me. She just stared at us, and I swear I was holding my breath for like a minute. Bracing for the worst. Finally she came out with it.

"Maybe it's a gift of some sort." There was a long, tense pause, as if she hated having to admit that. Then her expression softened a bit. "So who am I to say you aren't allowed to use it? But if there are any more ghost sightings or adventures in the future," she said, already starting to sound tough again, "I want to know about them. From the start. Amelia, you say you can't control whether or not you see ghosts. But you're going to have to control what you do about it. As long as you live under this roof, I'm the one who decides what risks you take." Her tone was pretty threatening. She was looking back and forth between me and Morris as though we were two bad kids, even though he's old enough to be my father.

"Jack could have died in that barn," she went on. "As it is, we don't know how long it'll be before he has full use of his legs again. And Ethan could have burned to death. Same with Kip. And you came close yourself."

She zoomed in on Morris. "I realize that ghosts are your obsession and you've done a lifetime of study, but if you can't keep Amelia absolutely safe when she's helping you with your research, leave her out of it. *You leave her alone.* Got it?" He winced, looking down at the table, then sideways at me. I couldn't tell what he was thinking, but he did look a little guilty.

I was so afraid she would try to break up our partnership. Because Morris's support and expertise have meant so much to me. Whatever's wrong with me, whatever allows me to see ghosts sometimes, I don't worry about it as much as I used to. But I wish I knew what I'm supposed to do about it. There are just so many unanswered questions.

Most of the time Joyce was talking, I was looking down, but when I did glance up I saw Ethan's eyes wide like crazy, his mouth open. Really, he seemed so thrilled. I guess he finally feels he's part of something exciting. And his facial twitch isn't as bad these past few days. Morris was pretty quiet, just listening to her and nodding as if he was totally okay with her being the boss of him.

Kip sat across from me saying nothing, but I could feel his eyes. I know he's been wondering what's up with me, because earlier that night it had seemed we were getting closer. Right up to the moment when I realized that, instead of following the rest of the ghosts out of the burning barn and off on their journey, Matthew had stayed behind. And with Matthew still around, the whole idea of me being with Kip seems wrong.

I've been avoiding contact with Kip ever since. I guess I'm afraid that if I look right into his eyes, he'll realize that something is up. That I have a secret that's tearing me in two.

Near the end of her little speech in the kitchen, there was a pause and it seemed like Joyce was done talking. That was when she turned to me.

"Is there anything you want to add, Amelia? Anything I've left out?" I was caught by surprise. It's hard getting used to the new Joyce, now that she's been forced to accept the whole ghost thing. I almost felt suspicious. But then I felt such a wave of self-consciousness and guilt, thinking about Matthew down the road on the Telford property. I caught Kip's eye, I couldn't help it. But I forced myself to look back at Joyce and I shook my head once, as if to say no.

Then Ethan jumped in and said maybe we should give ourselves a name, like a secret society. Jack laughed and put a hand on Ethan's shoulder and gave it a brotherly shake. "Like the Scooby-Doo Gang?" he asked.

I caught Kip smiling too, just for a second.

Joyce walked them outside while I stayed in the living room, by the window. I watched Joyce and Morris, their heads close, talking, before he and Kip got in their car. And I saw Kip look back at the house, pale and confused, as they drove off. We never even said goodbye.

Later, in my bedroom, my thoughts drifted back to that bottle of little white pills hidden in my old bedroom for so long. I'd found them in the medicine cabinet only a few days after my mother died. A prescription for tranquilizers filled months before, that she'd never opened. She never took even one. I know because I counted them. With so much going on around the funeral, nobody noticed that they went missing. That bottle of pills waited for me in the dark at the back of my closet at the end of every day for a year. They were my way out, if I couldn't stand to keep going. Then, when I met Matthew, I began to think of them less and less. And finally, one day, I told him about them. I just blurted it out. He looked at me sadly, and calmly said I should get rid of them. That night, I dumped the whole lot down the toilet, watching them whirl in the water as they flushed away, like a big bunch of maggots. I didn't need them anymore. Though I've kept the empty bottle as a twisted souvenir.

I remember imagining that maybe Matthew had been sent by my mother, from beyond the grave, to save me. Of course that makes no sense now, him winding up dead himself and all.

2

"*I*'m sorry I'm late!"

I scurry across the coffee shop floor and sit down in the seat opposite Morris. I wrestle off my coat while I try to read upside down from the page he's working on. He half raises a hand to wave hello, keeping his eyes on his papers. Then he shuffles them together and slides them into a folder, saying, "Oh, I got here early. Just wanted to go over a few things." He looks up and smiles, asking, "How are you?" in his usual cowboy drawl. It's been almost a week since Joyce's meeting, and three days since I set Matthew up in the Telford farmhouse. This is our first chance to talk privately since the barn burned down, about ten days ago now. Still, it's a coffee shop, so not really private. I'm worrying about how long I can keep Matthew's decision to stick around a secret from him.

"I'm okay," I say. "You look tired, though. Are you forgetting to sleep?"

Morris laughs, as if that's funny. True, I've never seen him *not* looking pretty tired. He may be old enough to be my father, but he looks even older. Picture an aging and world-weary sheriff who doesn't carry a gun, with grey scraggly shoulder-length hair and a scruffy beard. His face is drawn and gaunt, like he's been crossing a desert without much food. His hands even shake sometimes. If you met him, you'd see what I'm talking about. Of course, he's not a sheriff, he's a writer. He writes a newspaper column on local history. And when he's not doing that, he's researching ghost stories and tracking ghosts. And it's left him with this permanently haunted look. I could never have imagined when I met him that he'd have someone like Kip for a son. Kip is . . . gorgeous.

"I'm more worried about *you*," he says. "You didn't look well in the kitchen the other day. I know this has been hard on you, a terrible shock. And with Joyce putting things out in the open like that, you two must be wrestling with some serious issues."

"True. But nothing we're saying out loud."

"Anything I can help with? Or am I too much part of the problem right now?"

"No, Morris, really. It's been better than I would have thought. I mean, Joyce is leaving me alone most of the time. Nobody's said anything to me about you-know-what. She must have asked Ethan and Jack not to bring it up. So I'm not getting harassed or anything. It's almost creepy."

"But you're still traumatized. I can see it in your eyes. Like you're only half seeing what's in front of you. What happened was hard on all of us, with Dorothy Ross dying and . . . all the rest, but especially on you. You could see Matthew finally cross over. . . ." He doesn't finish the thought. He looks so sympathetic, and I feel a horrible wave of guilt again. How could I have lied to him about something so important? How can I keep the lie going?

He pauses, then adds cautiously, "I don't think Kip knew how to handle your e-mail after that meeting. He told me about it. He went back to Chicago in a dark mood, I'm afraid." He adds quickly, "He'll get over it, don't worry." He must read the pain in my face. "Honestly, Amelia, Kip will be fine. It's for the best. For both of you."

Last week Kip tried to get me on the phone, but I was so stressed about Matthew that I could hardly talk. I was a wreck. Finally I wrote to him, apologizing for avoiding him, and saying I just needed time alone. But I didn't mean for him to leave town or anything. Then I got a short e-mail a couple of days later, saying he'd enrolled in two new classes in Chicago for the winter term. He told me that he'd stay out of my way if I'd promise to "stay out of trouble," and that he'd check in to see how I was. Just like that, he was gone.

It makes me wonder if Morris encouraged him to leave Owen Sound. I look up at him sipping his coffee, eyes fixed on something outside the window in the nearby parking lot. He's hunched, his stringy grey hair falling forward, hiding his bony face. He knew there was something going on between Kip and me, and he didn't like the idea. As if we needed to be protected from getting too attached to each other, because it would never work between us and we'd both get hurt. Well, maybe he's right, but what he doesn't realize is that it's too late. I think about Kip all the time. I keep remembering things he said to me. Remembering every time we touched, even by accident.

Morris just wants to keep everything professional. I guess he stopped believing in things like romance a long time ago, when his family fell apart. He's had so much heartbreak that he's stopped believing in love, or anything much else that happens in the world of ordinary living people. He was an alcoholic for years, and this ghost research rescued him from his misery and gave his life a sense of purpose. Kind of what Matthew did for me after my mom died. Only Morris has never actually *seen* a ghost. That's why he needs me. I'm pretty good at that.

He turns back to me and lifts his eyebrows, like he's just remembered something.

"Guess who dropped by for a friendly visit yesterday?" Owen Sound's not a big town, and the number of people both Morris and I know is really, really small, so it must have something to do with the whole Telford barn thing. He tells me before I try to guess. "Grierson. Detective Grierson."

"Detective Grierson? So . . . are you in trouble or something?" I can't help but look around when I say that.

"Trouble? Always. No, that's not why he came over. I don't think so, anyway. He actually seemed to want to give me a tip. And you'll never guess what about." His voice drops. "Yeah"—he nods, seeing my disbelief, and leans in a bit—"he tells me that in the last few months he's been called three times to go down to 28th Sideroad, southeast of here, to check out a trespasser or burglar or something, twice in the middle of the night. It's a country inn run out of an old Victorian farmhouse. The Cornflower Country Inn, something like that. Just opened a couple of months ago. He tells me that each time he answers the call, the owner keeps him there for ages, and she's very friendly and he's been thinking that she's just lonely, but each time he finds her more distressed. And he's really stumped."

"Why? What's happening?"

"Well, according to Grierson, she hears noises in the house in the middle of the night. She thinks it's coming from a back staircase, one of those old servants' staircases that goes from a hall off the kitchen up to the second-floor bedrooms. She's been afraid someone is breaking into the house at the back and heading up those stairs. She's heard the creaking a half-dozen times, she says. More importantly, two overnight guests staying in the back bedroom have complained at breakfast about hearing things too."

"Hmm. And did Grierson actually say he suspects it's a"—I'd better choose my words carefully, public place and all—"*thing*?"

"Not exactly. He just said it's a bit of a mystery. That's as far as he'd go. But why else would he mention it to me? And make a point of dropping by in person to tell me? He also said there's never been any sign of a break-in on the property, and a few weeks ago both the owner and her guest heard steps on the stairs but, even though fresh snow had fallen earlier that evening, there were no footprints anywhere near the house."

"Interesting. Anything else?"

"One of the guests insisted she heard what sounded like gurgling or choking or something, outside their bedroom door."

"Ugh."

"Yeah. Not good for business."

"So—where is this place? Where on 28th Sideroad?"

"Well. . . ." Morris pulls some maps out of his folder and brings one to the top.

The geography of ghosts, that's what Morris calls his research. For a long while, he put his ghost-tracking research onto one huge map of Grey County that he kept in his basement office. But now he's made a kind of grid, dividing the map into a bunch of smaller sections, and he's slowly transferring his information onto these sections. All kinds of stuff, some of it you can't imagine why—like soil types and elevation and rock formations. They're on his computer at home, but he carries hard copies everywhere with him, and he's always scribbling little notes on them when he gets an idea. I can never make out his handwriting. He has these red dots on the maps, one for each ghost sighting he's heard about. In his spare time he's always got his head in old newspapers and local history publications, or even geology textbooks. He's mainly interested in the exact locations of the sightings. They're mostly in buildings like houses, or where houses used to be. But sometimes they're along old roads, or in farmers' fields. What matters most to him is figuring out why so many of those sightings seem to line up with each other, to form a kind of passageway through the county.

Morris calls these lineups *ley lines*, and he thinks they have as much to do with what's underground as what's on the surface. He goes on about some kind of "earth energy." But are ghosts drawn to certain places, or are they just easier to see in certain places? Some things we can't see but we know they exist. Like gravity, or radiation. That's how Morris thinks about ghosts. The mystery is why some people, like me, can see them, when most of the time most people can't. Not even Morris. So it feels good to put my freaky ghost vision to some practical use, in the interests of his research.

Now he runs a finger along a line of those red dots and stops at a particular point. Again I find myself glancing around, anxious that we may be watched. Then I look down and focus.

"It's heavily forested around there," Morris says. "There's a wetlands area too, a swampy stretch just in from the road. That's why it's never been developed. All old-growth. Anyway, the house property borders the forest. I haven't been able to find a record of any previous sightings. Not yet anyway. But that section of road runs right along the Line." He says *Line* with emphasis, and we both know what he means. "That doesn't happen often."

"It that just some kind of coincidence?"

"Maybe. But maybe not." He tells me about his research on 28th Sideroad. Turns out this stretch of road is the site of an ancient native trail. It's one of a few that have been identified by archeologists in Grey County, used for a thousand years or more by the First Nations peoples who lived in the woodlands here, up until only a few hundred years ago, when the Europeans came. "It wouldn't be the first time a ley line was both a pathway for the living and a ghost road for the dead, though this kind of phenomenon is getting harder and harder to find."

"But I don't get it. What does Grierson want from you?"

"Well, thanks to the Telford barn events, it's confirmed his suspicions about my sideline research. Let's just say he's caught me more than once over the years trespassing on abandoned property. I think he was wondering if I had anything prior on the house. Anyway, I acted casual and said I'd never heard anything about that house before. Then he said that if the owner ever calls him back, maybe he'll put her onto me, since he's not sure he wants to go back there. He says she's the kind of 'trouble' he doesn't need. That's how he put it."

"Wow. Weird. Why does he think she's trouble?"

"I think maybe his *wife* thinks she's trouble." That throws me for a second or two. "She's starting to get a little suspicious," he adds, seeing that I look confused.

Oh, she's jealous—I get it. "So what are you thinking?"

"Well, if I went over there at some point, to interview the owner, how would you feel about coming along? Doing a bit of a 'reading' of the place? Would you be interested?"

"To be totally honest, I think I need a break from meeting new ghosts. Just for a while. I'm not sure I can handle it yet."

Morris looks flustered. "Of course, of course. My God, you're right. I'm being insensitive, bringing this up so soon. Forget I mentioned it, okay? For a while, anyway. Until you're in the mood?"

I nod and tell him it's okay. Maybe next month.

"Actually," he says, tapping 28th Sideroad on his map, "I think that's the stretch of road where there was a car accident a couple of years ago. A guy lost control of his car and hit a tree."

"Died?" I ask. Morris nods.

Later, I hitch a ride home with Joyce and Jack, who's just had a medical checkup. He's had a lot of those since last Halloween, when he injured his back falling from the rafters of the Telford barn. His legs were paralyzed for a while, but he's slowly regaining use of them. I'm in the passenger seat and Joyce is at the wheel. I twist to face Jack sitting in the back.

"You good?" I ask.

"Could be worse," he says. Then I see his eyes flick over to Joyce, who's preoccupied with traffic lights up the road. He looks back at me and mouths a question, "Morris?" He's guessing I've been with Morris, and it's always best if Joyce doesn't know. I give him a slight nod and he smiles. He approves, and he doesn't mind covering for me when he can.

"How's Morgan these days?" he asks, out loud this time. Like that's who I've been with. I smile back at him.

"Could be better," I say. Morgan's my best friend at school. That's a bit of a joke between us, since Jack has had a mad crush on Morgan forever, and she kind of leads him on and jerks him around. She can't help it, I guess. She has too many romantic options to choose from. Joyce shoots me a look, then the light turns green and she's back to driving. Jack pulls out his phone to read a text message.

I decide to take a chance and ask her, just out of curiosity, whether she's ever heard of the Cornflower Inn on 28th Sideroad. She immediately gets suspicious, wanting to know why I'm asking, and I have to confess it's a place Morris mentioned to me.

"Let me guess why," she says sarcastically. "Anyway, the answer is no. I haven't heard of it. But I know 28th Sideroad. That's where I hit the deer about five years ago. One of the worst experiences of my life. It was right around sunset and I was taking a shortcut from somewhere. I'll never forget it. It reminded me of a young colt. Jumped out in front of the car. I nearly lost control. Came *this close* to crashing into a tree." She measures an inch between her thumb and finger.

The memory comes back to me—Joyce coming home that night. The car had a bad dent around the left headlight, and the side-view mirror was knocked off. She looked as if she'd been crying, and I'd never seen her like that before, so it really struck me. She sat on the porch with Mom all evening. It was when Mom was sick with cancer. Early on, when she still seemed okay.

"I saw the poor thing lying in the road in my rear-view mirror, flailing on its side. It was trying to get up but it couldn't. By the time I got out of the car, it was gone. Crawled back into the forest to die. Poor thing. Such a beautiful animal."

If the deer reminded her of a colt, I can understand why she was so upset. Joyce is horse-crazy. She's worked at riding stables south of town for years, and she owns two horses, Ponyboy and Marley. She keeps them in the paddock behind our house. They're the main reason she made us move out of town last fall.

"Jeez. That happened on 28th Sideroad? I'd forgotten about that."

"Well, it's not something you'd forget if you were in the car. Hitting a deer—it's a terrible experience."

"You're lucky it wasn't a moose," Jack says, looking up from his phone. "That's what everyone says. Hit a moose on the road and it'll take you out with it. So I wonder what happened to the deer?"

"In the forest? I don't know. Coyotes got it, I'd guess."

So here I am for the remainder of the drive home, thinking of the forest, dark and damp, dying deer and coyotes, until we turn into the driveway on 12th Line and Joyce lets the bomb drop.

"Hard to believe it," she says, "but I notice there's a Sold sign gone up on the Telford farm. They must have had to practically give it away."

3

I burst in through the kitchen door of the farmhouse, forgetting all about my boots leaving marks on the floor tiles. "Matthew?"

And that's when I see the words, fingerpainted in blood on the wall where the fridge used to go: BUYER BEWARE!

"What the hell? MATTHEW!"

He's standing in the hall, just beyond the kitchen entrance.

"Are you serious?" I yell at him, pointing at the bloody message. "What's that supposed to mean?"

He looks at me like maybe I can't read. "That's a saying. *Buyer beware.*"

"It sounds like you're trying to warn them that the roof leaks or something."

"Now that you mention it, the roof *does* leak."

"Matthew! You can't go around writing threats in blood and saying whatever comes into your head."

His face falls. "Well . . . I thought it was pretty cool."

"Where did you even get that blood?"

"I was bleeding from my pitchfork holes again, and I stuck a finger in. I know that's gross but, hey, next thing I knew—graffiti."

"Okay. That makes no sense, but fine. Whatever. Who's buying the farm? Did you see them?"

"I think so. A couple came through here with an older woman, and I'm pretty sure she was the agent. The couple seemed really negative about the place. They kept repeating how it would have to be gutted. I wish they'd use another word," he said, moving his hand over his belly. "The guy kept talking on his cellphone the whole time he was walking through the house and looking around. I think he might be a lawyer. I think she might be a lawyer too. They're looking for a weekend getaway or something. 'An old-fashioned hobby farm.' They're in for a surprise. This place has carpenter ants."

Oh my God. He just doesn't get it. "Forget the carpenter ants. This place has a *ghost*. And what were you doing while they were walking around? Trying to stay out of their way, at least?"

"Kind of. I followed them around a bit, as quietly as I could. I only noticed the woman look around once or twice. Suspiciously, like she felt a chill. We were upstairs in the front bedroom, one of my favourite places. I watch the road from that window. And maybe she heard a creak, too."

I remember my boots and take them off, putting them by the door.

"Matthew . . . what are we going to do? You can't stay here if people are moving in." Then something catches my eye. "And what's that on the stair? A doll?" It's old, and its body is made of soft cloth. The head looks hard, like china or porcelain, and it has no hair.

"Yeah, I found it in the attic. It's fantastic up there. You wouldn't believe the neat stuff."

"So what's it doing on the stair? Someone's going to step on that thing, and trip and break their neck."

Matthew is looking at me with a sullen, slightly exasperated expression. "You know, you're giving me mixed messages."

"What? What mixed messages?"

"You said I'm supposed to act like a ghost. Well, I've got news for you. Ghosts *do* that kind of thing." Then he gets all huffy. "By the way, moving that doll out of the attic was a bigger deal than you might think. I don't have the coordination I used to have, you know. I'm not sure, but I think it took me *all day*."

"Matthew, just . . . let's just think about this for a minute. I'm sorry if I'm mixing messages, but I've never coached a ghost before. And, I don't know, maybe I'm violating some important law of nature by trying to influence you at all. You're probably supposed to be crossed over to . . . somewhere . . . by now." I try to think. What are we going to do? "I guess we need to find you a new hangout."

"I don't want a new hangout. Why should I be the one to leave? I was here first."

"Are you serious? You want to stay?"

"Well, I think they're only weekenders. Maybe you can visit me here during the week."

"That doesn't sound practical. Not with a bunch of reno guys around." I look down the hallway and up the staircase. "Until I come up with a better plan, where's the best place for you to hide out—I mean, when the owners are around? So you have your own space and you can stay out of their way, more or less? How about the attic?"

"Sure. That would be okay. Unless they get a satellite dish. TV would be nice. It gets pretty boring, you know."

"Well, I don't think you should get your hopes up about watching TV. Can we agree that, until we think of something else, you stay in the attic when they're here? Why don't you show it to me now?"

"Fine. After you."

I head up the stairs, grabbing the worn-out doll from the step as I go. There are tiny pinholes all over its head where the hair used to be. But it still has eyelashes. Its round eyeballs look real, and it has a clueless little smile.

"Actually, I was thinking I might try to make her talk," he says behind me as I reach the second floor. I look back at him, shocked.

"You're kidding, right? A *talking doll* crosses the line. That's just . . . common knowledge." Even holding this doll in my hand is creeping me out—as if being alone with Matthew in this strange, empty house could feel anywhere near normal. The last thing I need from him is ghost tricks.

On the landing at the top of the stairs, I realize that I don't know where the attic is. I turn around to see Matthew still at the bottom of the stairs, looking up at me. He hasn't moved.

"What?" I ask.

"Nothing."

"Well, what are you waiting for?"

"Sorry, I lost my concentration." He starts slowly up the stairs. "It's just nice, that's all, thinking about you and me alone together in this empty old house. Kind of romantic."

"Look, your chance to get romantic was before you up and died. It's a little late for that now."

"I'm sorry. I thought I had more time."

At the top of the stairs he stops and faces me, standing only a few feet away. "Maybe it's *not* too late," he says.

I can't meet his eyes. "Believe me. It's . . . too late." It pains me to sound so negative, but sometimes I think he still doesn't totally get that he's dead.

"But maybe there's a way . . ."

"I don't want to talk about it. Please."

Something about his expression makes me vaguely uneasy so I change the subject. "Now, where is this attic?"

"There's a hatch in the ceiling in there." He points to one of the bedrooms.

"But it'll be pitch-dark up there with no electricity, right? How am I supposed to see anything?"

"Just you wait. Sometimes I can make lights go on, even when there's no power. There's an old lamp up there, not even plugged in, but I've made the light bulb light up—twice. It's wicked! Honestly, I have some kind of special powers." He looks quite pleased with himself.

"Okay, if you say so. As long as you aren't showing off, lighting things up near the front windows for someone driving by to see."

He looks at me like he's thinking, *Wow, give me some credit.*

In the bedroom I check out the hatch door in the ceiling of the closet. Then I look around for something to stand on. There's an old stool in the corner. I drag it over to the closet and glance back at Matthew. "I take it you don't need to stand on a stool?"

"Not really, but I'll use it anyway, just for fun. I kind of enjoy moving objects. Or opening and shutting doors. I don't know why but I'm good at that. It's just the more complicated actions where I lose my concentration. Uh . . . there are cobwebs, brace yourself. . . ."

"Oh, of course. Wonderful. Maybe you should go first. And do that thing you do with the light."

I step aside so he can get to the closet, but he gets too close to me and disappears, which makes me seriously uncomfortable. I feel a cool shiver all over like he's passed through me. I step back and I can see him again as he gets up onto the stool. He slowly opens the hatch and kind of floats up through it. *So creepy!* The hatch stays open and it's black up there, I can't see a thing. I wait for a minute or two and then start to feel impatient.

"Matthew?"

Silence . . . and then a drawn-out "Yesss?"

"Are you trying to sound spooky? 'Cause don't bother, if you don't mind. What's going on? Can you turn on some light or not?"

"It's not as easy as it sounds. Like I said, it takes concentration."

"Okay, fine." I wait, and my neck starts to get stiff from looking up. "It's just that I don't have forever." Finally I'm aware of a glow coming from above.

"Wow! Well done!"

His face appears in the hatch opening. He's grinning and holding a lamp under his chin to look ghoulish, the way kids do with flashlights when they're camping. Instead of creating spooky light and shadows, the lamp seems to glow right through him.

"Hey, don't be a jerk." *Honestly!* "Can you move so I can get up?" It's a struggle to hoist myself through the opening. Harder than I thought. I'm only in socks, so I don't want to walk around up here. It's probably full of mouse droppings and worse. Once I'm securely balanced, sitting on one beam with my feet up on the next, I look around. Boxes of old books, a red Singer sewing machine, some wooden chairs with busted cane seats, a cradle on rockers, a turquoise tin canister set—it's full of stuff.

Finally my eyes settle on Matthew. God, he looks strangely handsome up here, with his dark hair and narrow shining eyes and sharp features, holding that old desk lamp and smiling at me.

"You know, that lamplight is having a weird effect. It's like everything up here, including you, has a strange glow."

"This attic is supercharged." He glances around, beaming in an eerie way. "Like it's got traces of people in it. I went with my parents a few times to estate auctions, and I couldn't get why people wanted to buy such old stuff. But it's like past lives have rubbed off on it and there's something left behind."

"Sounds like germs to me. I don't really want to get into any deep talk about life and death right now. We've got more immediate problems. Now that the house is sold, you're not in such a great situation. You've got to promise me you'll try to keep your distance. This is serious. I don't want the media showing up at the door. You know, reality TV crews or something? Don't try to scare these people. It could backfire, badly."

"You worry too much. I don't see what could happen. It's not like I'm a vampire and they can put a stake through my heart."

"All the same, we don't know what we're playing with. Besides, what if I got caught coming into the house? Did you ever think of that? That could be bad news, for me and for us. For our . . . friendship. I mean, I could be charged with breaking and entering, for starters! Do you have any idea what Joyce would do to me? She'd friggin' kill me! So the first thing we have to do is clean up your blood and my boot marks in the kitchen. No more doing stuff that might make anyone suspicious, thinking the house has squatters or something. The bottom line is, if you're not prepared to leave this house right now, you've got to stay in the attic. I'm sorry, but you've *got* to."

"That's okay. I feel pretty at home here. Though I'd rather live in *your* attic."

"Well . . . maybe someday. Let's take things a step at a time."

I shouldn't have said that. Dumb mistake. The complications would be a nightmare. "Just lay low. Promise?"

"For how long?"

"For as long as I say."

"Jeez. You're bossy these days."

"I'm sorry. It's the new me."

"Well, I'd like to have the old you back."

Believe me, I know how you feel.

4

"This latest phone call takes our relationship to a whole new level. Grierson actually said, 'Why don't you see what you can do about this lady's goddamn ghost.' Word for word. He told me to give her a call."

I'm sitting in the passenger seat of Morris's car. We're on our way to see the lady who owns the inn on 28th Sideroad. Clarisse. A very old-fashioned sounding name. He says she's lived there less than six months. She inherited money from her wealthy grandmother, and picked up the old brick farmhouse for a steal. She arranged to have it restored and converted into a country inn.

My mind wanders a bit, thinking about the poor saps who bought the Telford farm. They probably think they scored a great real estate deal themselves. God knows what's going to happen when they move in. Then, as usual, I feel guilty about Matthew holed up in the attic there with Morris not having a clue. I wish I could tell him, I really do. But it's been seven weeks now. A little late for confessions. Besides, it's not just my secret. It's Matthew's.

It's late February, and more than a month since Morris and I last talked. He asks about my family, how everyone's doing. Especially Jack and how his broken back is healing. I tell him Jack's recovery is going well, though I don't get to see him as much as I used to. He's moved out of the house and in with his buddy Jeremy in Owen Sound until the end of the school year, to be closer to rehab. Jeremy's parents have a basement apartment. I miss him a ton, especially on weekend mornings, when we used to have little chats at breakfast about whatever and I could complain about stuff to him. I run into him almost every weekday at school, but it's not the same.

"And school? How's school?"

"It's okay. It's fine. I'm staying on top of things. I'm not seeing my friends so much outside of class, but it's hard anyway, living in the friggin' country and all."

Morris laughs. "Country living isn't so bad. I'd like to try it someday."

I get up the nerve to ask him about Kip, trying to sound as cool as I possibly can. He says they've only had short chats since Kip returned to Chicago in January. Then he says that what Kip went through in the barn, with the ghosts and all, left him pretty shaken. The idea of Kip being shaken makes me crazy, wanting so badly to put my arms around him. It feels like he's a million miles away.

Then he says something that totally makes my day. He says that with March break coming up, he's thinking of inviting Kip to Owen Sound for a visit. That is, unless Kip's already made plans to head south with his friends to some Mexican beach.

I say it would be nice to see him again. I feel my face heating up.

"So you haven't heard from him?" he asks, as if it's no big deal, but I know he's concerned.

I shake my head. Not even on my birthday a few weeks ago—though I never told Kip or Morris it was my birthday, I don't go around mentioning it like it's some big deal. Apart from Joyce, Jack, Ethan and Morgan, no one knows or cares I'm officially seventeen. That's only two years younger than Kip.

It's an effort but I change the subject, to calm myself down. I ask Morris about Clarisse, the inn owner, and he tells me she spent years working in the hotel business in the city but always dreamed of running her own little country inn, and the inherited cash, combined with a marriage breakup, convinced her to take a chance. So far, all her overnight guests have been friends and family. She's been practising on them, getting the hang of things. Then she started noticing that she had one overnight guest too many.

"You're sure you're up for this? You've had enough time off?"

"I think so."

We're driving west on 28th Sideroad, almost there, when Morris tells me this is the stretch where the fatal car accident happened a couple of years ago. I stare into the forest bordering the road, watching the trees blur past.

"Well, guess what?" I say. "Joyce hit a deer on this road, about five years ago."

"Really? They figure the guy who died was probably trying to avoid a deer. Because of the skid marks and all the swerving before he hit the tree."

We're both alert now, glancing left and right into the forest. Every family around here has someone who's done it—hit a deer, or nearly. The most dangerous seasons are late spring and early fall, when the deer are more likely to do something stupid like run into the road on account of it being mating season. The most common time of day is dawn or dusk, in the half-light. And of course everyone knows what deer do, once you've got them in your headlights.

It's only in the split second as I start to look away, while Morris is going on about how we're almost there and the inn should be coming up on our right just past the edge of the forest, that I catch sight of something moving among the trees. Deep in the green, there's an unexpected flash of pink.

The house is big and pretty—two storeys with a steep roof, and yellow brick with pale orange brick trim over the windows and down the corners. There are a few houses in town that look just like it. There's fancy wooden trim all along the porch roof, painted light purplish-blue. The front door is bright yellow wood with a bronze doorknob. The colours are repeated in a little sign with old-fashioned lettering that hangs on hooks from the porch: THE CORNFLOWER COUNTRY INN.

Morris parks the car at the beginning of the long driveway and we get out and walk toward the house. The upper-floor windows of old houses always catch my eye. Ghosts like rooms with a view, just like everyone else. Here, all I can see are curtains.

As we're taking in the front of the house, the door opens and a woman who reminds me a little of Marilyn Monroe, only older, comes out onto the porch. She's got big wavy blonde hair, about chin length, and a fake-looking smile. Her small waist is squeezed in tight with a wide belt, but otherwise she's slightly plump. You can tell from her big round eyes that she's totally stressed. We introduce ourselves and shake hands. Hers feels clammy to me. Then she invites us inside.

Everything looks perfect, like in a magazine—old and expensive and clean. She must be loaded with money, and I bet she isn't more than forty. Maybe forty-five, it's hard to tell. Maybe she's had Botox or something. She takes us into a sitting room with two sofas and a fireplace, and on the way I catch sight of her dining room. It's huge and has three tables, like a mini-restaurant.

She's looking at Morris pretty closely. Trying to size him up, I guess. He seems self-conscious. I expect him to break out in a sweat any minute. She's all focused on him and ignoring me, asking him about the column he writes for the local paper, sounding impressed. He must be enjoying that, but I've heard it all before. Quietly I get off the couch and walk around the room a bit and listen. I pretend I'm checking out some framed photographs on a side table, then wander a little outside the room and back into the big hallway. I listen some more. I can hear faint music coming from somewhere, maybe the kitchen. I look up the staircase. This isn't the staircase she's having trouble with, I know that. Anyway, I'm not picking up anything. I hear Morris call my name and figure I'd better head back in.

Clarisse waits until I join them on the couch and then starts telling us about her mystery resident. About how she first heard the noise only a few days after she moved in. The sound of shuffling footsteps, slow steps that sound small, as if the person is kind of dragging his feet. She says that since then, she's heard it every two weeks or so. It's not super-loud, and if it were just a creaking floor she could ignore it, the house being old and all. What makes it so spooky and impossible to ignore is that the creaking sounds like somebody moving *through* the house. You can hear it going up and down the back stairs, and back and forth in the upstairs hall. You can hear the steps getting closer or farther away, she says. And it's freaking out her guests.

"When you hear it, does it remind you of an old person?" I ask.

"Maybe," she says, then thinks some more. "Yes, I'd say so."

"Does it sound like someone in hard shoes, or maybe shoes with heels?"

"Not really. More like slippers on a creaky floor."

I think of something else to ask. "And then there's another sound?"

"Yes, like someone getting strangled. Almost like croaking. An awful sound. It raises the hair on the back of your neck."

"Like someone in pain?"

"That's hard to say. I've only heard it once, but my guests have reported it twice. Very low and deep. It's not like anything I've heard before. It's horrific."

I'm starting to feel a little sorry for Clarisse, even though she seems spoilt rich. Then she looks at me as if something just clicked.

"You're the medium?" she asks. She furrows her brow. "How old are you?"

"I'm seventeen," I say, catching Morris looking surprised. "But," I add, feeling I have to defend myself, "I've been seeing ghosts for years and years."

"Really?" I can't tell if she believes me or not. There's a moment of silence, then she turns to Morris. "So, can you help?"

"Well," he starts cautiously, looking from her to me for reassurance before launching into a pitch, "it's not as though we have a set service to provide or anything. We just have an interest in, well, paranormal activity, and we do have some experience dealing with these things. We've developed theories, over time, about ghost behaviour. And you could say we're interested in seeing how they can be helped—the ghosts, I mean. It seems that a lot of troublesome ghost behaviour is a cry for help."

Interesting. I've never heard him put it that way before. I can't help wondering what Joyce would say if she heard him talk about our partnership like this.

"But do you do a . . . a seance? Is that how you go about it?"

Morris glances over at me and keeps eye contact as he answers. "Well, uh, a seance . . . we *could* do a seance, perhaps." It's as if he's trying to read my reaction to the idea.

I don't know what to say. I don't have a clue how to do a seance. Morris must be picking up my thoughts, because he changes his tone.

"Look, there's something we should be clear about first. We are willing to see if we can discover your ghost's identity, maybe even help you do something about getting it to leave, and the only payment we ask is that you don't breathe a word of our involvement to anyone. If you do, you're on your own. No one in this county knows anything about our work except our immediate families and Detective Grierson. And that's the way it has to stay. If you don't think you can keep this confidential, then this is where it ends."

Wow! My jaw drops before I can catch it, and I'm pretty sure I'm blinking as badly as Ethan. Morris makes it sound like we're some kind of professionals who have been working together for years. Cool. Also scary—because he makes it sound like we know what we're doing, which we don't. We are definitely only guessing. I look over at Clarisse. She's nodding like crazy, and she touches a hand to his knee.

"Oh my goodness, I wouldn't dream of ever, ever telling anyone anything about this. Honestly! The last thing I'd want is for this to get around. You wouldn't believe how hard it was for me to call the police. Thank God it was Detective Grierson who responded. He's not like the others. Not so much 'by the book.'" Morris looks over at me when she says that. "If this got out, my business would be ruined before it even had a chance. I have big plans. *Big plans*. I'm a really great cook. My little inn will be in a Michelin Guide someday, I know it will. But not if it's being haunted by some horrible ghost!" Her face is getting red and she looks like she's about to lose it. "It's a nightmare. I don't know where else to turn."

As I listen to her, I find myself thinking about her ghost, somewhere inside this house right now, maybe even watching us. It must have a good reason for acting the way it is. For being . . . tormented. Something must be wrong.

I jump in and suggest we go upstairs, "So you can show us exactly where you think the footsteps are coming from." I figure that if we're going to act like this is a job, we'd better get to work.

She gets to her feet and asks us to follow her, taking us through the big front hall, around the main staircase and through the large kitchen at the back. *Wow*, I'm thinking. *There's a lot of chrome in here.* Along the far wall of the kitchen there's a door. She reaches for a ring of keys hanging on a hook off the side of a high cupboard and unlocks the door. It opens onto a short dark hallway with a side door leading outside and a narrow, steep staircase. She switches on a faint wall light and tells us that, most often, the mysterious footsteps can be heard on these stairs that lead to the back hall of the upper floor.

We start climbing, with Clarisse leading the way. The steps are definitely creaky. I'm trying to concentrate on what I'm feeling, but I'm not picking up anything. At the top of the staircase there's another door. It opens onto a hallway and we are facing entrances to two bedrooms. Again, very swank decor, like in a decorating magazine. The hallway turns a corner, then has a long stretch with more doors on one side, and windows facing the back garden on the other. She tells us the bedroom at the far end is hers.

We stand in the hallway for a bit. Morris keeps an eye on me, like maybe I'm going to start beeping if a ghost enters my radar. I give him a blank look. There's not much happening here. Morris tells Clarisse that we'd like to think about all she's told us, do some basic research on the history of the house, then get back to her. She nods but looks disappointed. Maybe she thought we'd offer a faster fix.

"Would you like to head down by the back staircase again?" she asks.

"Why not?" Morris says.

I'm on the top step, with Morris ahead of me behind Clarisse, when I feel it. A cold, cobwebby sensation over my face and arms. I freeze on the stair with a shudder, a feeling of remorse washing over me—so intense that it hurts. Then it's gone. A few steps below, Morris has heard me stop. He whips around and squints at me. Then he nods slightly and turns to continue down the staircase, pretending that nothing has happened.

5

I spent time this afternoon going through old records at the town hall, scribbling down a list of all the people who've ever owned Clarisse's house, and now I'm trying to read my awful handwriting, sitting at my desk in my bedroom, typing out names and dates on my computer. But more than that, I'm trying not to think so much about what happened last night. That's what's really on my mind.

Around eight o'clock my cellphone rang, which doesn't happen that often. I saw the long distance number and knew it was Kip. I could barely get out a "Hello."

"Just checking up on you," he said casually. "Seeing if you're still alive and all."

Hearing the sound of his voice brought everything back, as if he'd never left. But he sounded distant, and not just because of all the miles between us. Like he wasn't absolutely sure he wanted to talk to me. Anyway, I probably sounded like a stunned idiot at first, but I managed to pull myself together, and I asked him about school and his new classes and that kind of thing. Trying not to act giddy or immature.

We chatted for about fifteen minutes. Then he said, "I'm thinking of coming up to visit Dad over March break, so I thought maybe we could meet up sometime that week. If you . . . feel like it."

That's next week, I thought. *Oh my God!*

I wanted to beg him, "Please, please come!" Instead I was all "Oh, well . . . it would be nice to see you again. We could fill you in on our latest adventure." My heart was pounding and my mind played a flashback of his arms around me, his lips on mine. It's hopeless. Honestly, I can't wait to see him. *Please, please come!*

But right now, I should stick to business. Get these names and dates written down so I can show them to Morris. He said that if I found the names and looked up phone numbers, he'd make the calls. Like the old Telford farm, this place has changed hands a few times since it was built back in 1872. Looks like the first owners kept it in their family for three generations—the McNabbs. Then there were new owners, the Parsons, in 1934, and in 1976 the Carmichaels. But since 1994 there have been a whole bunch of owners. I'm counting six in all, including Clarisse.

I'm betting that one of the family members who lived in that house never actually left. But which one? Someone who died there probably. It is kind of suspicious that people moved in and out so much over the last twenty years or so.

Like maybe something was driving them out.

We figure we should start by tracking down the most recent past owner and then working backwards, asking each one if they ever heard strange noises in the house. Then maybe we can figure out who heard the noises first.

There's a light knock on my bedroom door. "Who is it?"

"Me. Can I come in?" It's Ethan.

"What do you want?"

"Nothing."

I let out a sigh. "Come in." And he does. I'm not crazy about him being in my room, period, but I've been trying to be nicer to him since that whole drama of him being possessed by a ghost a few months ago. I felt so sorry for him. But I can't shake the feeling that he's a natural-born spy. "What do you want, really?"

"*Nothing.* Just wondering what you're doing. I'm bored."

"Where's Joyce?"

"Out."

"Finished your homework?"

"Yes. Mostly." He hovers over my desk.

"Ethan, do you mind?" He's picked up a pen and he's clicking it to some dumb rhythm.

"I'm not hurting you, am I?"

"No. But you aren't helping me either."

"Well . . . I want to help."

"Good. Then leave me in peace. I'm trying to concentrate." I focus on my list.

"I mean it. I want to help. You're doing some ghost stuff for Morris, right? I can tell."

"Well, Joyce wouldn't want you to help, then, would she?"

"Maybe not. But maybe Mom would."

"Nice try," I say, not bothering to look up from my desk.

"I'm serious. Mom would. I know for a fact."

I spin in my chair to face him. "Are you kidding? You don't know what you're talking about."

"Mom told me I should help you more."

I look at him with disbelief. "Like I said, nice try. When? How old were you when she said that? Five?"

"Last year," he mumbles.

"WHAT?"

He mumbles again, "Last year."

"Come on, Mom's been gone more than three years. What are you talking about?"

"A dream I had."

"Uh . . . let's get this straight. You had a dream last year where Mom asked you to help me?"

"That's right." Now he sounds defensive and hurt.

"And you never said anything?" No surprise, I'm thinking. He only thought up the story just now.

"Because I thought she was talking about doing dishes and stuff, ALL RIGHT?" He's getting red-faced and angry.

"Well, I'd say you were right! She *was* talking about dishes and stuff. You should listen to your mother more, Ethan." Mean, I know, but sometimes he asks for this. He doesn't really do much of anything around the house. It's not my fault if this little fib has backfired on him.

"Fine, but I don't think so. Not since I got possessed by that ghost." I throw a surprised look at him and he straightens up in defiance. "Yeah. Everybody thinks I'm too dumb to know what happened in that barn. Well, I'm not so dumb, you know. I could hear that ghost. I could *feel* it."

His lower lip quivers but his jaw is clenched. The poor kid! And we all assumed that he had no idea what had happened. What has the experience done to him? And how did he keep it to himself all this time? I'm trying to think what to say when he turns his back and leaves the bedroom, slamming the door behind him, thumping down the stairs like he's twice his weight. The TV set turns on and a video game soundtrack kicks in. I sit at my desk and try to think. Ethan heard the ghost? He felt it inside him? *Is there more to Ethan than I realized?*

I get up and slowly, reluctantly, head downstairs and stand at the living room entrance. He's focused on the video game, his face intense and angry, his thumbs punching the controls like he's trying to break something. I just stand there and watch him. Finally I think of something to say. I know he can hear me above the sound effects, but he keeps his eyes on the screen.

"Ethan, I'm sorry. I didn't realize you knew about the possession. That must have been . . . scary. And you must still feel weird about it. But you didn't have to keep it to yourself."

"Why not?" he says, without looking up. "I can keep a secret too, you know." I'm starting to feel awful.

"Fine. Like I said, I'm sorry. But that doesn't mean you should say stuff about Mom like that. Just to get what you want."

"That was the truth," he shoots back, this time looking at me with hurt eyes.

I sigh. "Okay, if you say so. Then tell me about this so-called dream. What was Mom doing?"

He pauses as if he's remembering something, then starts playing the video again. "She was in the backyard, gardening," he says flatly, like he's tired of talking to me. "Happy?"

Now it's my turn for tears. Mom was gardening in the backyard? Just like every single time I saw her ghost, for more than two years, from the day after she died to the day we moved out of Owen Sound? The day she finally looked up at my bedroom window and raised her hand to say goodbye. Mom's ghost hanging out in the garden—that was my little secret.

———

47

An hour later, I call Ethan from the top of the stairs. He appears in the hallway and I ask if he'd mind coming upstairs for a minute. I want to ask him something.

He stands at my doorway, still sulking, distrustful. "Okay, Ethan. How would you like to help me with an investigation I'm doing for Morris? Top secret." Of course, his eyes light up and his mouth twitches into a smile.

"Yeah! What? What do I have to do? Is it about ghosts? I *knew* it! Did you find a new place that's haunted?"

"Wait—you know that if you ever tell anyone outside the family about this, you are dead, right?"

"Yeah, yeah. Joyce told me. I'm not talking, I swear. Are you kidding? No way. Never."

"Okay, fine, I believe you." Ugh. Trusting Ethan doesn't come easy to me. "Here's the deal. Do you think you could do an Internet search for me? All I need are addresses and phone numbers. If I give you a list of names, could you see how many people you can track down? And if it's a common name, list the addresses and phone numbers of all the people with that name. And focus on people living in Ontario, for now."

"Okay, sure. Um . . . sure. So what's this about? What do you need them for? Are you looking for something special? A ghost or something?" That's the only thing he cares about—whether this is about ghosts.

"Maybe." I give him the names of five owners, the most recent ones before Clarisse. I show him the website he can use to do the search, and I type in the first name on the list to show him what I mean. Three people show up. I tell him to put the ones with our area code, "519," first, and copy down the full addresses and phone numbers. It's not a big job, but it will make him feel he's helping. He's crazy excited.

"But be cool, okay? I'm not saying this is a big secret from Joyce—I'm going to tell her about it eventually—but I want to do it myself, when I have more information. So don't go all hyper, acting like there's some big fat mystery going on, or she'll get suspicious. Try not to even think about it around her. You know how she reads minds."

He practically runs out of my room with the list. I jump up and call after him, "Ethan, did Joyce say where she was going?"

"Yeah, she's visiting her friend with the hip surgery."

I haven't dropped in on Matthew for a week. Maybe this is an okay time to slip out, while Joyce is away and Ethan's got something to do.

"I'm going for a bike ride, for some exercise," I yell.

That's been my line for a while now. It works quite well. I've been riding south on 12th Line and making my way over to 11th Line, and then north to 18th Sideroad and back home. It's a really good workout and, best of all, everybody seems to buy it. What they don't know is that, each time, I stop at the Telford farm and check on Matthew. I never stay too long because I'm nervous about someone driving by and seeing me. It's lucky there are so few cars on this road.

Although the place is sold, it should be a while before anyone moves in. Matthew says they're going to totally renovate the house first, so there could be months of contractors banging around. I honestly don't know how that's going to go, and whether Matthew will behave himself. One thing's obvious: he's determined to stay.

I hear the bulldozer before I see it, moving leftover debris from the barn fire into a huge pile, then scooping it up and dumping it into big bins with the name of some haulage company on the side. Looks like they've been at it for a while. When they're done, the new people can plant a vegetable garden or something and no one will ever guess what awful stuff happened there. It's hallowed ground now, Morris says. Hallowed as in *Halloween*. I slow down on my bike, trying to decide if I should even stop. Obviously I can't go inside to see Matthew, not with this guy working outside.

Once I'm directly in front of the farm, I decide to get off my bike and make like I'm trying to fix something on the back wheel. The guy riding the bulldozer pays no attention to me. He's too busy working up a cloud of ash, scraping up and dumping heaps of black junk into those bins, making a racket. I peer at the upstairs bedroom window, Matthew's favourite lookout. Sure enough, he's standing there at the glass, staring down at me. He lifts a hand slowly and gives me a little wave with his fingers. I check that the bulldozer guy isn't looking my way, and I give him a quick wave back. Then I see that he's holding something. It's that stupid doll— and she's waving too. *Ugh!* That gives me a cold shiver. I shake my head disapprovingly, point to the guy riding the bulldozer, and get back on my bike and ride south down 12th Line.

Sometimes I worry that being a ghost is seriously messing with Matthew's judgment.

I'm helping to clear up the dishes from breakfast when Kip calls and asks if I'm free to go for a drive this afternoon. I actually drop a bowl, which thank God doesn't break.

"What was that?" he asks.

"Oh, nothing." He's calling from Morris's house. He arrived in town last night. I try to answer him nonchalantly, as if I'm just another friend from college. "A drive? Uh . . . sure!"

After I hang up, all I can think about is what to wear. Why is it that every time I try to dress for something with Kip, I end up feeling that my clothes look like hand-me-downs from my brothers? I turn my closet upside down, trying to find something remotely sexy. *Remotely.* I come up with nothing. So I do what I usually do when I'm desperate. I call Morgan, asking for some female guidance. Besides, I can't not tell her Kip is in town. Anyway, she guesses right away.

"The gorgeous Kip Dyson? How did I know?" she teases me. "So far, he's the only reason you've ever asked me for fashion advice." And then she lays into me. "Okay, Amelia. I thought you'd totally blown it, but apparently not. The gods are giving you one more chance. And you've got a lot of ground to cover, my dear. I'm thinking red. Your red sweater with the long sleeves. The one you wore at the school assembly. Very nice. The tightest jeans you own. Skip lunch if you have to. Padded push-up bra if possible, as long as it's not beige."

I manage to cut in. "Morgan, you're reading way too much into this."

"Don't interrupt. Matching panties if you've got. Or any colour but beige. Now please don't get distracted this time. Stay focused."

I have to laugh. Considering that Morgan doesn't know anything about my secret life, she seems to get the big picture accurately enough. She's absolutely right. I've got to avoid getting distracted. By thoughts of Matthew . . . or ghosts . . . or girls at Kip's university, because I can't help wondering if he's involved with any of them.

"I've got to tell you, Morgan, now I'm *really* feeling the pressure."

"Good. Pressure is a part of life. Embrace it."

Usually when we talk, it's all about her adventures, which is fine with me. For one thing, her life is so entertaining, and for another, I can't tell her about most of mine. I'm always grateful that she talks to me at all, since she has lots of other friends to choose from. Maybe she likes the variety. I'm her "weird" friend. Of course, she doesn't know the half of it.

It's been a long time since the topic of Kip came up between us. She always used to say he was waiting for a sign from me. The ball was in my court, she'd say. She figured I was just stalling because of my lack of experience, and my being such a coward. Which was partly true, but not the whole picture. How could she know that Matthew was still in my life, and that things with him were becoming more complicated all the time?

What she *did* know was that things had been heating up between me and Kip around Christmas, but then something bad had happened. She knew that he had moved back to Chicago early in January, and that I had suffered from major heartache that was too awful to talk about. She always tells me that I'm still in love with Kip.

"In case you didn't know," she says. "Don't even try to deny it. It's so obvious."

I thank her and promise to report back. "But—reality check—he's only asked if I want to go for a drive. This could go absolutely nowhere. I'm not sure I need special *underwear*."

"It's not for him, it's for you. For your confidence. And don't be so negative," she says before hanging up. "A drive is perfect."

"Joyce?" I call from upstairs as I hear her come into the kitchen from the back porch. She's been out with the horses, as usual. "Have you seen my red sweater? The one with the really long sleeves? I haven't seen it in weeks." I'm responsible for handwashing my own stuff, but Joyce does the washing-machine laundry for the family. I hope I didn't put that sweater in the hamper. I hope she didn't stick it in the dryer and shrink it.

She comes to the bottom of the stairs and looks up at me. "No, young lady. I did not see your red sweater with the sleeves so long you can't eat without dipping the ends in your food."

That's so Joyce. But it's good news. I've put it somewhere and it must still be there. *It didn't get up and walk off by itself, did it?* That's one of her favourite lines. And that reminds me of Matthew thinking how clever he is, getting his doll to move by itself. Oh my God, is he practising the art of possession? *Matthew, don't go rogue on me.*

"What's the special occasion?" Joyce calls up as I head back to my room to search again.

"What do you mean?"

"Why are you suddenly anxious about your red sweater? What's up?"

See what I mean? And when she catches you trying to pretend nothing's up when something definitely is, she really enjoys it. You can tell. I've learned that sometimes there's no point in denying it.

"I'm seeing Kip this afternoon," I answer from inside my bedroom, trying to sound casual. "He's up from Chicago for a few days visiting his dad, and he phoned and asked if I wanted to go for a drive." *Happy?* I almost add, but I don't want to sound like Ethan.

"Ah. Kip. And how is Kip?"

"I don't know yet, but I'll ask when I see him."

I finally find my red sweater. It's on the floor at the back of my closet, where it must have fallen. It's still on the hanger. Morgan's right, it's the closest thing I've got to something nice. Now I have to figure out which jeans to wear, and that's going to affect which shoes I wear. Or should I wear my boots? Mid-March and it's still pretty cold, though there's hardly any snow on the ground. But there are some icy patches. I'm sure we'll have at least one more big winter storm before spring arrives, but I hope it's not today. I don't want anything to interfere with this drive.

I'm sitting on my bed, thinking about boots versus shoes, when there's a knock. It's Ethan.

"What next?" he asks, handing me two sheets of lined paper with about twenty names, addresses and phone numbers hand-written in pencil.

I look at the list. He really did do a good job. Maybe he can be useful after all.

"Thanks, Ethan."

"Now what happens?" he prods.

"Nothing happens. I give it to Morris, that's all. Good job. Thanks."

"But is there anything else I can do?"

"Not really. Not now. But this is good. I'll let you know if there's anything else. Honest."

He looks disappointed. "Where are you going?" he asks.

"Out," I say, and gently shut the door on him.

I'd better go with the boots.

6

As we drive south on 12th Line, I steal a sideways glance. His hair is still thick and longish and dark gold. Eyes crystal blue. The shadow of a beard. The face of an angel. Chicago hasn't changed him much. He's still . . . perfect.

I was so happy to see Kip when he came to the door that at first I thought I would start crying. But I didn't. It was one of those fast hugs through winter coats. No eye contact. A little awkward. He stepped inside the house just long enough to say hi to Ethan and Joyce, and ask after Jack.

We approach the Telford farm down the hill on our left, and I feel myself go tense. He asks me if it bothers me to see it.

I try to relax and shrug. "Not really. I don't know." I add, "I ride my bike past here all the time." I think about Matthew in the attic, or maybe in the upper bedroom.

"Wow, I see they've bulldozed the barn. You wouldn't guess it was ever even there."

"Yeah. The new owners are going to start renovating any day."
He glances my way and I wonder if he's asking himself how I know
that. "That's what I've heard, anyway," I add. "From Joyce."

He drives by the farmhouse, hardly slowing down or even looking at it. But then, why would the house mean anything to him?
I focus on the road ahead. I couldn't handle seeing Matthew in the
window right now.

"So where are we going?"

He looks across at me and smiles. "Well, where do you want to
go? You're the Grey County tour guide."

I think fast. "Well, um . . . we could drive by our latest haunted
house. Did your dad tell you about it? It's a country inn. Only
about fifteen minutes from here."

It's hard to read his face. I can't tell if he's interested. After a
moment he says, "Sure. Why not?"

I give him the general directions. "And then maybe we could
go for a walk." I'm flashing back to the last time we took a walk,
on the Bruce Trail. We kissed. It was a high point of my life, is all.

"Sure," he says again.

I hope he's not just saying that, and already feeling bored. There's
another pause before he speaks again. He keeps his eyes on the road.

"So what's new, Amelia? What's happening?"

I smirk. "You're kidding, right? Can't you tell there's nothing
new? Nothing's happening."

"That's not true. I don't believe you." He smiles again. "You
look good. New boyfriend at school?"

I can feel myself blush. "Yeah, right." Not a very witty response.
"Besides, you know those boys in my school are too young for me.
Not enough life experience."

"Not enough *death* experience, you mean?"

"Not nice," I say.

"You're right. Not nice."

There's silence, and a sigh slips out of me. It's so frustrating having to play games with Kip and hide my feelings. *Exasperating—* that's the word. He glances at me with a perplexed expression, then looks back out at the road.

"Ah, maybe you're right. Not much has changed. Same old enigmatic Amelia."

"What about you, Mr. Dyson? What's new with you? New girlfriend at school?"

It took some nerve to ask, but I figure we have to clear the air somehow. When there's another long pause, I get a sinking feeling that I've nailed it. I feel that familiar heartache, but at the same time I tell myself to hurry up and accept it. *At least we're still friends. That's better than nothing. Way better.*

"Kind of." Another pause. "An Amelia substitute," he adds.

"Really?" I look at him. "You mean . . . she's like me?"

"No. She's nothing like you."

Right. More embarrassment. I give my head a spastic shake, trying to make sense of him. Okay, fine.

"I'm kidding!" He laughs, reaches out and pokes my shoulder. "She's just a nice person, that's all. A good friend."

"With benefits?" Again, I'm cringing at my own words. I wish I'd just shut up sometimes.

He looks over at me, saying nothing, with a half-smile turning into something less comfortable. Does he think I'm being crass? Immature? Pointing out the obvious? Time to change the subject.

"So, turn right here," I say. "It's just a few minutes down this road."

"If I wanted them." His voice drops and he looks away. "Benefits, I mean."

"Ah." I knew it, I just knew it. But it still feels like a shock to the heart.

"But . . . no," he mumbles, so I can barely hear.

"Oh." I suddenly feel depressed. Face it, it's only a matter of time. My eyes sting a little and I can't hear anymore. My fault for getting into territory I can't handle.

There's an awkward silence till we reach the property.

"So, this Cornflower Inn," I say, with forced cheerfulness. "It's really beautiful, like in a magazine. The problem is that she's got this ghost wandering around, scaring her overnight guests. It's not only spooky, it's a major problem for her business. She's afraid that rumours will spread and no one will want to stay in a haunted house."

"Maybe she should just go with it. Like a theme park. She could call it The Haunted Bed and Breakfast."

I laugh. "Well, maybe that's plan B, but for now she wants it to pack its bags and leave. Besides, it's not a happy ghost. All moaning and groaning and shuffling around in the middle of the night."

"Creepy. So how are you going to get rid of this guy? You'll have to pull an overnighter here. Stay up with a flashlight."

"Right—I can just see Joyce letting me do a sleepover with Morris at a haunted house." The very idea of asking her makes me laugh.

He laughs too. "Maybe I could stand in for Morris," he adds.

Somehow, that strikes me as less funny. He once said I was mean, but sometimes I think he's the mean one. As if spending the night together would be no big deal. Maybe not for him.

Just past the forest there's a meadow and then the big house. I suggest he stop the car out front for a minute. He pulls over to the side of the road.

"She says the ghost wanders around in the hallway on the second floor, toward the back of the house. And the back staircase. A door in the kitchen opens onto a staircase that was originally for servants, leading to the upstairs hall. The second floor hallway's an L shape, and her own bedroom is down at one far end, with the staircase opening up around the corner at the other end."

"Sounds like the ghost of a murdered servant. I'm guessing the butler did it. Knife, kitchen, butler."

"Possible. Likely, even. Mystery solved. Well done."

"It was nothing."

We both grin, catching each other's eye, then quickly look away.

"But solving the mystery might be the easy part. Getting the guy to leave the house, that's trickier. Did I mention that the owner looks like an aging Marilyn Monroe?"

"No, but you should have mentioned that first." I'm pretty sure he's joking, but it's still slightly unnerving to think about him and Clarisse. Him and . . . anyone.

"Yeah. I think your poor dad was having trouble concentrating on her story. Didn't he mention it?"

Kip laughs. "No. But Dad gave up on women years ago. My mom said he was already pretty seriously negative when she met him, and I think, when she left him, that was the nail in the coffin, romantically speaking. Anyway, if he was a pessimist when he met Mom, he's a total non-believer now. With one exception, maybe. I think he had a crush on your mother."

"Oh God, I don't want to hear about that. But there's something kind of sad about him. Like his heart got permanently broken. No wonder he seems to live for ghost-tracking."

"Yeah. His one true love."

"Anyway, he actually suggested to Clarisse that we might hold a seance. Can you believe it? To summon the ghost."

"Damn, I want to be there for that. Can you do it soon, before I have to leave?"

"I don't know. I mean, what do I know about holding a seance? Nothing, except from the movies."

"That's probably all there is to know."

After a few minutes we've had enough of looking at the house. Kip does a U-turn and heads back in the direction we came from. There's thick forest on either side of us, and I'm scanning for a sign marking an entry point into the Bruce Trail, but there isn't one. Instead, I see something lying by the side of the road. At first I think it's a large dog, then I realize it's a deer.

"Oh!"

"What?"

"Stop the car! I think we just passed an injured deer. It must have been hit by a car. I think it's still moving. We should call somebody."

Kip is looking in his rear-view mirror. "Nobody else has been by this way since we came. I don't see anything. Where? Which side?"

"There, on the right, back there! On the gravel by the edge of the trees. I didn't notice it when we drove past the first time."

Kip pulls the car over and stops. "Where? I still don't see anything."

I get out of the car. There it is, about two hundred feet back. A deer lying on its side, front legs flailing, head lifting off the ground, then falling back. Now it's struggling to move along the gravel. Dragging itself toward the trees, back into the woods. Pulling itself along with its front legs, its back legs trailing behind. I see it disappearing into the woods.

"Where is it?" Kip's out of the car and standing beside me.

"You didn't see it?"

He shakes his head.

I point down the road. "It kind of dragged itself away on its belly. It's . . . it's gone now." I strain my eyes. In my last glimpse of the animal pulling itself along the ground, I saw something strange.

"I know this is going to sound crazy, but I think it was wearing a pink jacket."

7

ip is looking at me with his mouth open in disbelief, slowly forming a smile. "Come on. You're not serious. You're *not* serious, are you?"

"What? I'm just telling you what I saw. A pink jacket. Okay, maybe it wasn't a deer wearing a pink jacket. But . . . it looked like a deer to me. And I could swear I saw a pink jacket."

"Amelia, if you saw a four-legged animal wearing a pink jacket, that can only mean one thing. It was a *dog*, escaped from downtown Toronto. I'm pretty sure I saw a dog in a pink jacket there. With matching boots, as I recall."

"I'm serious. Okay, maybe it wasn't a deer, but it sure looked like one. At least, it did right up until . . ."

"Until when?"

"Now I'm not sure. But . . . it was moving strangely along the ground."

We stand there on the side of the road. I'm slowly realizing the truth of the situation: either that deer was an apparition, or the pink jacket was. Something had to be.

"Kip?"

"Yes, Amelia?" He says my name as if he's expecting the worst.

"How would you feel about taking a short walk into the forest?"

"And leave the car at the side of the road?"

"Yeah. Just for a minute. I need to check something out."

"It wasn't really a deer, was it?"

I look at him, feeling I owe him an apology. "Maybe not."

"Well, what the hell. I guess I asked for this." He turns back to the car and locks it.

Most of the trees in the forest are pine and spruce, but the undergrowth isn't thick, on account of the winter. There's still some snow on the ground, and even a bit of ice. But there's no sign of any injured animal, no tracks where it might have dragged itself along, and nothing pink, either, for as far as I can see. I'd say I was imagining things, except . . . didn't I see a flash of pink as I drove by here with Morris last week?

Kip suddenly points to something in the distance, through an opening in the trees. "What's that?"

I jump. "What? Where?"

"Looks like an old tree fort."

I see what he's pointing at. "Oh, that. No, that's just a deer stand. Deer hunters hang out on those, waiting for deer to pass by below them. The deer travel in little groups, like family clans, and they usually walk in single file, and the hunters shoot at them as they go past. Deer stands are pretty common in the woods around here. They can be a hundred years old, some of them. That's a really old one."

I look around and realize we're on the edge of a swamp. You almost wouldn't know, because the ground is mostly still frozen with a thin layer of snow on it. You can tell from how the trees standing in it are all thin and dark and dead. Long dead. The deer stand is about ten feet inside the swamp.

"Well, it looks like a tree fort to me. So the poor deer get picked off by snipers in front of their kin. That's cruel."

"You like venison stew, don't you?"

"You're cruel too."

We take a few more steps and I realize we're now standing on ice. Frozen swampland. I stop. "Probably isn't very thick at this time of year," I say, looking down. The swamp water may not be deep, and I wore boots, after all, but Kip is in trainers.

"I've never seen a live deer close up," he says. "That would be amazing. I'd like to hang out on that deer stand till some come by. Do you think we'd have to wait long?"

"Yes. If they come this way, it's probably only once a day."

As he takes a few more steps toward the stand, I hear a cracking sound.

"Kip, I don't think this ice is going to hold you, and who knows how deep the water is?"

"Can't we just—" and with a crunch his right foot breaks through, plunging into frigid water up to his knee. "Damn!" he yells, "COLD!" As he struggles to lift his leg out of the ice water, the other foot breaks through, and he turns back to me, knee-deep in the freezing water, yelling, "Friggin' freezing COLD!"

"Oh my God!" I can't help it, I start laughing. I have to cover my face with my hands to try to compose myself. "I am *so sorry* for laughing. It's not funny. Believe me, I know." I'm trying desperately to stop. "Okay, don't move. Let's think what's the best way to get you out." I'm backing off the ice myself, to the edge of the frozen swamp.

"What? You're going to leave me in here like this?" He's laughing too, but swearing under his breath. "Friggin' cold."

"There's a rock behind you. If you can get onto that, maybe you can get back to solid ground a little farther along. Maybe the ice is thicker that way. Can you try to get over there, onto that rock?" With each step the ice around him breaks. It's hopeless. I hold up my hands to my face, half alarmed, half laughing. "Oh my God, Kip, I'm so sorry." I hate myself for being so amused. I'd be dying if that were me.

"What rock?" he asks, and starts to twist around, but he loses his balance and falls backwards over something in the water, crashing through more thin ice, flat onto his backside in the icy swamp. He's on his feet again in a nanosecond, but not fast enough. He's drenched to the waist.

Now I'm really horrified, and he's letting loose a string of curses, not angry so much as surprised, like he can't believe this is happening to him. In jeans soaked and heavy with freezing swamp water, and his jacket pretty wet too, he wades toward me, crunching ice with every step until he's out and standing beside me, soaked and shivering like crazy.

"Why is it that when I'm with you, something bad always happens to me?" He's gritting his teeth, his arms held out from his sides, and looking down at his jeans. "Why is that?" He clasps his frozen, wet hands to the sides of my head and gives me a playful shake.

"Ooh, that's cold!" I shriek.

I grasp his shoulders. I'm trying so hard to keep a straight face. "Kip, we've got to get you back to my place. I'm sure there'll be some old clothes of Jack's that you can change into."

We hurry through the forest to the road and head for Morris's car, poor Kip making sloshing noises with each step.

"I can't get into the car like this," he says. "Cloth seats. I'll soak them."

"You can sit on my coat." I'm pulling it off. "Is there anything in the back that you can . . . change into?"

He opens the doors, sticks his head in the back seat and pulls out an old blanket.

"I guess this is it." He looks at me, lifting his eyebrows. "A little privacy?"

I quickly turn my back to him, and hear him cursing, struggling to peel off the soaked denim. I'm fighting not to look at him, eyes focused down 28th Sideroad. There are no cars in sight, thank goodness.

"Damn. Got to get the shoes off," he mutters, and he curses some more, hopping on one foot—his shoes are stuck in the legs of his jeans, I figure—and then leaning against the car door.

"Can I help?"

"I can manage, thanks anyway."

I hear the back door open and the heavy jeans hit the floor, then his jacket with soaked sleeves, and I hear him open the driver's door and get in. I turn and open the passenger door and slip in, finally looking over at him, a scratchy-looking brown wool blanket wrapped around his narrow hips like a towel. I start to take off my coat again.

"Put this around your shoulders?"

"No thanks. It'll only get wet. You keep it, I'm okay."

"Oh." I don't know what else to say. "Did I tell you how sorry I am?" I'm looking him in the face, trying not to look down. No matter how sincere I am, I'm still fighting this smile. He looks adorable.

"If you really feel sorry for me, prove it by putting on the other blanket back there. If we're stopped by the cops, I don't want to be the only one wearing a blanket."

I laugh nervously and glance at the back seat. There's no other blanket there. He's just teasing.

He starts the engine and cranks up the heater.

"I swear I never saw that coming," I say.

His face goes serious. "You aren't a witch or something, are you? I mean, on top of everything else?"

I grin and shake my head. "I honestly don't think so. What did you trip over, anyway? A branch?"

"No, something metal . . . You're not going to upload pictures of me, my ass in the swamp, on Facebook, I hope."

"Never! I would never do that to you. Besides, I hate that stuff." I have a flashback to party pictures someone in Chicago posted last year, a college girl with her eyes on Kip, looking hungry like a vampire.

When we pull into the driveway back home, I ask him what he wants to do—stay in the car while I run in and bring out some pants, or come inside and change in Jack's room.

"Can you bring something out to me? I'm really not keen to walk around Joyce's house in a blanket." He's still shivering. I check that the heater's on high.

"Got it. I'll be quick." I get out and run into the house.

Ethan jumps up from the TV to meet me. "What's happening?"

"A little emergency. Kip is outside in the car and he needs to borrow a pair of jeans."

"Really? Where are his own jeans?"

I search through Jack's drawers, pull out a pair of denims. "They got soaked. He went through the ice in a swamp in the woods." Jack's pretty heavy-set compared to Kip. The kids at school call him the Hulk. Will these jeans even stay up? I run back out and Kip rolls down the window. He looks really cold. His lips are turning blue. I shove Jack's pair of jeans through.

"They're probably a bit big and too short for you, but they're dry."

67

"Thanks." He loosens the blanket and I spin around to put my back to him. Take a deep breath.

"Um . . . would you like to come inside to warm up for a bit? I could make you some tea or hot chocolate? Find you some dry socks?" I hear his fly zip up.

"You know what? Thanks anyway, but I'd like to get home and into a hot shower. How about I call you tomorrow?"

"Sure. Okay. I mean, I'm off school this week too, so I'm free anytime. If you are. When do you have to get back? To Chicago?"

"Oh, in a few days. I've got an open bus ticket to Buffalo."

"Oh. Well, I guess I'll talk to you tomorrow, then?" I touch his shoulder through the open window. I wish I could do more, but he's still shivering. He smiles and nods, and when I pull back my hand he rolls up the window.

As he backs out of the driveway he waves, then takes off up the road, leaving me full of regret, as usual.

This was definitely *not* Morgan's idea of a romantic afternoon.

8

I talked to Morgan last night and filled her in on our disaster date. It was nothing like a date, I had to tell her.

"Did he actually call her his *girlfriend*?"

"Not exactly, no. 'A good friend' is how he described her. I asked if they were friends 'with benefits.' He said no, but he sounded like he's thought about it."

"Hmm. Well, I'm impressed you had the nerve to ask. Well done."

"I'm trying to get real about Kip. I hate getting my hopes up for nothing."

"I don't know. I think getting your hopes up is good for you."

"Well, like I said, he's got someone he's . . . hanging out with."

"His problem. You let him worry about that."

That's Morgan. She's very practical.

Since there's no school this week, I don't know why I'm so awake at eight a.m. As I lie in bed, part of me can't stop thinking about Kip in his underwear under his brown blanket in the car, and the other part of me is thinking about that injured deer by the side of the road. It sure looked injured. Unless it was faking it.

I talked to Morris last night too. He knew what state Kip had returned home in, and he wanted to know what the heck we'd gotten up to. He laughed about it. But he doesn't approve of there being anything too personal between me and Kip, I realize that now. It's obvious he thinks it would end badly. He's just one of those people who don't believe in happy endings. I understand where he's coming from, believe me, 'cause I've often felt like that myself. But that doesn't mean I don't want to risk getting hurt by Kip. I think Morris is trying to protect both of us, which is nice of him, I guess.

Anyway, the reason Morris called was to tell me about a few of the phone calls he's made to former owners of the inn. He only managed to get hold of three people on the list, but he says that was enough, because one of the guys happened to be the first of those owners—the guy who bought the place in 1994.

"And he was the most direct of the three," he said. "He didn't hesitate, didn't care who I was or why I wanted to know. He said the place was haunted—'Damn right,' he said, just like that. So that means we can keep trying to track down the later owners if we want, for research, to gather more info about the ghost, but now we know that the ghost predates all of them."

"So it's going to come down to three families, then," I say. "The McNabbs, the Parsons and"—I double-check the list in front of me—"the Carmichaels. That makes it a little easier. I wonder if any of them had servants or housekeepers."

"Yep. House like that, probably. I'm guessing there's something fishy with the Carmichaels, 'cause all hell breaks loose after *they* sell the house, with later owners coming and going on a yearly basis."

"So . . . what next?"

"Well, that's up to you. How would you feel about going back to the inn? See if you can establish communication with this ghost? You've already had some kind of contact."

"Yeah, I felt a presence. But do you mean like in a seance? You know I've never done anything like that."

"It might be worth a try. There's a long tradition of holding seances in places thought to be haunted. Presumably it sometimes works."

I'm listening to that energy he gets in his voice when he talks about ghosts. I take a deep breath and sigh. I'd feel bad turning him down. "I'm not against holding a seance. I just don't know how."

Morris says there's really nothing to know, and I should just follow my gut. What's the worst that could happen? Then he says Kip is keen to come along. *Flashback: Kip wrapped in a blanket.* He asks if I'd mind.

"Uh, no. Of course not." *Hardly.*

"The only question is whether we should say anything to Joyce first. We more or less promised we would."

I don't answer that. I just know I don't want to be the one to talk to her.

There's a pause.

"Morris, there's another thing I want to mention. I think something strange is going on in that forest, along the road, just before you get to the inn."

"Like what?"

"I'm not sure. But something . . . pink. I don't know. Maybe nothing. I've just seen something pink, a couple of times. It caught my eye. And a deer lying by the side of the road that seemed, well, kind of unnatural."

"Pink? Pink what? A deer?"

"I really don't know." I'm embarrassed by how crazy this sounds, and I decide to drop it for now and concentrate on the ghost at hand. "Anyway, forget it. Probably nothing."

Except after we hang up, I realize that I'm more interested in whatever I saw beside the road than in some ancient servant walking the back stairs at Clarisse's inn.

I phone Morris back and Kip answers. I ask him a bit shyly if he's warmed up. He just groans and reminds me that he almost went to Mexico this week instead of coming here. I feel better when he admits that freezing his ass off is a small price to pay if we're going to have an honest-to-God seance. "I can't wait!" he says.

"Yeah, well, could you do me a favour? Tell Morris not to bother coming by to pick me up. I'd rather meet you guys there. I'm going to ride my bike over."

"Really? That's a long hike. Are you sure?"

"Yep. I'm in training. For a bike marathon. So it's a good work-out. I figure I can do it in under an hour."

"Does that mean you're going to arrive all hot and breathing heavy?"

I laugh. "Cold and shivering, more likely."

I'm not really in training, but I've been doing so much bike riding these last few months that I'm thinking I might as well try a marathon. As for Kip, it seems he's still a bit flirty with me. Is he a hopeless flirt with all girls, or does it mean he still likes me, even just a little?

After lunch, I find Joyce upstairs at her computer and tell her I'm going for a long bike ride. I may even ride into town, I say. She mutters something about exercise being good. I'm sure she figures I can't get into too much trouble on a bike. As I'm heading out the door, she calls, "I hope you're watching for cars on those country roads. Don't assume those drivers are looking out for you. Got it?"

"Got it," I say.

My plan is to go back into the woods near the inn. By myself. I have a funny feeling about what I saw the other day, and I need to check it out. That'll be a lot easier without Kip hanging around, distracting me. And Morris doesn't need to know. He's focused on Clarisse and her ghost. I've figured out a route I can take, travelling south on 12th Line and then catching a sideroad west. From there, if I zigzag west and south, I'll eventually hit 28th Sideroad.

But first things first. It's been more than a week—I've got to check on Matthew.

Thank goodness there's no one around. I knock gently on the side door of the Telford farmhouse. "Matthew?" I know it's weird to wait for a ghost to let you into a house, but what isn't weird about this?

The door opens slowly and I step inside, but Matthew isn't there. "Hello? Matthew?" I'm wearing my high rubber boots, on account of the swamp, so I take them off at the door. "Matthew?" I hear creaking on the stairs. "Is that you?"

I've got a bad feeling. I peek into the hall and up the staircase. Matthew is sitting near the top step, his chin resting on his chest. His jet-black hair is hanging over his forehead and into his eyes. His eyes look black too, like charcoal. He's holding that dumb doll under one arm. It seems like he's in a bad mood. He just looks at me, not moving his head, his brows pinched in a scowl.

"There you are. Hi." He doesn't answer. "Is something wrong?" I'm trying not to show I'm worried, trying to ignore the doll thing.

His face relaxes a bit and he straightens his legs out on the stairs, and leans back until his whole body is straight like a board. He slides down slowly and smoothly on his back, totally rigid, practically skimming the stairs, until he hits the hallway floor. It's plain creepy. Then he gets to his feet, doll in hand.

"Matthew? Is everything okay?" He walks slowly past me, fading a bit as he goes by, then getting more visible once he's in the living room.

"What could be wrong?"

"Seriously."

"Oh, you mean *seriously*?"

This is what I've been noticing about him lately. He's acting a little cranky, sarcastic, even. I think maybe it's the idea of new owners invading his territory.

"Oh, apart from the fact that I'm dead, and you're off living your life like nothing's changed . . . ?"

"How can you say that? That's not fair."

"Well, let's see. How come you look like you're going on a date?"

"What? I don't know what you mean."

"Yes you do." He's standing at the window, looking out. That dumb doll is tucked under his arm. It's true. I'm wearing makeup, and my red sweater again.

I change the subject. "What's with the doll?"

The doll's head turns with a jerk to face me and I jump at the shock. Its eyes look so real. Did I see them . . . blink? Matthew's half-hidden face breaks into a smile. Is he cracking up on me?

"What about it?" he asks, and he turns to me. At first he looks amused, but when he sees how freaked I am, plastered against the wall, his face falls. "I'm sorry. I'm lonely, that's all. And *bored*."

I pull myself together. "I thought you didn't have much sense of time passing. I mean, do you even know how many days it's been since I saw you?"

"I guess not. Let me think—don't tell me. An eternity?"

"At least you haven't lost your sense of humour."

He lets out a bit of a grunt, then slumps against the wall and sits down.

"She's all I've got between your visits. Maybe, when the new owners move in, I can play with *them*."

"I don't like the sound of that." I watch him take the doll's hand and examine it closely. Neither of us says anything for a while. How do I get him back to normal conversation? I have an idea.

"You know, I need some advice. I've been asked to hold a seance in a haunted house." He looks up at me, his eyes brightening. "Not *this* haunted house. Another haunted house." His face darkens again and he looks back down at the doll's hand.

"The thing is, I don't know how to do it. Any . . . advice? I mean, about communicating with a . . . with a ghost?"

He shrugs.

I try again. "Well, if some stranger came here and wanted to make contact with you—to ask you questions, say—what would make you want to talk to them?"

He thinks about that for a few moments. When he finally looks up at me, his eyes are shining with tears.

"If they could tell me how to get back to my life. Back where I used to be. Hanging out in the library with you. Then I'd talk to them."

"Matthew. . . ." I have to stop there, remembering how I used to feel sitting beside him at school. I never got the chance to put my arms around him and hold him tight. Hold his face close to mine. Feel his warm breath. And now—now it's too late.

There's a long silence while we just look at each other across the empty living room. Before I know it, I'm blinking and wiping my eyes with my sleeves and probably smearing my mascara. I slide down to sit near him on the floor.

"Matthew, if I could get you back your life, believe me, I would. If I could do something, anything, to make it happen, I would. If I only knew how." I cover my eyes for what feels like an hour.

When at last I look up, Matthew is staring at the doll again, gently stroking its bald head. That brings me back to reality. Matthew is a freaking ghost, and he's getting spookier all the time. And there's nothing I can do about it.

"I've got to go," I say with a sigh, and I stagger to my feet.

"Sure she does," he whispers to the doll.

He follows me to the side door and watches as I put on my boots. "Just ask the ghost what's wrong," he says. "Something's bothering him. Something's on his mind."

I turn back to him and nod. "Okay. Thank you."

"With me, it's you."

I take a deep breath and try to pretend I didn't catch that. I look at the doll under his arm. "So what's her name?"

"You have to ask?" He lifts the doll to his lips and plants a light kiss on its forehead.

Oh God, I think, as I get back on my bike and head for the road. Why did I have to ask?

9

 pedal uphill, struggling a bit, and think about how unfair everything is. I used to want so much for Matthew to like me. Now that he's all mine, I don't know what to do about it. Because whether we like it or not, death changes everything. Is it really only because of me that he stays behind? Is it me that's keeping him here?

And then there's my guilt about the way I fantasize about Kip, wishing I could be his girlfriend when I'm not even in his league. Is it only because he seems more real than Matthew? But who's to say what's real? I feel like I don't know anymore.

Riding toward 28th Sideroad, I try to imagine how it might have been if Matthew had lived, if he'd been able to finish high school and maybe go to college and get a job. But it's hard to imagine much beyond that, like being married to him or anything. We've always been so different. Maybe best friends is all we'd ever have been anyway. Friends with benefits? Who am I kidding? Matthew was too religious for that, and me, I'm chicken.

When I'm on 28th Sideroad, approaching the part where the forest gets thick on either side, I check my watch. I still have about twenty minutes before I meet Morris and Kip at the inn. That gives me about fifteen minutes to slip into the forest for a quick look. I ride onto the gravel, stop and drag my bike into the trees so it's not visible from the road, in case Morris drives by this way. Then I set off by foot, farther into the woods. Five minutes later, I reach the edge of the swamp.

I can make out the area where poor Kip fell in. The ice is still broken, not quite refrozen and not melting much either. I flash back to him flailing and going down in the water. Maybe I'm a little mean after all, because I feel the twitch of a smile coming on. I decide to stay right where I am, and just look around and listen. And only a few minutes pass before I see her.

She's sitting up on the deer stand, her legs dangling over the edge. She's looking down into the swamp. A girl about twelve years old, wearing a pink ski jacket.

I take a few steps toward her along the edge of the swamp, being careful where I walk, and for a moment I glance down at the slippery tangle of snowy undergrowth at my feet. When I look up again, she's gone. I stop and look around, seeing nothing but a few silent deer watching me from the other side of the swamp before they turn and run deep into the trees beyond.

A haunted wood alongside a haunted house. I wonder if there's a connection? And what is this girl doing alone in the forest anyway? That's what I'd like to know.

Morris's car is parked beside the inn, in a space set aside for guests. I wonder how long they've been here. I leave my bike leaning against a lamppost and go up to the front door.

Through the glass of the door I can see Morris and Kip standing with Clarisse in the hallway, talking. Clarisse is wearing a sweater and skirt and shoes with heels. She's showing serious cleavage. I suddenly feel like a little kid. I dig into my shoulder bag for my lip gloss and quickly smear some on. Then I take a deep breath and ring the doorbell.

After we all say hello, Kip and Morris pull a round table into the middle of the kitchen while Clarisse runs back and forth carrying chairs, placing them around it. I give her a hand. She's opened the door that leads to the back stairs, and from the table we'll be able to see the bottom steps. Morris turns to me.

"What do you think, Amelia? Should we kill the lights?"

I look at him. "Kill" the lights? Really? He's way too excited. But I don't know. Have I ever seen a ghost in daylight? Of course. But if this ghost has only been heard at night, maybe that means something. Meanwhile, Clarisse is flapping around the kitchen like a bird, gathering up candles, rummaging in a drawer for matches, hitting the lights. The room falls into shadow. Is it my imagination or is she checking Kip out? She's old enough to be his mother! As she runs around the table, positioning the chairs *just so*, she accidentally steps on his toe and makes a big deal of apologizing and checking that he's okay. I catch Kip's face. He's looking down trying not to smile. He finds this amusing, obviously. She lights a big candle, puts it in the middle of the table and invites us to take our seats. We do, and they look at me. That's when it really sinks in. They're expecting me to *do* something.

"Can we just sit in silence for a while?" It's all I can think to say right now, but I also have a feeling it's important. I need to listen. To the house.

They're quick to say *Sure, yes of course,* and we all fall silent. I can hear the refrigerator running. And somewhere a clock is ticking. I'm working hard at not looking at anyone, keeping my eyes on the open door leading to the back stairs. A car goes by on the road outside. Clarisse asks if we should be holding hands or anything and I tell her I don't think so. Then Kip asks if I'm sure. Could it hurt? He looks at me with a mischievous smile. "Couldn't hurt," Clarisse says with enthusiasm, and takes hold of Kip's hand, and then Morris's on her other side. I exhale and shrug.

"Okay, fine," I say, "but I don't think it makes any difference."

Kip takes hold of my hand, smirking slightly. I give Morris a look that says *Thanks for getting me into this.* He reluctantly reaches for my hand, as if he's trying to apologize with telepathy or something. We sit in silence a little longer, only now all I can think about is the feel of Kip's hand in mine on my right, and the awkward, nervous clutch of Morris's hand on my left. Our eyes gravitate to the candle flame on the table between us. It's better than looking into each other's faces. I try to block Kip's touch from my mind and concentrate on the ghost. This is getting ridiculous.

Finally, Morris speaks up.

"Do you think maybe you should say something?"

I look at him, feeling more embarrassed and resentful by the minute. Another deep breath, and here goes.

"Hello? Are . . . you there?" I look toward the back staircase again, and flinch.

Sure enough, someone is sitting in shadow, a few steps up from the bottom. A spasm of fear runs through me. My hands twitch involuntarily and both Morris and Kip respond, their hands tightening around mine. *It's okay,* I tell myself. *You're safe.* It's a pale, thin figure, almost white, hunched and leaning against the staircase banister, head lowered, with bony hands covering its face. It looks like an old man, frail and bald-headed. I can't make out the face at all, like he's hiding it from me. I have the feeling he is very sad, or upset, or ashamed. Or full of regret—I'm not sure which, exactly. I've been holding my breath, and now I let it out slowly. I try to sound calm.

"Are you okay?" I wait. Nothing. "Is something wrong?"

The ghost doesn't seem to hear me. I wait some more, and watch him. He doesn't move. I take another deep breath.

"Can you hear me?"

There's no response.

I steal a glance at Morris, who's looking at me like he's about to burst with curiosity. I realize that I'm not afraid anymore. I'm starting to relax.

"He's sitting on the stair," I say. "He looks . . . unhappy." I watch the ghost some more. "He doesn't look well, either. Like maybe he's sick."

We sit in silence a little longer, then Morris whispers, "Do you think he knows we're here?"

"I don't know." I gently wrestle my hands out of Morris's and Kip's grips, and I make quick eye contact with Kip as I rise from my chair. "Maybe you guys should stay where you are. I just want to get a closer look."

I walk around the table and toward the door. I stop about six feet away, keeping my eye on the ghost, and wait some more, until something brushes against my leg and I jump. Clarisse gasps "Pumpkin!" in panic, and an orange tabby cat meows and circles my feet and crosses the floor toward the open door. It stops there, sits and watches the stair. "Pumpkin, no!" Clarisse hisses under her breath, as if she's afraid this ghost is a cat-killer.

There's silence again. Then the ghost rises slowly to his feet, hands still held up to his face, and turns his back to us. He takes a step up the stairs.

"Is there anything we can do . . . to help you?"

For the first time it seems the ghost has heard me, because he stops. He keeps his back to me but he lowers his hands from his face. I see the bony bald head give the slightest shake, and the hands return to his face and he shuffles away, one stair at a time. I hear the stairs creak with his footsteps.

At first I feel frozen, then I lunge forward—I'm not sure what I'm planning to do—but it's too late. He's gone.

I stand facing the door for another minute or so, thinking about what I just saw. Again I feel a terrible weight—of regret, or guilt? Finally I turn to face Morris, Kip and Clarisse, no longer holding hands, sitting on the edge of their seats.

"Did you hear anything?" I ask. All three nod. Clarisse looks white enough to be a ghost herself.

Feeling a little dizzy, I head back to my chair. "He's gone."

"Wow," Clarisse whispers. "Well . . . could anyone use a drink?"

Morris ignores that and turns to me. "What did you see?"

"I couldn't see the face at all. But it looked like an old guy, frail and weak. Bald. Wearing pyjamas, I think. And a thin robe. Like a hospital patient, maybe. Or just out of bed."

"A night walker. That's a well-documented ghost behaviour," Morris says. "Stuck in a dying stage, not realizing he's already dead."

"He seems bothered by something. I couldn't see his expression, his hands were covering his face most of the time. Like he didn't want to show it. Like he was ashamed, maybe. The only time he dropped his hands, he had his back to me. But he heard me, I'm sure he did. He stopped on the stair and shook his head when I asked if we could help."

As I talk to Morris I see Clarisse, out of the corner of my eye, lean in closer to Kip. Then she falls into him, sideways, right out of her chair. We jump to our feet and Kip manages to catch her before she hits the kitchen floor—she's fainted. We lay her down on her back and I run into the living room for some throw cushions for her head.

As Kip takes a cushion from me and gently lifts her head to slide it under, her eyes half open, eyelids all fluttery. She clutches his arm.

"Oh my," she says. "Oh wow."

"A bit of a shock, I'm sure," Morris says sympathetically.

"What am I going to do?" she whimpers.

"Well, he didn't look dangerous or hostile or anything," I say, hoping that makes her feel better. She looks at me as if I'm crazy.

"A ghost?" It's like the reality is sinking in. She starts to panic again, her voice rising. "In my house? In my inn?" She tries to sit up, then gets dizzy and lies down again, looking up at Kip with big pleading eyes. "What am I going to *do*?"

It occurs to me that she's wearing a ton of eye makeup.

"I can't stay here alone. Just me and that . . . whatever it is. *Who*ever it is." She's holding onto Kip's arm like she'll never let go.

Morris tries to calm her. "I'm sure you aren't in any danger. No reason why the ghost would try to harm you now when it's never tried before."

Her eyes look like they're about to pop.

"Um, well . . . I guess Kip and I could spend the night in one of the spare rooms. There's a book launch I have to attend in town tonight, but I could come back when it's over." Morris looks at Kip. "Maybe Kip could keep you company in the meantime." He looks back at Clarisse and adds, "If that would make you feel better."

83

"Oh my God, yes! Would you really?" She's still got ahold of Kip's arm.

"Uh, sure. Sure." He doesn't look sure at all. Trapped, more like.

"I'd be so grateful. I can't stay here alone after that." She sits up again. "I'm packing my bags. Tomorrow, I'll go stay with my sister in Orangeville. I need to get away from here, I need to think."

Morris hands her a glass of water and she takes a sip. "And if you want," he says, "while you're gone, we can try to make some progress here, see if we can . . . improve the situation. Usually ghosts hang around for a reason. It's almost like they get emotionally stuck in a place. We'll try to find out why this one's stuck."

Listening to Morris and Clarisse, I feel warm with irritation. I'm a little jealous of her getting to spend the night with Kip. I mean, it's perfectly natural that she doesn't want to be alone here. And it's very chivalrous of Morris and Kip to come to her rescue. She's still going on about how "You've no idea how much this means to me . . . *blah, blah, blah*," and I can't help thinking maybe it's a bad idea. If they're going to stay over, maybe I should too.

For a second Kip and I lock eyes, and I have to admit that he looks more afraid than happy. I lean in and whisper, "Maybe I should stay too. I'm just saying."

He shakes his head. "Joyce would kill you. You said so yourself."

"But you look nervous."

"Well . . . maybe a little. Any advice?"

"Yes. Beware of Clarisse. She's the one you'll hear moaning outside your bedroom door."

He laughs. "Thanks. Big help."

Why is Kip at his most irresistible when he looks uncomfortable?

Call me. I mouth the words, making like I'm holding a phone to my ear, as Morris comes out onto the porch. I don't want to let him know how worried I am about leaving him here with that ghost hanging around. Who knows what it could get up to?

Kip steps back inside, and stands in the doorway with Clarisse as Morris puts my bike in the trunk. We get in the car and Morris starts the engine.

"Morris, I didn't want to say anything in front of Clarisse, but I'm not crazy about Kip being alone in that house with a mysterious ghost. We don't know anything about it. Whether it could cause trouble. I think, if you guys are spending the night, I should too."

"Forget it."

"But . . ."

"'Nough said." He backs out of the driveway. "You think you're the only one afraid of your grandmother?"

On the drive home I think about telling Morris about the girl in the forest, but all he wants to talk about is the ghost at the inn, so I figure I'll tell him later. He talks about how a haunted house is the classic ghost story. How sometimes a ghost can come to feel such complete ownership of the house that the walls, the floors, everything becomes an extension of his disturbed spirit. It can get so extreme that the ghost inhabits every inch of the house. The walls breathe, the floors shake, the windows rattle—direct expressions of the ghost's emotional state. By that time the haunting has gone too far, and the only solution is to destroy the house.

But this particular case seems far from that. A single ghost who doesn't take up more space than he needs, Morris says, no more than he might have occupied while he was living. Morris is determined to see if we can uncover this ghost's problem. Get him to leave the house and take that journey to wherever ghosts are supposed to go. Then Clarisse can have her dream house back.

There are three families left to check, and that'll take us back to the year when the house was built, in the late 1800s. He suggests we split up the research, with me taking the two more recent sets of owners and him taking the three generations of the first family of owners. We'll start by gathering the names of all the family members, and their birth and death dates, and we'll eliminate candidates from there.

"One thing really helps," Morris says. "How many males who lived in that house were bald? It's a head start, so to speak." He laughs. He's in a good mood.

Later, when I'm lying in bed trying to fall asleep, I think about Kip spending hours alone in that big house with Clarisse and the old ghost. But eventually my mind wanders back into the forest, to the girl in the pink ski jacket.

Who was she? How did she die? And why is she wandering the land of the living?

Does she need our help too?

10

As I'm rinsing off my cereal bowl at the sink, Joyce walks in and says she's heard how Kip and I got into some trouble in a forest swamp the other day. Ethan told her about it. Of course. She asks how Kip is doing, saying she didn't think we'd see him back around here so soon.

So soon? Seems to me he's been gone for ages. Even yesterday seems like a week ago. I've been trying not to freak about what may have happened at the inn overnight. He hasn't called yet.

I dreamt about the forest last night. When I woke up, I remembered the injured deer I'd seen when I drove out there with Kip. It wasn't only the glimpse of a pink jacket that stuck with me. It was the way the deer was dragging itself along the ground, almost like a human.

I ask Joyce if she remembers hearing about a young girl being killed in Grey County, if she's ever read about anything like that in the papers. She looks at me sideways. She reads stuff into everything I say, looking for evidence that I'm up to no good—which, to her, means messing with ghosts.

"No," she says. "What do you mean, *killed*? Murdered? Why do you ask?" Typical Joyce.

"Oh, nothing. Not murdered, necessarily. In an accident, maybe," I say. "Just . . . I heard something about a girl who may have died on 28th Sideroad. A sixth- or seventh-grader, maybe?"

Her eyes narrow. I knew she'd be suspicious. It's impossible to ask an innocent question in this house anymore.

I try to sound casual. "I heard somebody mention it, I forget who. I was just curious, is all."

Joyce smirks like she thinks something's fishy, but she gets up and starts making coffee, talking about how it's going to be a nice day today, looking through the kitchen window at Marley and Ponyboy in the paddock out back. She must have decided to let me off the hook for now. Not that she's stupid. She's probably guessed that I've seen the girl's ghost.

It's early afternoon before the phone rings and Joyce calls upstairs to me. Kip is on the line. *Finally.*

"Where *are* you?" I ask, trying not to sound too anxious.

"Back home. We just got here."

"Oh. Wow. So you spent a lot of time with Clarisse. Did you see a ghost? Or hear one, at least?"

"No, nothing at all. And that's fine with me." He laughs. "Clarisse can be pretty scary all by herself."

Oh, great. "I take it you don't mean 'scary' scary. Spare me the details."

"I'm kidding. We just stayed up pretty late, that's all. Talking. She wanted company while she made her way through a bottle of red wine. For her nerves."

"I thought Morris didn't drink."

"He doesn't. He just watched."

"Got it. Well, then." I try not to think about Kip and Clarisse together. "So the main thing is, no apparitions."

"Well, if anything happened, I slept through it and so did Dad. Clarisse didn't hear anything either. By the time we got up today she was all packed. She gave us a set of keys to the house, and she and Pumpkin hit the highway. I think Dad wants to spend the night there again tomorrow."

"But if anyone should be sleeping at the inn, it's me. *I* should stay over." I mean, what good are these guys going to be when they can't see a ghost standing right in front of them?

"Well, I'll mention it to him. See what he says."

I hang up and stare at the wall. I was relieved hearing Kip's voice, but now I'm anxious again. Why did I go and say that? As if Joyce would let me stay overnight at a strange place, especially one with a ghost. I'd have to tell her I was spending the night at Morgan's. Ugh. Lying to Joyce is so stressful.

Do I even want to spend the night in a haunted house? Who would? But it's got to be me. I'm the only practical choice.

It was Morgan's idea, but it didn't take much. I just had to hint that I could use an excuse to spend the night away from home. Next thing I know, I'm tagging along with her and three other friends to the Galaxy Cinema to catch a movie that opened last weekend. A rom-com but with some gross-out scenes.

When it was over, I phoned Joyce on my cell and said I'd probably do a sleepover—Morgan hovering over me and coaching me—*'cause we're going out for a bite and it'll be too late, by the time we're through, to get a ride back home.* Since moving out of town was Joyce's idea, she can't complain when the distance from Owen Sound isn't convenient.

So now she thinks I'm spending the night at Morgan's. And actually it turned out to be a fun evening. I don't hang out with school friends that much, and without Morgan I'd hardly ever get a chance, so I'm pretty grateful to her. Sometimes I get the feeling Joyce is too.

Meanwhile, I'm sure Morgan thinks I'm spending the night with Kip at a motel somewhere. Her eyes popped out of her head when he came by her place to pick me up. She gave my hand a squeeze when we said goodbye, a look of concern on her face. I don't think she thought I was dressed for this.

"It's not what it looks like," I said. "He's just dropping me off at some lady's place for the night. I'm house-sitting for her."

Morgan obviously didn't believe me, though it wasn't far off the truth. Her eyes flitted back and forth between me and Kip and I could feel myself blushing, thinking about spending a bit of time alone with him. As it turned out, Morris was parked down the road, waiting for us, so that put an end to any fantasies.

On the way to the car, Kip explains that Morris thought the idea of me sleeping at the inn made sense, but not alone. And he didn't think it would look good if he stayed over with me, and he didn't like the idea of Kip staying either. So this is the compromise: all three of us will sleep there tonight.

Once we get into the car, Kip falls silent. It's like he and Morris have had an argument or something.

It's a dark evening with a cloudy night sky, and Morris flips on his high beams, lighting up the bordering bushes and trees far down 28th Sideroad. We're approaching the Cornflower Inn from the west this time, so we won't be driving past the forest where I've seen the girl three times now—that is, if you count what I thought was a deer at the side of the road. The car slows and we turn into the long driveway leading up to the big yellow house. Except for the porch light, the place is dark.

We sit in the car for a minute, saying nothing, just looking up at the house. I scan the upstairs windows. I guess I'm a little nervous. Then we get out.

Morris has the key and walks up the front steps ahead of us. He's got a big black canvas case that I've seen him with before. It must be fifty years old. I'm travelling light, with just a few necessities in my handbag. I'm planning on sleeping in my clothes.

Morris fusses with the lock.

"Dad brought hot cocoa," says Kip.

"No kidding? Perfect."

We're being playful, more or less mocking Morris for treating us like kids, but later, sitting around the fire that he lit in the living room fireplace, sipping hot chocolate in big mugs, it's pretty wonderful. As usual when I'm with Kip, I want to look at him the whole time, which is hard to do without being creepy. Fortunately, Morris has mostly left us alone while he wanders the house.

I'm not sure what he's hoping to find, but he seems to be conducting some kind of inspector's survey. Every once in a while we hear him on the back stairs or in the halls upstairs, pacing. It's almost funny, and we look at each other and giggle. I half expect him to accidentally break something valuable, like an antique vase, before he's through.

Finally he comes back downstairs to the living room, saying he's going to read in bed. He's taking the front bedroom, next to Clarisse's room. He suggests I take the bedroom closest to the back-stairs door and Kip the next one down the hall. He gives Kip an extra-long look when he says that. Then he turns to me.

"Amelia, obviously you're calling the shots tonight. So wake us up without hesitation, for any reason. And if you think waking us up will only interfere and you'd rather not, that's okay too. Just give us the details in the morning. Is there anything you'd like from us?"

"Uh . . . I can't think of anything. Honestly, the ghost I saw didn't look like too much trouble. I'm not worried. I'm just going to try to find out what his problem is, and whether there's anything we can do to help. But yeah, I'll holler if things get ugly, for sure."

Morris says good night and heads upstairs. Once he's gone, I look over at Kip, and he's staring at me like he's about to say something that's been on his mind. Like he's been holding back, waiting for Morris to go to bed.

"What?" I ask, when I can't take the tension anymore.

"I just wanted you to know, it wasn't easy getting Dad to let me come tonight."

"Well, he's probably trying to protect you from another bad ghost experience. You remember what happened to you in the barn."

"Vaguely." He nods. "But no, it's not ghosts he's worried about."

I have a feeling I know where this is going. I look away from him, into the flames in the fireplace. After a moment he continues.

"I had to reassure him that everything's cool between us, you know? Wounds all healed. Just friends."

I look at him again, unable to read his expression. "Kip, I . . . I don't know what to say."

"I've noticed."

"I don't feel that way. Like *just* friends."

"You have a strange way of showing it."

He's talking about the way I've been with him ever since the barn burned down, ever since I found out Matthew had decided to stick around. I catch myself heaving a sigh of hopelessness.

"I'm so sorry, Kip. I can't explain. . . ."

"Or won't."

His eyes look calm and sad, like he's weary. We sit in silence and I feel a lump growing in my throat. I look back into the fire.

"I felt so close to you that night, Amelia. I didn't care if my dad was going to have trouble with it. That was his problem. I thought the person who stood between us was finally out of the picture—this guy I couldn't even see. So imagine my surprise when you suddenly push me away, just when I thought . . ." He doesn't finish.

Silence again, and then he asks, "Do you know what that was like?"

I can't answer. The flames are going all blurry, becoming a red and yellow haze.

"Look, I'd rather be a friend to you than nothing at all," he says. "I really would. It's just that, if we're going to be friends, I need some kind of explanation. As a friend you owe me that. I mean, I need to be able to trust you. Trust that you aren't just . . . just a little wacko."

A tear rolls down my cheek. It's at my jaw before I can brush it away.

"I'm sorry. You're not. I know that. But . . . I need to hear something from you."

"All right." I take a deep breath. Here I go. "He's . . . he's still here."

"What?"

"Matthew. He's still here. He didn't leave."

"*What!*" He jumps to his feet and stands over me. "You . . . you said he *left*. You said they *all* left. All the ghosts in the barn walked away, you said." He has raised his voice, and now he lifts his eyes to the ceiling like he's looking for something.

Oh God. He's going to bring Morris down here.

"Please, Kip."

93

"What are you saying? He's still *where*? Where is he?" He begins pacing, hands holding the sides of his head like a vise.

"Kip, Morris will hear you."

"I don't care." He stops over me again. "He should know. How could you keep this from us? From both of us? We're supposed to be"—his voice drops—"in this together. I can't believe you didn't tell me."

"I couldn't. I was in shock myself."

"You could have." He shakes his head, almost whispering now. "You made a choice not to tell me."

I try to stay calm, desperately hoping that Morris hasn't heard us. "I was so confused when I realized he was still around. Just standing by a tree as the barn burned down, watching us. I couldn't believe my eyes. I didn't know for sure until days later, when I got a chance to sneak back. I didn't know what to expect, but . . . there he was."

"Just hanging out?" He says the words like he doesn't trust me.

"Yes, believe it or not. He's moved into the empty house now. He's . . . *haunting* the Telford farmhouse."

Kip drops to the couch, head in hands. "I don't believe it," he says. "I don't bloody believe it."

We sit in silence on opposite couches. The distance is killing me. I finally get up and sit down beside him.

"And we drove by there just yesterday and you didn't say anything?" His shrug is like a small spasm. "I give up," he mutters.

"Don't. Don't give up."

"Why not? I hate to admit it, but this explains everything. I have better things to do than compete with a guy I can't even see. Or be kept in the dark by you."

"I'm not in control of the situation."

"Not good enough."

"But what am I supposed to do? It wasn't my secret to tell, you know, it was *his* secret. I mean, he passed up going to the promised land, or some damn place, to be with me. What am I supposed to do with that?"

"Maybe you don't want him to leave. Maybe that's why he stayed. Why not admit it?"

"It's more complicated than that. You know it is."

"Too complicated for me. I'm not interested in getting screwed around like this, I'm not. My dad's right."

"Kip, I don't know how to explain it. But . . . there's this bottle of pills I kind of stole, that I held onto for ages."

"What pills? What are you talking about?"

"Tranquilizers, sixty of them. *Enough*, I figured. They were my mother's prescription. I hid them in my closet for a year."

"What's your point? What the hell are you trying to say?"

"I think I would have taken them—all at once, I mean—if not for Matthew. I needed someone to tell me to throw them away, and I had no one. Not until him. I threw them away because of him."

Kip shakes his head slowly and rises to his feet as though he's very tired. I could wrap my arms around his knees if I only had the nerve. *Forgive me!* Instead I say, "He's got to cross over eventually, doesn't he?"

"Yeah, whatever." There's a long pause. "You know what's ironic? It was Clarisse who talked me into confronting you. Yeah. She said we were obviously 'in love.'" He's straining to control his voice. I look up at him but his eyes are looking straight down, almost shut. His lashes are wet. "I'm going to bed."

I stay paralyzed on the couch as he leaves the room. In the hallway, at the foot of the stairs, he stops. He comes back to the doorway, focusing on the red embers in the fireplace.

"Wake me if you need any help or . . . anything," he says, his voice flat. Then he disappears again.

I listen to his footsteps on the stairs and along the second floor hallway. A door closes.

11

id I just hear something?

It's two a.m. and I haven't been able to sleep. I've taken my shoes and socks off and I'm lying on the bed, on top of the covers. I've left my door open about six inches. I've put an extra pillow under my head, and at this angle I can look through the gap and see the knob of the door to the back staircase. I'm not afraid of ghosts tonight, because nothing worse could possibly happen to me.

Kip has given up on us for good. I just know it.

What will it be like in the morning? Will he even talk to me? Will he tell Morris, first chance he gets? After he leaves tomorrow, will I ever see him again? Will he ever forgive me? *I'd like to see what you would have done, Kip. If you could have betrayed your best friend's secret so fast. Especially if you used to be in love. And if you owe him your life.*

Did I just see something? I'm not sure. I don't even know if I heard anything. Sitting on the edge of the bed, straining my eyes and ears, I'm getting nothing. Was there something there or not? I wait a while.

Then, reluctantly, I stand up and tiptoe to the door. A weak light in the hallway casts a small yellow halo. I stare at the door to the back staircase, focusing on the doorknob. Is it moving? No. I watch for a few minutes, then quietly turn away, casting a quick eye down the hall to Kip's closed door before returning to my bed. I lie back down, carefully adjusting the pillows to keep my head propped up facing the doorknob. Something tells me there's someone on the other side. Lying there, I begin thinking again about Kip . . . and Matthew.

I sit up again. *Is someone there?*

I wait and listen. This time I definitely heard a faint creaking sound. A minute goes by and I hear it again. Someone is on the back stairs.

I take a deep breath to steady myself, then swing my legs off the bed and stand up. There's a lamp beside the bed on a small table— I switch it on. I wait and listen some more, then walk to the door as quietly as possible and out into the hall. I stand before the back-stairs door and stare at the doorknob.

I hear something on the other side, a muffled sound. I touch the knob, then slowly turn it, my hand shaking a little. I hold my breath and pull the door open. Faint light from the hallway reaches only halfway down the stairs. The bottom of the stairs is in total darkness. I see nothing, but I stand still and wait.

Nothing.

Leaving the door open behind me, I take a step down, and then another. I stare into the darkness at the bottom. Carefully I descend three more stairs, then stop. That's as far as I'll go for now. I stand perfectly still.

That's when I feel something wash over me, cold and familiar— like dry cobwebs or a thin veil. It takes my breath away and makes me shiver. What was I thinking? I really don't want to do this. I slowly climb backwards up the stairs, still facing the darkness below.

At the top of the stairs I slip back into the hallway and shut the stair door as quietly as I can, then scurry back into my bedroom, closing my door behind me. Get back into bed.

That's all I can handle tonight, so go away.

Someone's knocking on my bedroom door—four weak knocks. I'm on my feet before I'm fully awake, weaving slightly on unsure legs. Where am I, again? I was in a deep sleep, finally, after hours of fretting and anxious listening. Now my heart is pounding.

"Is that you, Kip?" There's no answer. Of course it's not Kip. *Dreamer.*

I check my watch. It's 5:15 a.m. I stand up close to the door and listen some more.

"Hello?" I whisper. No answer. I turn on my bedroom light and slowly open my door. There's no one there. I listen.

There's a faint sound coming from the back stairs again. I'm thinking about whether to check it out when I hear knocking. Four weak knocks, exactly as before, but this time from behind the staircase door. I look along the hall toward Kip's bedroom, and peek around the corner and down the main hall toward Morris's door, open an inch. All silent. As I look back at the stair door I hear four more knocks, even fainter this time. I take a deep breath, stand before the stair door and reach for the doorknob.

This time, as I open the door and the pale hall light reaches down the stairs, I see the hunched figure, its back to me, sitting on a step in the shadow near the bottom. Just as I saw him during the seance. It even looks as though he's still covering his face with his hands. I steady myself and take a step down, leaving the door open a bit behind me—for a little light and, just in case, a quick escape.

"Are you okay?" I realize how ludicrous this sounds even as I whisper it. He's a friggin' ghost and he's obviously upset, so of course he's not okay.

I wait but there's no response. I take another step and slowly sit down about six stairs above him. Why not? This is something I've got to deal with. And it may take a while.

"You knocked on my door," I say tentatively. "Why? Do you want something from me?"

The bald head lifts slightly.

"Is there anything I can do?"

The head bows low again.

"I know you can hear me. Can you talk?"

There's a slight turn, a half-shake.

Maybe he *can't* talk. I look at the back of his head. The bony skull, the narrow shoulder blades poking from under a thin dressing gown. The whole apparition is pale, nearly white.

"Have you been ill? Do you feel ill now?"

No response.

"Or are you sad? Are you . . . ?" I'm trying to think. "Are you grieving about something?"

The head nods, slowly.

Then the figure rises to his feet, still with his back to me. He's making a noise. At first it sounds like moaning, but then it takes on a distinctive sound, "*F-f-f* . . . ," struggling like someone with a stammer. It's painful to listen to but I try to be patient. Finally I hear what sounds like the word *four*.

"Four? Four what?"

His hands suddenly drop from his face and reach out behind him, twisted at an unnatural angle in the shoulder sockets. His bony fingers are outstretched, arms reaching toward me, fingers trembling like worms. Okay, I'm getting the hell out of here. I scramble to my feet as the ghost starts moving backwards up the stairs, the back of his bald head getting closer and closer. Terrified, I trip back through the partly opened door and fall into the hall, my head hitting the wall behind me. I feel a sharp pain—and the hallway goes dark.

I hear Kip's door bang open and out of the shadows he lunges at me, bare-chested, in blue jeans. He drops to the floor and sits me up. I hear Morris running down the hall toward us. *Where am I?* I'm sitting slouched against the wall, on the floor outside my room. They're asking me questions—*What happened? Are you hurt? Can you stand up?*

But I'm okay. I hit the back of my head but not too hard. I touch it and it hurts but there's no blood.

Kip disappears and Morris kneels down, pulling my shoulders to straighten me up. Kip comes back with a cold wet cloth. "Do you want to talk about it?" he asks.

"I don't think so." I can't look either of them in the eye. "I'm sorry . . . sorry I woke you up. I just need to lie down for a while. I'm going back to bed. I'll be fine." I don't want to tell them what I saw—not now. I don't want to talk about it to anyone.

I hold the wet cloth to the back of my head and get to my feet, showing them that I'm okay. "Really. Let's talk in the morning. It was no big deal. I tripped."

I leave them standing in the hall, looking at each other with stunned expressions, as I close the door to my bedroom. I lie on my bed until my heart settles down, and then I get under the covers.

Okay, that was scary.

Try not to think about it, I tell myself. *Sooner or later you'll fall asleep.*

"I need to talk to you about something," I tell Morris.

We've just seen Kip off on the bus, waiting until the big grey coach pulled out of the terminal parking lot. I watched Kip's shaggy bronze head at the window as the bus passed by. He turned to face us with unfocused eyes.

"What's going on?" Morris asks, sounding worried. I feel a huge weight on my chest, and a fog in my brain. Kip decided to leave town two days early, and it's all my fault.

"What is it, Amelia? What's going on? Is it about what you saw last night?"

I've already told them about my paranormal adventure, including the final bone-chilling creepiness that sent me bursting through the back-stairs door in a panic. Somehow, in the morning light, I was able to convince myself that the ghost hadn't actually been trying to scare me to death. It seemed more determined to communicate than to kill. I told them that the only message I could make out was the number four. Three times I heard four faint knocks on the door, and the one word the ghost struggled to say sounded like *four*.

It made no sense to any of us, and we are no better off than before we spent the night. It seemed to me, from the weird way the apparition reached out to me as he moved backwards up the stairs, that he desperately *wanted me to give him something*. Yes, if I had to describe it, that's what it felt like.

But, ghost aside, I woke up feeling heavy with sadness. Kip no longer seemed angry, just withdrawn. As if he really had given up last night. Given up on us.

He didn't say anything to Morris about Matthew, but when we said goodbye he gave me this dead-eyed look, then gestured toward Morris with the slightest movement of his head. I knew he was telling me to 'fess up and tell Morris the truth. Then he bent forward and brushed my cheek with a kiss. It made my heart sink, feeling him that close and yet so distant. "Take care of yourself," he said, and he turned away.

"You too," I whispered, longing to say more. *Please forgive me.*

"Amelia?" Morris's voice jerks me back to the present. "You said you had something to tell me. Why don't we drive down to Harrison Park, grab a park bench?"

I nod.

Harrison Park is right in the middle of town. It's a big, beautiful park about a hundred years old. The river runs through it, and so do hiking trails. It's set in a kind of river basin, with a winding road leading down from a main street, so it feels secluded, surrounded by hills and open in the middle. We used to toboggan here as kids. I usually love it here, but today I feel too sick to feel anything but dread.

"Now," begins Morris. We sit side by side on a cold wooden park bench, facing the river. "What's up?"

Oh God.

"There's something I haven't told you. I've wanted to but I didn't feel I could. I've been keeping it to myself since the night the barn burned down."

"Uh-oh," he says under his breath.

"You know how I said all the ghosts headed west out of the burning barn?"

He looks at me, eyes narrowing, like he's bracing himself. I'd better just plow through this.

"Well, that's what I thought I saw. At first. But when it was all over—after the fire trucks and ambulance and police came, and just before we were all released and about to go home—I saw something, someone, standing off in the distance, watching us." I pause, take a deep breath. "It was Matthew. At the last minute, he had broken away from the other ghosts and stayed behind." I see Morris frowning and I rush on. "I had no idea, honest. I was in such shock when I saw him, I . . . didn't say anything. I didn't know if I could believe my eyes. And he motioned to me not to tell anyone. So I . . . I didn't. Until last night. Last night I told Kip."

There's a pained look on his face. Not anger, more like serious disappointment. He raises his eyebrows. Finally he speaks, quietly.

"Matthew's ghost? He's still around?"

I nod.

"You . . . you've been seeing him? Since the barn burned down?"

I nod again. "I'm sorry, Morris. I'm sorry I didn't tell you sooner."

"Well. That explains Kip's mood this morning. And the dark circles you both had under your eyes. Like matching raccoons."

"Oh God, Morris. This is the last thing I wanted to do. To upset Kip . . . and you."

"I'm not upset. I'm sure you had your reasons. I'm not standing in your shoes. I can't speak for Kip. He takes things a little more personally."

"I just hope he can forgive me." I can barely get the words out.

There's a long silence. Morris stares straight ahead. I look down, my hands clasped together, feeling cold. Finally I take a deep, shuddering breath and try to straighten up.

"Can we not tell Joyce about this?"

Morris sighs. "I'll have to think about that."

"I can take you to him. He's staying in the farmhouse."

Morris turns toward me on the bench. "Yeah?" I can feel the adrenalin kicking back into him. He can't resist a ghost encounter.

"Well, I'd be lying if I said I wasn't interested," he says.

12

"Don't freak out or anything," Morgan says. "I just thought I'd warn you, that's all. I know how you hate surprises."

I'm sitting next to Morgan in English class. It's been over a week since March break but I still feel stunned, so this bit of news from her isn't sinking in. It's not every day that I get invited to a weekend party, but more than that, Morgan's just floored me by telling me that a guy in my math class is going to be there and, according to her, he's interested in me. He told her himself. His name is Lester, Lester somebody. She says his family has money. I hardly know who she's talking about. I don't remember him ever even opening his mouth.

Now that she's dropped this little bomb, my brain has flown straight out the window. Thank God I did all my English homework last night—that probably means I won't be asked any questions in class today. That's the odds, anyway.

It's been such an effort getting back into school mode after March break. Hellish. My concentration sucked, and I felt so tired.

That awful night at the Cornflower Inn did me in, partly because of lack of sleep and partly because of how depressed I felt afterwards. Morgan noticed how down I was, and asked me if Kip was still in town. I had a hard time responding, my throat got so choked up. I finally said, "Don't ask." So it's a big change of tone, her chatting about Lester what's-his-name.

Joyce has been giving me hard looks too, though she hasn't asked what's going on, thank God.

On Sunday I finally took Morris on a visit to see Matthew. We were taking a big chance, now that the new owners have possession of the house. But they haven't moved in yet or anything. A renovations crew began working there last week. They've been ripping off old roof tiles, and a big stack of new ones was sitting in the driveway when we arrived. I thought of Matthew up in the attic, with roofers making all kinds of noise above his phantom head.

There was no one working on Sunday, though. Morris parked his car on the road in front, and as we approached the house I could see Matthew in the upper window, looking down at us. At the side door Morris asked me how we got in, and he was surprised when I just knocked. The door slowly opened about a half-minute later, by itself. Except it was Matthew, of course. I could only see him once we were inside and he'd stepped back a bit. Turns out that was as much hospitality as he intended to show.

I'd come prepared for a real meeting between Matthew and Morris. I had brought paper and a pen and set them on the kitchen counter, and I'd explained to Morris how Matthew can communicate by writing. I was eager for Morris to get a demonstration, partly as proof that Matthew was there. But Matthew just looked at me like he found me slightly amusing, and walked out of the room. It was embarrassing. Here I was, thinking the two of them could finally get to know each other, become friends, even. But no, Matthew wasn't interested. Instead, he made snarky comments like, "If he came for a scare, he should check out the wiring in the basement."

It's always weird talking to Matthew in front of someone who can't see him. I tried to tell him that Morris was key to his survival. A crucial ally. Told him he should offer some gesture of friendship. But he would hardly glance at Morris, and kept giving me these looks, like it was me who didn't quite get it.

Poor Morris just stood by, looking awkward but patient. I decided to ignore Matthew and take Morris on a tour of the house. Matthew followed us around at a distance, smirking. I even got Morris to peek up into the attic. Matthew's stupid doll was there, propped up near the opening. All I could think was, *Please don't make that thing move and give poor Morris a heart attack.*

It didn't, so I guess our visit could have gone worse.

Finally Morris said he thought we ought to be going, and we headed back downstairs. He stopped at the bottom and asked me where Matthew was, exactly. I told him Matthew was still standing on the landing at the top of the stairs. Morris looked up the staircase and began talking.

He told Matthew that he believed he was standing there, because I'd said he was and he trusts me. He said that he had decided a long time ago that ghosts exist, even though he's never seen one. He said that if Matthew was going to stick around Grey County, they should try to be friends, because any friend of mine was a friend of his, and that meant he and Matthew had something in common. He said that he's one of the few people determined to support me and help me cope with my ghost vision, and added that Matthew could be a huge help to him personally, to his ghost research, and then he said, "Who knows? Maybe, just maybe, we could help each other."

Morris looked back at me and gave a little shrug, as if to say *It was worth a try,* and said we should be off.

As we left, I shot Matthew one last *Gee, thanks a lot for all your help* look. Then, standing outside on the porch, Morris reached into his coat pocket for his car keys and found the piece of paper I'd put on the kitchen counter. It was a message from Matthew: *Tell me, Uncle Morris, can you make me a real boy again?*

I've never seen Morris that moved before. Standing there with that note in his hand, he didn't speak. He just stared at it for a long time, then put it in his shirt pocket very carefully, with the glassy-eyed look of a five-year-old who just caught Santa in his living room on Christmas Eve.

Morris had his very own personally addressed message from beyond the grave.

I have to admit, Matthew, that was a nice touch.

Morris called the next day, still excited, talking about how he thinks Matthew is evolving into a "mischievous" ghost. Apparently that's a recognized ghost type—not intentionally harmful or hostile, but unappreciative of the feelings of the living. Amusing himself at their expense, even. To a degree, Morris explained, Matthew is still struggling to grasp the truth of his existence, his separation from the people around him. He's almost experimenting with the effect he has on them, trying to understand the nature of the relationship that remains. Morris thinks things could be a lot worse. As for me, I find it difficult to think of Matthew as a particular type of ghost. He's Matthew—not exactly the guy I hung out with in the school library, but who can blame him for feeling out of sorts?

Mr. Chambers has just asked me a question in front of the class. Unfortunately I have to ask him to repeat it, because I didn't quite hear him the first time. Turns out I know the answer, but that doesn't keep me from looking like a daydreaming idiot.

After class, Morgan congratulates me on my quick recovery. Then she asks me again about the party. Am I going to go? How do I feel about Lester? His dad's a surgeon. And he's kind of cute, she says. The shy type. I tell her I'm not sure. And is he shy or does he just have nothing to say? She thinks I'm being a little negative, and maybe she's right. Though I've never even noticed him before, I suppose I should keep an open mind. There can be more to a guy than whether he's the kind who gets noticed right away. And if everyone went on first impressions, lots of us would be in trouble. But seriously, how can I be remotely interested? Is she kidding?

After school I run into Jack hanging around in the hall with some friends in grade twelve, waiting for the start of a basketball game in the gym. He looks good these days. He's still walking with crutches, the kind that wrap around your arms, but he almost looks like he doesn't need them, he's gotten so much stronger. He's getting his old super-athlete swagger back.

"Hey, what's Jeremy's mom feeding you?" I ask. "You've put on a few pounds."

He just grins and lifts his eyebrows like it's a secret. That's our inside joke, because none of us likes Joyce's cooking much. Too healthy. I'm sure that since Jack's moved out he doesn't miss it at all. He pulls me aside and lowers his voice.

"By the way, letting Ethan help you with a bit of research? That really made his day."

"Yeah, well, he wasn't supposed to tell anyone. That's the problem with Ethan."

"Oh, I don't think he'd tell anyone but me. Well, and maybe Joyce. But it's good for him. You should use him more often."

Jack's got a bigger heart than me—always has had. But I suppose he's right. I've promised Morris to do some serious research on the Carmichael family, who owned Clarisse's house from 1976 to 1994. Maybe there's some way Ethan can help there too. I tell Jack I'll think about it.

"And by the way, when are you moving back home? At the end of the school year, I hope. Please don't tell me you're spending the summer in town. It's not fair leaving me out on 12th Line with only Joyce and Ethan. Ethan's improved lately, I admit that. But Joyce is still Joyce. I don't have anyone to talk to—anyone *normal*."

Jack laughs. "Gee, thanks. Normal? Since when do you like *normal*?"

"Okay, not normal. A superstar. I don't have a superstar to talk to."

He puts an arm around my neck in a rough little hug and then lets me go. "Call me anytime," he says, swinging down the hall on his crutches.

I head home on the school bus, wondering if I've got it straight. I mean, whether Lester is the guy I think he is. A shortish guy with a buzz cut. I guess you could say he has a cute face. With Matthew getting a little stranger every time I see him, and Kip hundreds of miles away and probably never wanting to see me again, maybe I should give Lester a chance. If only to see how many more ways I can be a total loser with guys.

On second thought, I don't need to know.

13

*Y*esterday evening, I was doing a bit of research on the Internet. I'd promised Morris I would, before Clarisse got back from staying with her sister. He wants to be able to give her an update and reassure her we're making progress. I feel sorry for her, I really do. It's hard enough dealing with a messed-up ghost who's your best friend. A ghost who's a total stranger is so much worse.

My mind kept drifting back to Kip. It took all my self-control not to put his name in the search engine instead. The last time I did that, I regretted it. I wonder how he and his new "friend" are making out. And *if* they're making out. By now, they probably are. It's been three weeks since I last saw him, leaving town on the regional bus. But mostly, when I think of him, I see him bursting out of the Cornflower Inn bedroom in the middle of the night wearing nothing but his jeans. If only I'd been clear-headed enough to take a picture. Then at least I'd have something worth staring at.

It turns out that Eric Carmichael was a big shot. A local politician. He was on the town council for years, like about thirty, one of the longest-serving councillors in Grey County. He was born and raised here and lived in town most of his life. He only moved into the big house on 28th Sideroad in his later years. He died in 1994, in his mid-seventies, which is when the house was sold. I decided I'd head over to the county archives after school to find out more. This morning, sitting on the school bus with Ethan, I broke down and asked if he wanted to help me with more research. Joyce was going to swing by Owen Sound on her way home from the riding stables, so that would give us an hour free before hitching a lift back home with her. Ethan, of course, said, "Cool," grinning all the way into town.

I got through the school day okay. Morgan reminded me about tomorrow's party and I asked if I could come to her house first so we could go together. I've been trying not to think about it. I've seen Lester a couple of times since she first mentioned him, and both times were awkward. I guess we're on each other's radar now, whether we like it or not. Our eyes kind of met in the cafeteria but I looked away fast. I couldn't help it. I was tempted to look back but I didn't want to risk it. He probably already regrets mentioning me to anyone.

After school, Ethan and I walked over to the archives office. I wanted him to find whatever he could in the local newspaper about Carmichael, and hopefully his obituary too. In the back of my mind, I had already decided I was going to spend a bit of time looking up something quite different. I wanted to find anything at all about the death of a young girl in the county. I mean, how many girls die at that age? Not many, in any given year. So I figured it would be a big news story. But I spent ages looking and I couldn't find anything. I went through the last ten years, then the ten before that, and the ten before that. Nothing.

Ethan, who'd been reading files on-line at another workstation, called me over, saying he'd found a ton of stuff. Most important was a long obituary for Eric Carmichael. It had a picture of him, taken when he was younger, smiling at his desk with a mouthful of big teeth—and a shining bald forehead. *Bingo,* I thought. Okay, that's not absolute proof, but it's pretty key. This guy was already seriously bald, and the picture was from 1978. The other thing the obituary said was that he'd died after a lengthy illness, during which he was cared for at home by his wife. His *fourth* wife.

Ethan found out a few other things, too. Like how he had two drunk-driving charges back in the mid-1980s. One was dropped. Also, he'd been investigated by authorities twice, once for financial irregularities during a campaign and once for accepting bribes—he had gotten an extra-good deal on a new car from a dealership in Springmount, which might have been connected with some road construction done near there at the time. At least, those were the accusations from a reporter on the local paper. Carmichael was never charged. In fact, when he retired, he was celebrated like some kind of local hero. Whether he was ever guilty of anything or not, by the time he died, nobody seemed to care. But I can't help thinking that a ghost who doesn't want to show his face might have a guilty conscience about something. And then there's that awful feeling of remorse I pick up from him.

We were about to leave when Ethan said something that made me stop and think. He said that if we were much later, Joyce would file a missing persons report. It gave me this idea to do one last search, not of girls who had died but of girls who had simply gone missing.

That's when I found her.

Jenny Barton.

She was twelve years old, just as I thought. She disappeared from her hometown of Hanover on a Thursday afternoon, March 25, 1986. The last time anyone saw her was at about four p.m, after school. She was riding her bike north on Highway 6. She was wearing a pink ski jacket.

It was a huge story at the time, and it led to a province-wide manhunt. At first everyone assumed she'd run away from home, but soon the big fear was that she'd been abducted. People thought maybe someone had convinced her to get into a car, and had thrown her bike in the trunk, because they never found a trace of her, or her bike, for that matter. That's who's hanging out in that forest along 28th Sideroad. Jenny Barton.

A second search of her name brought up a few articles following up on the disappearance, but after several years there was nothing more. As far as everybody knew, she'd just vanished.

On the drive home, Joyce puts me through the third degree. I've been wondering when that was going to happen. She wants to know what we were up to at the archives, and why Ethan was with me. And what this has to do with school, which is the only thing I should be spending time doing research for. Of course she's already guessed that the research is for Morris, but she wants to hear me confess. So I have to admit that it's about the Cornflower Inn—the owner thinks there's a ghost haunting the place, and she told Detective Grierson, and he told Morris and actually asked Morris if we could do something to help the woman. That's Clarisse, I explain, the woman who owns the inn. And a *direct request* from Detective Grierson, I repeat.

Joyce turns and looks at me with her steely eyes for so long that I wonder if I should remind her that she's driving, and shouldn't she be looking at the road once in a while? I think it totally caught her off guard, though, me mentioning Detective Grierson. I make a mental note that his name is the one to drop when I'm in these tricky situations. He makes the whole thing sound more legit, and there's also something a bit unusual about him, for a cop, and she has a weakness for unusual people.

"Clarisse who?" she finally asks, sounding irritated, so I tell her what I know. "She's really nice," I assure her. "Very classy," I add, wondering if that's a word Joyce would like. Maybe not so much. "She's really hard-working." That goes over better. "I was just trying to give her some help figuring out who the ghost might be. Checking the archives."

"And why is that?"

"Because if she knows more about the identity of the ghost, maybe she can get it to leave her house. Find out what's keeping it from moving on to, you know, wherever, and see if there's anything she can do about it."

"And what's 'wherever'?" she says, sounding skeptical as can be.

"I don't know, but there's something that happens when people die, and if something goes wrong they seem to get stuck between their past lives and something else. That's what ghosts are—they're stuck." I think of Matthew. "Sometimes by choice." Then I think of my mom. Why was she stuck? She always seemed worried.

"And something 'goes wrong' how?"

"I'm not sure."

Ethan's been strangely quiet the whole ride home, but he's paying attention. Now he speaks up.

"I think it's 'cause they get to be invisible and they don't have to go to school or work or anything else. They have total freedom. Just hang out all day and no one can even see them. Except Amelia." He grins at me.

Joyce says nothing to that. It may be the first time ever, at least in my memory, that she hasn't grabbed the last word in a conversation. It's like she doesn't know what else to say.

But just when I think I'm safe, as we turn into the driveway, she thinks of something.

"I don't like the sound of this. It's time your friend Morris and I had another little talk."

14

I find Joyce at the sink in a blue shower cap and bath-robe, making her morning coffee. It's Saturday and she's getting around to it a little late. She smacks the spoonfuls of coffee into the little basket with such sharp whacks that I wonder if she's suffering from serious caffeine withdrawal. Should I give her some time to drink down a cup, or just take my chances?

"Would you mind if I spent the night at Clarisse's inn? Tonight?" I'm cringing inside. I don't know where I'm getting the nerve to ask, but there goes.

"I would." *Whack.*

"It's just that I have this party tonight, I told you about it. I'm going with Morgan. So I'll be kind of late anyway. And Morris"—Joyce stiffens—"Morris is seeing Clarisse in town tonight and she said she could pick me up from the party and we could go back to her place for the night. She'll bring me home in the morning."

"No. I don't like the sound of that."

"But why? Morris thinks she's nice. And Detective Grierson is practically friends with her."

"She's a total stranger who just happens to think she has a ghost in her house. I don't think so. I can pick you up from your party."

Ugh. I go up to my bedroom, sit at my computer desk and phone Morris to tell him what we've learned about Carmichael.

"Interesting, eh?" I say. "I'm getting a definite feeling about this ghost. I think he's a guy with a guilty conscience. But the question is, why?"

"So you're already convinced the ghost is Carmichael?"

"Well . . . yeah. He was bald, for one thing. And he was a corrupt politician. Oh, and a cheater. That's what I'm reading between the lines."

"Lots of men are bald," Morris says. He thinks I'm jumping to conclusions, and tries to convince me to keep an open mind. "If every corrupt, womanizing politician became a troubled ghost, we'd have quite a crowd of them on our hands. I'm just saying maybe there's more to it than that."

Then I tell him that I don't think Joyce is going to let me go to the inn tonight. (I should have let her have that cup of coffee first.) He says maybe he should try talking to her.

"Be my guest. She does want to talk to you. But—warning—I don't think it'll be friendly."

"Well, here's an idea. What if I bring Clarisse over there to meet Joyce in person? Clarisse is wild about horses too, so they'd have something in common. We could say it's because she wants to talk horses."

I think about that. I suppose it's worth a try. "Fine. Good luck with that."

I've got something else to think about—this party tonight. It's at Kristen's place. She's another of Morgan's best friends. And this guy Lester will be there. Probably nothing will come of it. I bet he'll avoid me all night. I don't care. Only I'm afraid it will be awkward, and maybe even embarrassing. Especially if he told people he's interested in me and now he's changed his mind. Which is probably what happened. I mean, why else has he not made the tiniest move to talk to me or even come within twenty feet of me all week? So fine. I hope to look as decent for the party as I can, and act as natural as possible, which is always tough, and just try to enjoy myself. How horrible can it be, compared to everything else that's happened this year?

I'm in my room most of the afternoon, doing homework and psyching myself up to go out tonight, when through my window I catch sight of Morris and Joyce and Clarisse walking toward the paddock to see the horses. Holy crap, that was fast. I keep an eye on them without being obvious about it. Won't it be odd if Clarisse and Joyce hit it off? They're kind of opposites. Clarisse is wearing ankle boots with heels and tight purple jeans. Not exactly Joyce's style.

They're out there stroking Marley and Ponyboy and talking for at least an hour, and when I catch them finally walking back toward the kitchen I have to think. I hear the back door open and shut and now they're in the kitchen. Should I go downstairs and say hello? Or should I stay out of it? I decide I'd better head down and, taking a deep breath at the kitchen entrance, I walk in as casually as I can fake.

Morris and Clarisse are sitting at the table and Joyce is making tea. Morris looks up first, with a big hello like he'd forgotten I live here. Right. And Clarisse smiles and says hello too, but she's a lot cooler about it. Joyce barely looks up, acknowledging me with a lift of one of her bushy eyebrows. She looks a little worried, so they must have gotten somewhere with her. Clarisse confirms my suspicion.

"Your grandmother says that if you want to spend a night at the Cornflower Inn, it's up to you."

Really? What did they have to tell her to get her to agree to that? But all I can think to say is "Oh. Okay."

"Yeah . . . so anytime would be fine with me. Tonight, even."

Clarisse doesn't want to spend another night in that place alone, so no kidding, *tonight*. I glance at Joyce but she's looking down, concentrating on her boiling kettle. I look at Morris, who widens his eyes as if he's surprised too.

"Well, uh, great. I mean, why not? I'm in town tonight, over on 8th Avenue. Should we say tonight, then? Joyce? Are you sure?"

Joyce throws me a look to let me know she's not happy, then stops what she's doing and shuts her eyes for a second. When she opens them, she shrugs and says, "It's your decision, I guess." She brings two cups of tea to the table, spilling one of them a bit as she sets it down.

"I've got it," Morris says, jumping up to grab the dishcloth hanging over the faucet.

She lets him clear up the spill, and sits down with a third cup in her hand.

"Now, where was I? Oh yes, that's when I heard this awful bang coming from the engine . . . ," Clarisse is saying, and she proceeds to tell Joyce all about some bad experience she once had trying to start up a gas-powered chainsaw or something.

I decide to back slowly out of the room and head upstairs.

Sitting at my computer, I think about e-mailing Kip. I flash back to the two of us at the Cornflower Inn, in the living room, sipping hot chocolate. I've got this image of him in my mind, sitting across from me on the couch, and I hold it steady, trying to recall every part of him. Everything he said, every little gesture. Before he changed his tone and decided to call me on everything.

Dear Kip, I type, *Please forgive me.*

I hit the delete key.

15

I drag my bike out from behind the garage and head down the driveway and south on 12th Line. I've told Joyce I'm off on one of my marathon bike rides. Of course, she asked me how last night was, the party and then the sleepover at the inn, and I told her both were pretty uneventful, which is about half true.

There's a heavy, grey sky today. It could start raining any minute. I'm really hoping it holds off, at least for another couple of hours. Until I've done what I have to do.

As I ride, I think about the party, which could have been a lot worse, I guess. Lester finally walked up to me, about thirty minutes before I had to leave, and said hello. He looked embarrassed and I'm sure it wasn't easy for him. I'd been anxious about whether we were ever going to talk, so it was kind of a relief when we did. I just wanted something *normal* to happen, like a chat or whatever. I wasn't going to track him down or anything. I figured he'd started this whole awkward thing so it was his job to make the first move.

And we did talk, about our math teacher. Then he mentioned how my brother Jack seemed to be doing well after his "broken back" drama. I also found out that we used to live only about a block away from each other years ago, before his family moved to a bigger house in town. He asked me if I downhill ski, and he seemed disappointed when I said no. Then we ran out of things to say. So much for normal.

The truth is, he seemed really nervous. But I've decided he's not such a bad guy. Maybe he really is shy, like Morgan said. Maybe I'm the first girl in school he's talked to outside of class. Maybe he thought I would be a good person to practise on.

As I reach the top of the hill, I can see that the Telford farm has a shiny black car parked out front. *Damn.* I slow down but I don't dare stop. As I ride by, I look up at the second-floor windows but I can't see anyone. There are lights on inside the house. Maybe they've finally finished the rewiring.

There's another huge trash bin outside, the size of a shed, filled with ripped-out kitchen cupboards and all kinds of debris, looking like the wreckage from a tornado. Big chunks of wallboard and wood and old carpet. The car in the driveway doesn't look like it belongs to one of the renovators. It looks like the kind of car lawyers would drive. A Mercedes or something. *Matthew, I don't want to even think about what you're up to in there. I understand you're frustrated, but please, please behave.*

Who am I kidding, that I can understand anything about how ghosts feel? Or that I can get through to Matthew better than I can to the ghost at the inn? Which is not at all.

Clarisse picked me up from the party, as we'd planned, and we drove back to her place. I'll admit that heading back to the inn made me think much more about Kip than about Clarisse's ghost.

In fact, she came right out and asked me about him, which was really unnerving.

"How's your friend Kip?"

"All right, I guess. I mean, I'm not sure. We haven't talked in a while." I remembered what Kip had said, about her suggesting that he confront me.

"Oh, that's a shame. I thought you two had something going on."

"Not exactly." I really didn't want to talk about him to her, like she was some older sister or something. An older sister you couldn't trust not to steal your boyfriend if she had half a chance.

She just shrugged and said she'd had a hunch. "Something's going on between you two. Am I not right? Lots of something." She paused, looking at me, then said, "Which is really sweet. So why all the pain? What could be so complicated at your age?" She told me she thought he was *just adorable*. No kidding. Then she went into a big thing about how lots of promising relationships never get off the ground because each person is waiting for the other to make the first move.

"By the time you reach my age," she said, "you could be filled with regrets about that. Don't let it happen. It'll make you miserable."

"Did that ever happen to you?" I asked her, vaguely curious. She was the one getting personal, after all.

She laughed out loud. "Me? Hardly. No, I never waste time waiting. Not if I can do something about it."

"And how has that worked out for you? I hope I don't sound rude."

"Not at all. Well . . . life has been interesting, so far. Lots of chapters. Some up, some down. All interesting. To me anyway." She smiled as if maybe she had a few good secrets of her own.

"Anyway, as I said, too bad about you and Kip. Not one I'd toss back, if I were you."

Maybe my concentration was off, from thinking too much about Kip, or maybe I've just got a lot to learn about talking to ghosts. But I'm not sure last night's encounter was a success. This ghost is such a hard read. After I'd slept a few hours in the same bedroom I'd stayed in before, I woke up with that same feeling that the ghost was nearby, and I decided to try to get through to him again. I found him on the back stairs, just like before, sitting on one of the lower steps in the shadow, with his back to me.

I started by talking to him in a quiet voice, saying he seemed really unhappy. Was there anything I could do for him? He didn't move, didn't lower his hands from his face, but I could hear this weak and raspy *g-g-g-g* coming from him. I waited to see if it would turn into a word. I was wondering if maybe he was trying to say *Go away*. He seemed to give up in frustration. There was a long silence and then the sound started up again, *g-g-g*.

Strange how some ghosts can talk and talk, and others can't or won't. This one was desperately struggling to say something but he couldn't get it out. That was my impression, anyway. And I was starting to feel frustrated too.

Finally the bony hands dropped from the face and slowly started to reach back and up the stairs toward me, just like before. I went on high alert on account of last time. But this time only the hands moved, twisting behind the ghost's back and bending in the shoulder sockets like the arms of a circus freak, the palms reaching out to me. In a raspy voice he said, "G-g-give."

"You want me to give you something? What can I give you? Do I have something you want?" I watched the fingers trembling as if straining for something just beyond reach. I decided to take a chance.

"Mr. Carmichael?" No answer. "Is it you, Mr. Carmichael?"

The hands coiled into fists and pulled back in front to cover the face again. *Aha!* I thought.

"Look, I know a bit about you," I said, trying to put it as gently as possible. "I know that you weren't exactly a saint during your lifetime. That there were a few political scandals. Four wives. Maybe you weren't a very faithful husband, or a devoted father." The ghost slowly rose to his feet. I braced myself. "I'm not judging you or anything. Not at all."

Just in case, I took a careful step backwards, closer to the half-opened door.

"Because no one's perfect, right? So . . . Mr. Carmichael, if you're feeling bad about yourself or how you lived your life, maybe some of the decisions you made, you should try to get over it. Cut yourself some slack, you know?" The ghost seemed frozen, listening. I figured maybe I was on a roll. "Besides, it's all over now. Your life, I mean. Not much you can do about the past. You should just move on. I mean literally. You should leave this house and move on. Head west, or whatever. What's done is done."

And that's when I realized I couldn't see him anymore. He'd just faded away.

Now what? Had I made any impression at all? I waited to see if he'd reappear, for maybe fifteen minutes, and then I gave up and went back to bed. Who knows? Maybe it worked. Maybe the ghost is gone.

Over breakfast in her fancy dining room this morning, I told Clarisse about my encounter with her ghost. She doesn't like it when I refer to him as "her" ghost. Anyway, I told her how I had a little talk with him and suggested he let go or move on, whatever you call it when ghosts go away, and he hadn't really responded.

Now all we can do is wait to see what happens next. But from the minute I woke up this morning it's not her ghost who's been on my mind. It's *my* ghosts, Matthew and Jenny. Ghosts I can relate to. I have a strong desire to see them both.

When I reach that stretch of 28th Sideroad, I check that there are no cars or people anywhere in sight and come to a stop. I drag my bike into the trees along the side, pulling it over the rough forest floor, over roots and rocks, trying to keep it from getting tangled in branches and bushes. As I stop to look back, asking myself if I've taken it far enough from the road, I hear her.

"Are you going to drag it all the way to the swamp?" She's standing about twenty feet away, drenched from head to toe and shivering. Her face is greyish white like the belly of a fish. Her hair, her pink jacket, her blue jeans are dripping wet.

"Pardon me?"

"Are you going to put your bike in the swamp?" Her eyes are wide and intense. Her wet bangs are stuck to her forehead.

"You must be so cold," I say. "Freezing. Why are you all wet?"

"That's where *my* bike is. In the swamp." She says this as if she's trying to sound brave.

"Why is it in the swamp?"

"A man put it there."

"What do you mean? A man put your bike in the swamp? What man?"

"He put it in the swamp. It broke through the ice and sank. The ice just broke."

Oh my God, why would someone do that to her bike?

"Is your name Jenny?" She nods. "Jenny, did something bad happen to you? Did somebody do something to you? The man who put your bike in the swamp?"

"The girls in my class, they did something bad. They ran away when I came. They lied and said they had to go home. Then they went to Martha's house. And they laughed at me. They said mean things. The girls at my school hate me."

"But. . . ." I'm confused. "Did the girls at your school hurt you? Did they do this to you?"

She hangs her head, her hair in clumps dripping down her face. She looks away, folding her arms tightly, holding onto herself. She looks freezing cold.

"My bike is in the swamp" is all she says, and she starts walking away, deeper into the trees, toward the swamp.

At first I don't move, I just watch her walk through the trees, but then I lose sight of her. I drop my bike and follow her, but when I get to the edge of the swamp she's nowhere.

The swamp has thawed since I was last here. Now it's just dark water full of rotted wood and algae. I look up at the deer stand. She's not there. I look beyond the swamp to the trees on the other side, where I last saw deer—empty and still. I listen but hear only the usual birds calling.

Looking down into the swamp water, I remember something Kip said when he fell through the ice. He said that whatever he fell backwards over felt like metal. I walk along the edge of the swamp until I'm as close as I can get to the place where he fell. I look around for a broken tree branch I can use to test the water's depth. Then I check out the height of my rubber boots and slowly wade in, testing the soggy bottom with each step. After about six steps the water's near the top of my boots, and I don't want to go any deeper. I take the tree branch and cast it out in front of me, using it to feel around in the dark water for anything under the surface.

There's something there, all right. I try to push it but it won't budge. I try to lift it by locking the branch into it and pulling up. Something moves and breaks the surface. It's ancient and rusted, in the shape of a bicycle wheel.

"Jenny?" I call out, and listen. There's no answer. I let the wheel go and it disappears underwater again.

I back out of the swamp and onto dry land, then slowly turn full circle, scanning the trees for anything pink, anything unnatural, anything moving. Finally I give up. It's going to start raining any minute, and I've got to head home.

I make my way to where I left my bike and that's when I see her pale little face. She's sitting on the ground at a distance. She's not wet anymore.

"Jenny?"

"I like your bike."

"Jenny, what happened to you?"

"I ran away."

"I know, but what happened then?"

She's staring at my bike. "It's because the girls at my school hate me. They say mean things."

"But what happened here?"

"The man put my bike in the swamp."

She's fading, so I ask quickly, "Jenny, did the man . . . hurt you?"

"He put my bike in the swamp," she repeats, and now I can barely see her.

"Jenny?"

Nothing. She's gone.

I think about her the whole ride home. She was only twelve, two years younger than Ethan. Still a child, young and innocent. Something very bad happened to her and no one ever knew, except for the guy who did it. I have to sit back on my bike seat and wipe a few tears from my eyes before I can go on.

There's a rainstorm banging against my bedroom window, and every few minutes a lightning flash and then a crack of thunder. I'm lucky I made it home before it got this bad. I call Morris from my cellphone, hoping Joyce is preoccupied with making dinner down in the kitchen.

"Morris, I think I've uncovered a crime."

"A crime? Does this have something to do with Clarisse's place?" He lowers his voice. "Because all hell's breaking loose."

"What do you mean? She was fine when she dropped me off this morning."

"Well, she's not fine now," he whispers in his hoarse, raspy voice. "She's upstairs taking a bath."

"WHAT?"

"She called me a few hours ago saying she couldn't stay another night at the inn until that ghost is gone, and asking if she could crash here until she can arrange some temporary living space. So what could I say?"

"She's moved into your house? This sounds like a set-up for a sitcom."

"Glad you're amused. She's using Kip's bedroom. Just for a few nights, that's the deal." He pauses. "No smart remarks, please." It's true that I'm laughing on the inside, but I wouldn't dare say anything out loud.

"Apparently, whatever you said to the ghost last night didn't work. She says it made things worse. She's been hearing moaning through the walls all day. Wherever she goes in the house, she hears the floors creaking somewhere else. Shuffling, creaking, groaning, you name it. Once the thunder and lightning started, that was it. She'd already finished packing when she called me. She says it's like you touched a nerve, and now the ghost is having a total meltdown."

"Gosh . . . I don't know what to say. The last thing I wanted to do was make him more upset."

"I know, I know. Look, it's not your fault. Just tell me what you said to it. Then we can think about what to do next."

After I tell Morris exactly what happened between me and the ghost, word for word, and describe every gesture, there's a long silence on the other end of the phone. Finally he says, "Well, damned if I know what went wrong. Sounds like you were friendly enough."

"Maybe this is the darkness before the dawn. Like he's on the verge of a breakthrough, and just getting some stuff out of his system before he moves on to a better place."

"Yeah . . . or maybe he's losing control and he's about to get completely impossible. It'll be such a shame if she has to abandon her inn over this."

Now I feel guilty. "What should we do?"

"Well, until Clarisse makes some kind of arrangement to move in with her sister, we shouldn't do anything. I don't think she'll be here long."

"Is she really upset?"

"She arrived this afternoon with a big bottle of Chilean red, and let's say she was disappointed that I wouldn't help her drink it. But . . . what did you mean earlier, about a crime?"

"Oh . . . never mind. That can wait."

"What can wait? What's happened?"

"Nothing. Not recently, anyway. I'll tell you later."

Morris isn't happy about being put off, but we say goodbye and I hang up. The lights flicker, then go out. Damn. My computer screen goes black. I walk over to my bedroom door and peek out.

"Hey!" Ethan comes out of the living room, where he's been playing a video game. "What the hell? Joyce! Candles!"

Ethan loves power outages, let's face it.

"Just chill out." Joyce appears at the kitchen entrance. "The power will probably come back on in a minute. It better," she adds. "I've got a chicken in the oven."

I wonder if the power failure has affected Owen Sound. I can't help but find the thought of Morris stuck in the dark with Clarisse pretty amusing. But then my mind wanders down the road to the Telford farm, and I have a flashback to Matthew's doll on the dark stairs. I worry about whether Matthew understands how threatening his behaviour could seem to ordinary people. I really hope the new owners weren't planning on spending the night.

16

*L*ast night's storm was like the Apocalypse. The worst thing about a power outage isn't that the lights go out, or even that the oven doesn't work. We just lit candles and Joyce took the half-cooked chicken out onto the back porch and threw it on the gas barbecue. The worst thing is that the pump for the well stops working. This time we had no running water for, like, eighteen hours. That sucked. No water for washing up, no flushing toilets.

This morning was school, but instead of making us take the bus, Joyce drove Ethan and me to the Tim Hortons restaurant in town for their breakfast special, and the bathrooms.

The second-worst thing about power outages is no Internet. We finally get power back at 4:32 this afternoon, just after I get home from school, and at 4:35 I'm reading my e-mail.

Checking out the Owen Sound Daily News online tonight, as usual, for Dad's latest column (and the obits for you), when I read about Grey County's big power failure. Luckily, candlelight suits you. —Kip

This e-mail is my first contact from Kip in almost six weeks. I sit like an idiot, as usual, staring at the computer with my hands on my heart, trying to breathe. Panic and excitement and longing—the feelings are as strong as ever.

As soon as I stop shaking enough to type, I write back. I figure that's okay, since he started it. I tell him that the power is finally back on (obviously, or I wouldn't be on my computer) and that I've always been more the flashlight type. I tell him that I've been thinking about him, on account of finding an old bike in the swamp.

That thing you tripped over? It was the dead girl's bike. And here's the really disturbing part. She told me a man dragged her bike into the swamp. Why would anyone do that? Unless they wanted to hide it. And why would they want to hide her bike when it happened to belong to a girl who died soon after she went missing? This mystery man obviously had something to do with her death and he was covering up the tracks. It's a cold-case murder mystery. It has to be.

I also mention that the Cornflower Inn ghost isn't doing so well, and has driven poor Clarisse out of the house again. I tell him I'm hoping it wasn't something I said to the ghost that sent him over the edge.

And you'll never guess where it drove her to! To your dad's place! No kidding! In fact, she's sleeping in YOUR bed! It's supposed to be for a few days, but what if she decides she doesn't ever want to leave????

I look at everything I've written. It's quite a lot. Too much, maybe. Should I shorten it? I finally hit send, but not before I've signed off.

I hope you are enjoying your classes and Chicago and life in general.

Not exactly what I wanted to say, but it's been sent. Now I just need to not get all hung up on whether he'll write back.

Morris and I have agreed to meet up after school on Wednesday to review our strategy. In the meantime, I want to check in on Matthew. I'm worried about him. I haven't been able to get in to see him in almost two weeks. Anything could be going on up the road, and I have no way of knowing unless I can get into the house. It sucks that Matthew can't use a cellphone or anything like that. Yet he *can* write with a pen. Weird. There's no use in me trying to make sense of it. I just can't.

The days are getting a little longer, which means I can sneak away after supper to visit Matthew and be back before dark. That's what I'll try to do tonight.

Before supper is on the table, I track down Ethan at his computer. I remind him about the research he did on Carmichael. I've got an idea.

"Ethan, remember how his obituary said he had four wives? It's a long shot, but I'm wondering if any of the wives is still alive. Especially the last one, the one who nursed him when he was dying. Did you happen to write down her name? Do you think you could see what you can find on her, see if she's in the phone book or anything?" The truth is, I could do this myself, but I'm starting to think it's a good idea to give Ethan little research jobs. It's good practice for him, and it makes him happy.

"Totally," he says, and pulls out some lined paper with the notes he took when he was at the archives office. He's made a point-form list of a whole bunch of details about Carmichael. Impressive. He grabs a pencil and runs it down the edge, scanning. "Here she is," he says. "The last wife. Edith Bartlett. She was his office assistant when he was a town councillor. See, it says here. For like seven years before they got married."

"That's interesting. So she would have known him really well. Can you see if you can track down her address and phone number?"

"Sure. What are you trying to find out?"

"I don't know. I'll know when I see it, I guess."

As I leave the room, I stop and look back at Ethan. "You're good at this. You're a really good researcher." He beams. I admit I'm surprised myself. Who'd have guessed? He's only fourteen, and he's not even doing that well at school. Maybe there's hope for him yet.

If Carmichael had anything on his mind on his deathbed—maybe dirty secrets that were bothering him—who'd know better than the person who was nursing him day and night? It could be a big help to talk to her, if she's still alive.

That's what I'm thinking about as I head south on 12th Line toward the Telford farm.

Fingers crossed that no one's home this evening. No one but Matthew, that is. It's a weekday, so I'm assuming that the owners won't be around, and that the reno crew are done for the day. Sure enough, the driveway is empty and the house looks quiet. Thank goodness no other houses have a view of the place, that's all I can say.

As I approach the side door, I can see it's already opened a crack, as if Matthew's been waiting for me.

"Matthew?"

I enter and close the door behind me, then look around. The kitchen is stripped back to the slats behind the plaster. There's shiny new copper plumbing where the sink used to be. Thick wiring and metal boxes for wall plugs and switches are attached every few feet along the walls. Otherwise, the room is an empty shell.

"Matthew, where are you? Are you okay?"

"Compared to what?"

Now I see him, sitting on the lowest step in the staircase.

"What's wrong? Did something happen?" He's not answering. He's just staring down at the floor, bare wood planks now that the old carpet has been ripped up. Everything must be even creakier with the carpets gone.

"Matthew? Talk to me."

"About what?" He's still not looking at me.

I stare at him in silence a little longer. Finally he turns to face me, and his eyes slowly focus.

"They took Amelia from me."

"What?"

"They took my . . . doll. My Amelia doll."

"Oh God, Matthew. What are you saying? What do you mean, they took it from you? Did you leave it hanging around? How did they find it?"

"It's in the garbage bin by the side of the house. She threw it in there. She really is some kind of freak, you know. You wouldn't believe how she reacted after she'd come across it a few times. It was like watching someone go completely mental before your eyes. It would have been funny . . . if it hadn't ended the way it did."

"Oh, Matthew! This is *exactly* what I was afraid of! You *cannot* leave things lying around in this house. You cannot do *anything* in this house that can be seen or heard by the owners. They will catch on to you, and before you know it you'll have priests, TV producers, who knows what else, harassing you. You have to *think* before you do anything! Anything at all!" I'm sick at the thought of what might happen now. "So what you're saying is that the owners suspect the house is haunted?"

"I don't know."

"But did they actually spend time here on the weekend? Overnight?"

"Yes, in a sleeping bag in one of the bedrooms. Like camping. They had a picnic basket. And a bottle of wine."

"So where did they see the doll?"

"Ummm. Well, first time was on the stairs. So she stuck it in a garbage bag in the kitchen. And later, on the window ledge in the bathroom. That's when she started getting freaked. Blaming him. It was like World War Three."

I'm beginning to get the picture. Poor woman. "Was that all? Or was there more?" This is a side of Matthew I haven't seen before. I'm bracing myself.

"Well, she stuck it in a garbage bag again, so of course I had to get it out."

"And what did you do with it?"

"Well . . . I guess I was a little irritated at her."

"And?"

"I just put it somewhere they'd find it later in the day. I think that put her over the edge."

"Where?"

"I mean, how could I know about the thunder and lightning and the power going out?"

"*Where?*"

"In the sleeping bag."

"You *didn't!*" I stare at him in disbelief, and he stifles a smile. "How *could* you? What were you thinking?"

"I don't know. What am I, a mind reader? Anyway, they left soon after that. In the middle of the thunderstorm. But first they dumped her in the bin outside. Where I can't get her."

Crap! That does it. Now they know. Question is, what are they going to do about it?

"Congratulations, Matthew. You officially announced your presence on their very first sleepover."

"Well, I was here first."

"You're not serious. You didn't buy this place, remember? You just broke in." I feel like I'm talking to a crazy person.

"But it was your idea, or have you forgotten? And it feels like my home now."

He stands up and turns to walk slowly up the stairs. His attitude is making me very nervous, but he's right—this was my idea. I follow him. He stops on the second-floor landing and looks out a window that opens onto the side of the property. You can see the big dumpster below. He leans his face against the glass, sideways, his eyes on the bin.

"I've never seen you like this before, Matthew. You've got to pull yourself together. I think you're taking this too hard."

He turns his head toward me with a jerk. "Is that what you *think*? Well, easy for you. You don't know what it's like. You don't have a clue."

I cringe at that. I've never heard him so angry. I close my eyes for a moment, trying to think.

"You're right, I don't know what it's like. And you can't just go out and rescue the doll yourself?"

"No, I can't. Don't ask me why. I can't leave the house, for some reason. Not these days, anyway."

Strange. It's like what Morris said about the barn—that a haunted space takes on a quality of its own that can affect the ghost. That's what he means by "hallowed." It's the reason the ghosts couldn't leave the barn until it burned down. Unless you're talking about

Jimmy, who could leave so long as he was possessing some poor guy. Morris says possessing someone is the ultimate achievement for ghosts. It gives them so many options.

"If it'll help, I guess I could fish your doll out. But only if you'll hide it somewhere, *really* hide it and keep it hidden. Somewhere in the attic where they'll never ever find it. Will you do that?"

His face softens and he nods like a child.

"Fine, then," I say, trying to suppress my annoyance. I head downstairs and outside. It's awful seeing him this upset. He's got me worried. But am I just asking for more trouble? I walk up to the bin, wondering if I can even reach inside. No, the sides are too high. I find an old wooden chair in the backyard; it's rotting but I think it'll take my weight. I bring it to the back of the bin, step up onto it and peer inside. The doll is right on top of a heap of junk. Weird. Her round, human-like eyes are looking up at me and her slightly open little mouth has a dumb smile, as if she's saying, *Oh! It's you!*

I take a deep breath, bend at the waist, reach down and grab her by the leg. As I lift her out, I glance up at the window. Matthew is watching me, his cheek still pressed against the glass. I lift the doll high and give it a little shake in his direction, then head back inside and run up the stairs two steps at a time with the doll in my hand.

"Mission accomplished," I say. "Safe and sound. No damage done." I balance her on the banister at the top of the staircase. "But only on condition that you hide her. Let's find a place right now, okay?"

He gives me a little smile and moves toward her as I back away, into the bedroom with the attic hatch.

Up in the attic, Matthew lightens up, literally. He's got that soft glow again, as if something under his skin is shining through. It's pretty eerie but I don't really mind, because at least he's happier now. He hides the doll under some insulation in the far corner of the attic, then moves the old sewing machine over the spot.

"Has anyone been up here lately?"

"Only the roofers. They didn't seem to care about any of the stuff. They were just checking the rafters for rot." He's calming down now, settling into an old chair like it's his favourite. "So what's new with you?"

"Uh . . . not much. I've been trying to communicate with a couple of other ghosts lately. An old guy who hangs out in a country inn on 28th Sideroad. He's all miserable and moany and I'm trying to find out what his problem is, but he's terrible at talking. I've managed to get two lousy words out of him. I can barely make them out and they make no sense at all."

"What are they? Maybe I can help."

"Well, the first time I saw him, all I could get out of him was one word, the number four. And I only guessed that because he kept knocking four times to get my attention. And so far, the only thing that relates to the number four is the number of marriages the guy had. The second time I saw him, about six weeks later, again he only said one word. He was holding his hands out in the creepiest way imaginable, and what he said sounded like *give*, like he wanted me to give him something. God knows what."

"Hmm."

"What?"

"So he's only said two words, *four* and *give*?"

"That's right."

He doesn't say anything for the longest time, just stares at something across the attic floor. Finally he looks at me. "And you're sure it was two words?"

"Yeah, just two words."

"Not one word?"

I've been sitting hunched on one crossbeam, feet resting on the next, arms wrapped around my knees. Now I drop my head down between my arms, embarrassed. *Forgive?* Why didn't I think of that?

"My God, Matthew, that didn't occur to me. Wow! You may be right. It kind of makes sense that he was trying to say *forgive*. He wants forgiveness. He certainly looks like a guy with regrets."

It's almost seven now and I've got to get back home, so Matthew and I head downstairs. I want to part with him on an upbeat. The last thing I need is to leave him in a bad mood, so I thank him for his help with Clarisse's ghost.

"Really, that's very helpful. I still can't figure out why the four knocks, though. Maybe it was just another way to say *for*. Like he was searching for different ways to express it."

"It's hard to say what you mean," says Matthew. "You do your best, try everything you can think of, because sometimes words don't work. For ghosts, anyway."

"For everyone."

Once outside, I remember to put the old chair at the back of the house where I found it. I wonder if it was smart to give him back his doll.

This little solution, Matthew? The farmhouse? It's not working out so well. But I don't know what else to do, where else in this world you can belong.

How do I talk to him about this? I can't even begin to think of the right words.

17

orris and I are heading back toward Owen Sound, driving south through Wiarton. I'm in the passenger seat, trying to write down some of the more interesting things Edith Bartlett told us, before I forget them. Edith's probably already forgotten them, because she was a little drunk.

I've already filled Morris in on the details of my latest visit with Matthew. The first was how Matthew pointed out to me that the two words spoken by Clarisse's ghost might have been two halves of one word: *for-give*.

Morris was impressed.

The second was that the new owners of the farm have probably figured out by now that the house they've bought is friggin' haunted. Unfortunately, Matthew is way too fond of that doll he found in the attic, and that's what's causing the problems.

"How do you mean 'fond'?" Morris asked.

"Well, he's named it Amelia. And he's been leaving it all over the house for them to find. On purpose."

Morris ran a hand through his straggly grey hair. "Great. Just great. Does the doll look like you?"

I laughed. "Hardly. For one thing, it has no hair. And its eyes look more real than mine." Then I remembered to ask him about Clarisse. "Still hanging around your house, taking baths and stuff?"

He muttered, "Don't ask."

"All right. If you don't want to talk about it," I tease him. "Really. I understand."

"Thank you," he said, trying to sound firm. Embarrassed, more like.

Edith Bartlett was pretty interesting. She lives by herself in a small cottage up the Bruce Peninsula coast. She's in her mid-seventies, which means she was about twenty years younger than her husband, Eric Carmichael, when they married. Wife number four. All Morris had to do to get her to agree to an interview was tell her that he's working on a column about famous local politicians. He said he was hoping for some personal background on her husband, because he was such a colourful character and all. He introduced me as a student intern helping him with research.

She greeted us on her front porch with a glass of what looked like water with ice in it, but we figured out pretty fast that she wasn't drinking water. For one thing, she clutched it close to her chest. She asked if she could get us a drink and Morris asked for tea. But she stuck to her glass the whole time we were there, and disappeared to refill it, too, weaving a bit as she walked inside.

We settled down on her back porch, facing Lake Huron. That part of the shore is flat and marshy, not sandy like Sauble Beach or anything, but on this beautiful spring day it seemed like an amazing place to live, the air filled with the sound of birds. Edith's a big woman with a fleshy red face, and she owns a big dog, one of those huge black ones with a large head and long hair. It lay on the porch with us the whole time, with its head resting on her feet as if they were a pillow. Every once in a while she talked baby talk to it.

She spoke in a loud voice, hooting and laughing a lot, sometimes almost singing her words. A bit loony, really. All about how her Eric was such a natural politician and had a great way with people. She did imitations of him, full of drama and dumb jokes. He'd been involved in local politics and community affairs for years, was a bit of a local celebrity before she got to know him personally. He gave so much to the people of Grey County, she said. He'd hired her to help run his office back in 1982. Her eyes were pink and glassy as she remembered those years, calling them "the good old days."

Morris asked her who Eric was married to at that time.

She cleared her throat. "Rose," she said. "His third wife." She must have realized that this sounded a little weird. We were talking Owen Sound here, not bloody Hollywood.

Morris asked what she knew about the first two wives.

"Not much," she said. "He'd married very young. Had two children right away. He had a third child with his second wife, in the early 1970s. Unfortunately, he was never close to his kids. Too much of a workaholic. Didn't see any of them much once the marriages broke up. He and Rose married in the late seventies. He broke up his second marriage for her. She was a sweet, shy gal and he'd fallen in love with her, but he regretted it soon enough. Not the best choice for a politician's wife. Her nerves were bad. She was *fragile*, you might say." Edith gave us a look as if she'd almost felt sorry for her. As if Rose had been pretty pathetic.

"She'd wanted children too," Edith added, "but it never happened. She died of cancer in 1987. Horrible ordeal."

"And what was it like, working for him during the 1980s?" Morris asked.

She got this smug look on her face and took another sip from her glass. "Well, we didn't have your typical working relationship, I can admit that now. We were . . . very close, right from the start. For many years. We knew how to have a good time." She paused, smiling to herself. "And he leaned on me a lot, for the kind of support a better wife might have given. And when Rose died, well, we didn't waste any time. We married the following September, and he retired soon after. We enjoyed what we had of his retirement years, before he got too ill."

Once we had let her sing his praises for a while longer, I asked Edith how he had died. "It was Alzheimer's," she said. "That was rough."

"I can imagine." Morris nodded sympathetically.

"You know what it's like," she went on. "The disease ran its course. His mind became increasingly somewhere else, stuck in the past. He would have these imaginary conversations with people who weren't there. He would get very moody and agitated. He was always wandering around upstairs, talking to himself."

"I hope you don't mind me asking, but did he die at home?"

"Oh, I don't mind," she said. "Yes, he did. From a fall. He got so weak and disoriented toward the end, and it was hard to keep an eye on him around the clock. He managed to sneak out of bed one night. He fell down a flight of stairs and hit his head. The paramedics couldn't revive him."

Morris and I looked at each other. I was the one to ask, "He died on the staircase?"

"Not the central staircase. The back staircase," she said. "The one we never used. I don't know where he thought he was going. He'd always kept the bottom door locked on the kitchen side."

Well, that was all we needed to hear. We thanked her very much, and Morris looked ready to leave, but she seemed so loose and relaxed by that time that I decided to ask her one more thing. It was pretty personal, and I didn't know if she'd be offended. I asked her if she thought Rose had suspected how close she and Eric really were. I was trying to figure out how guilty this Carmichael guy might feel.

We sat there in her wicker porch chairs, looking out at the lake, waiting for her to answer.

"I don't know. She was a very private person. If she ever confronted Eric about it, he never told me." She paused, looking into her drink, and a shadow of concern came over her face, pinching her forehead. "There was one time when I thought she'd figured us out. A political fundraiser at the bingo one Thursday evening. She and Eric had separate cars, because he'd come straight from the office. It was quite a party atmosphere, and I guess we'd all had a few beers. Anyway, Eric and I may have let down our guard a bit. He stole a kiss in a backroom, and I swore at the time that she caught sight of it."

For the first time, I noticed a slight tremor in her hand. She took another sip of her drink.

"Anyway, she left suddenly, looking pale, saying she wasn't feeling well. It turned out that she'd been diagnosed with cancer not long before that, had just had her first chemo treatment, and no one in the office even knew yet. But I remember Eric taking Friday off, and coming into the office Monday morning looking pretty rough himself, saying she'd been in a car accident on the way home that night. Hit a deer, he said. I remember asking if maybe she'd been too upset to be driving alone. It kind of weighed on me. But he wouldn't talk about it." She mumbled under her breath, "Poor gal."

Now, as we enter the strip-mall area on the outskirts of Owen Sound, Morris admits that he's coming around to my theory—that

Carmichael is our ghost and he died with a bad conscience. But he's still not convinced that we have the whole picture. The gritty details.

"But he was obviously a jerk," I point out. "He was a failure as a father and a husband. And it sounds like he and Edith were having an affair through most of that marriage. Rose *must* have known about it. And who knows how he behaved in the first two marriages?"

"It sounds bad, I agree, but not that unusual. Not that extreme, I'm afraid. Would that turn him into this tortured soul stuck in his old home, unable to let go? There must be more to it."

"Maybe there is, and Edith just wants to protect his reputation."

We both sit in silence, thinking about what to do next.

Later, as Morris turns onto 12th Line to drop me off, he speaks up again. "The practical question is, if this guy is hanging around because he needs forgiveness, how do we get it for him? Do we bring a priest to the house, maybe? Not to hear his confession, since he's not much of a talker. But to perform some kind of absolution? I don't know. Maybe that could be arranged. I know the parish priest at St. Timothy's quite well."

"Absolution?" I ask.

"Just a fancy church word for forgiveness. The priest acts on behalf of God, absolving you of your sins. It's a little ritual. It means that God forgives you."

"Oh. I suppose that might work . . . except he'd want to be forgiven by the actual person he hurt, wouldn't he? Like Rose, or maybe his kids."

"Much more difficult, obviously."

"It's just that his pain seems to be about something specific. But hey"—I picture a priest in black flowing robes like in the movies—"whatever works."

18

Sitting in the cafeteria with Morgan and Brittany, I see my brother Jack across the room, putting a lunch tray back on a trolley, and decide to go over and say hi. Now that he's staying at Jeremy's house, I miss having him around. He's always been the only person I can share frustrations with about Joyce, often without having to say much at all. Even a look can do it. So things aren't the same without him.

He asks what I'm up to, and if there's anything he should know. I try to sum up Clarisse's ghost problem as neatly as possible.

"Forgiveness?" Jack says. "The guy wants to be forgiven for being an asshole? Is that why he's a ghost?"

I wish he'd keep his voice down. "I don't know. Just because I see ghosts more easily than most people doesn't mean they make sense to me," I whisper.

"So now what?"

"I'm not sure. I think we have to dig a little deeper. See if there's something really rotten about him that we still don't know. Because we need to be pretty specific when it comes to arranging forgiveness. I don't think it'll do much good, somebody forgiving him for just being an asshole, period."

"Boy, I know some real assholes myself. Will they be ghosts when they die?"

"It's got to be more complicated than that. I mean, Matthew became a ghost and he was practically perfect—when he was living, anyway."

"You mean he's not perfect anymore?" Jack looks amused and then confused. "Hey, didn't all those barn ghosts 'cross over'? Isn't he in the happy hunting ground or somewhere by now?"

"Well . . . something like that . . . anyway, death kind of changes people. I don't think you can judge them by their behaviour once they're ghosts." I realize I'd better drop this before Jack suspects that something's up. I give him a hug and tell him I'd better get ready for my next class, math.

"Math class? Ah, Lester."

"What do you mean? Who *told* you?" I'm indignant. "Not that there's anything to tell."

"Don't worry, everybody knows that."

"What do you mean? You sound like Ethan. Everybody knows what?"

"That there's nothing to tell. No sparks or whatever. Poor Lester."

"Oh my God. Don't tell me that. I'll start feeling sorry for him."

Jack just laughs and says, "Yeah, his dad's going to have to buy him a new car. See ya around."

What was *that* supposed to mean? This is my first math class since the party, and since then, I've only seen Lester from a distance. We kind of smiled at each other a few times, and once he waved, sort of. He looked unsure but not heartbroken.

So when I walk into my math class, I can't tell if I'm just imagining that everyone's looking at me. And when I go to my usual seat, I realize that Lester is sitting directly in front of me. He wasn't there before. He turns around in his chair as I sit down and he smiles stiffly. It's the same smile I've been getting all along, impossible to figure out. Is he being polite, or is that what he looks like when he's in love? I can't tell. Anyway, he doesn't say anything, and once the math teacher starts talking I try to put Lester out of my mind, even if his head is kind of blocking my view of the blackboard.

An idea hits me in the middle of class, and as soon as the bell rings, I rush out into the hall as fast as I can and pull out my cellphone. I make a speedy call to Morris, stepping outside the school's side entrance as he answers.

"Morris, I think you should phone Detective Grierson and ask him if he could look up police records from the mid-1980s. What I'm wondering about is that car accident. The one where Carmichael's third wife, Rose, supposedly hit a deer on her way home from that bingo fundraiser? If she really had an accident, wouldn't she have reported it? It must be recorded somewhere. I know that when my grandmother hit the deer a few years ago, she reported it. I don't know if people did that twenty-five years ago, but I think the police would want to know about accidents caused by deer, don't you? So could you see if there's anything on the record? I'm assuming she took his last name when they married, but maybe not, since she'd be the third Mrs. Carmichael. But who knows? And I'm guessing it was on 28th Sideroad. The accident, I mean."

"Okay, slow down. Not a problem. I'll call him. I'm not sure why this is so urgent, though. What's it about?"

I realize I've still told Morris hardly anything about the girl in the forest.

"Well . . . maybe it's nothing. I'm just curious because—remember I told you there's another ghost in the forest near the inn? I mean, I told you I'd seen something pink? Well, it's the ghost of a girl who died when she was twelve years old. She wears a pink ski jacket. And she's in the forest. I think she hangs out with the deer. Anyway, I have a feeling she sometimes takes possession of a deer herself, though I haven't quite figured that part out. I'm just curious about what's behind all these cars hitting deer on that road."

"Okay, okay. I'll call Grierson. No problem. Aren't you in school today?"

"Between classes. Anyway, gotta go." I hang up feeling a strange relief. Like it's about time I stood up for the ghost of Jenny Barton.

After school, just before I get on the school bus heading out of town, Morgan grabs me.

"I heard you ran for your life out of math class today. Poor Lester! Is he really that repulsive to you? I think he's kind of cute. In his own way. He's just a little shy, that's all. You're killing him!"

"Holy crap, Morgan! For one thing, I only ran out because I had to make a quick phone call, and for another, if he's so hot for me, he doesn't show it much. And really, I've got nothing against the guy. Nothing. Except . . ."

"Except he's not Kip Dyson. Or is it Matthew Sorenson you're still stuck on? Look, I get it. I'm not saying sleep with him. Don't even 'friend' him on Facebook if you don't want to. But . . ." She stops, smiles and gives me a hug. "Oh, whatever. You do whatever feels right. But it's nice to be wanted, don't you think? Enjoy that, at least!"

Morgan. If she only knew how complicated my life is.

When I get home, there's an e-mail from Kip. Which, of course, immediately starts my heart racing. But it's only one line.

What? So now you're a cold-case detective?

That's it. Better than nothing. Way better.

19

orris called this morning. Detective Grierson says there was a report filed, all right. On the evening of March 25, 1986, Rose Carmichael had a car accident on 28th Sideroad. Hit a deer. No injuries to driver, minimal damage to vehicle and no insurance claim made on the repairs. The report was filed in person at the police station the following day, by Eric Carmichael, her husband. His signature only.

I had to go back over my notes from the day Ethan and I went to the archives to be sure I was right about the date. And I was.

"That was the same day Jenny was last seen alive. The girl in the forest? She was reported missing by her parents in Hanover on March 25, 1986. Last seen after school, riding her bike north on Highway 6. Wearing a pink ski jacket. Her ghost is hanging out in the same area where Carmichael's wife supposedly hit a deer."

"Okay," Morris said. "I admit that's a very interesting coincidence. But Hanover's a long bike ride away."

"Not really. Four or five hours. The timing works out. And

here's my other hunch," I said, feeling like I was on a roll. "I think it was Eric Carmichael who had that accident. Not Rose. I think he blamed it on his wife to protect his own reputation. To cover up drunk driving, maybe, not to mention a hit and run. He was a politician, remember. It wasn't a deer he hit, and he knew it."

"Wait a minute. You're guessing all this just because he's the one who filed the report?"

"No, there's more to it. I've left out the best part, believe me. You've got to come with me to that swamp. There's something you need to see."

Less than two hours later, Morris and I are on our way. We drive south on 12th Line, slowing down as we pass the Telford farm, only to see four cars in the driveway. One of them is the shiny black one I saw last time. The owners' car. That's not good.

"Looks like trouble," I say. "Why so many cars on a Saturday?"

"A housewarming party?"

"I doubt it. They don't even have a kitchen sink, last I saw."

I think of Matthew all alone up in the attic, and feel anxious.

On our way to 28th Sideroad, I give Morris more background on Jenny. I remind him of the little adventure Kip and I had over March break, when Kip came home soaking wet. I tell him that's where we're headed. The swamp isn't that far from the road, just a few minutes on foot. Back in mid-March it was still covered with a layer of ice, although it was getting too thin to walk on. Then I remember what Jenny said about her bike—how, when the man threw it in the swamp, it broke through the ice. March 25. The ice must have been the same in 1986 as it was this year. Anyway, I tell Morris about Kip falling backwards over something in the swamp that day, and describing it as something metal. And that's what I want to show Morris.

I told him to wear the highest rubber boots he's got, and I'm wearing the same. We pull over on the side of the road, as far off the gravel as possible. There's nothing but woods on either side, and the road is empty in both directions as far as we can see. I tell him to follow me, and I lead the way into the forest, taking roughly the same route I've taken each time. It's not a path, exactly, but it's not too overgrown either. Somebody or something goes through here once in a while. Deer, probably.

When we get to the edge of the swamp, I see them on the other side. Five or six deer, frozen like lawn statues, staring at us from across the dark water through the black skeletons of a few dead trees. I point the deer out and we stop to look, barely breathing. They're such beautiful creatures. Who could shoot one? Suddenly, as if they've heard a silent whistle, they're off, leaping in single file along the line of trees and then deep into the forest.

We move on. I find a large branch on the ground, probably the one I used before.

"We just need to wade out a few feet and I'll be able to reach it." I haven't told him what "it" is yet. "It's about halfway between here and the deer stand over there." I get a good grip on one end of the tree branch and start working the other end into the swampy bottom. It takes longer than before to wrestle the bike wheel up above the waterline, and in the end Morris has to give me a hand.

"This had better be good," he says, straining. Then the wheel breaks the surface. "Okay," he says. "And this is what?"

"Jenny's bike."

"And you know that how?"

"She told me her bike was in the swamp. About a dozen times. It looks like a twelve-year-old girl's bike to me. Isn't that what it looks like to you?"

"Maybe." We tug and tug and finally manage to free the bike from whatever muck and slimy weeds it was caught in. We pull it up out of the swamp and drag it onto dry ground.

"Definitely a girl's bike, one that's been underwater for ages," I say.

Morris bends over to take a better look at the wheels. "Those wheels are a mess. Nobody would be riding a bike in that shape. It's possible it was just dumped here as trash. People do that, you know. Dump their trash in woods sometimes. It's against the law, but some still do it."

"Okay, well, there's another part of the story I've been saving for last. I knew this bike was here because Jenny told me it was. But here's the thing. She told me that *a man* dragged her bike through the forest and dumped it in the swamp. She watched him do it. See what I'm getting at? Why would she lie about something like that? And why would anyone do such a thing? Except for the fact that a busted bike is *evidence*. Evidence that a girl on a bike was hit by a car, and it was covered up."

It's so obvious to me what happened that I'm starting to think Morris isn't as smart as I thought he was. Because he's hesitating, like there's something he still doesn't get.

"Are you saying that Carmichael dumped Jenny's bike in the swamp after killing her with his car? And what? Hid her body? Is that what you're saying?"

"Well, why would he put her bike in the swamp except to hide the fact that she was on this road? Why would he want to hide it unless he didn't want people to know what happened to her? Because she definitely died, Morris. One way or another, this girl died here."

He runs his hands through his hair. "Did this ghost *say* that a man hit her with his car? The same man who put her bike in the swamp? I mean, how do you know for sure the man is Carmichael and not someone else?"

"But who else? Don't you see? This crime could be the reason Clarisse's house is haunted. The crime her ghost wants to be forgiven for. Remember what Edith said about the bingo gathering that night? There was booze, and he'd been drinking."

"But if what you're saying is true, what happened to the body? Where are her bones?"

"Well, I know where I'd look." I nod toward the swamp.

"These are serious allegations, Amelia. I mean, if what you're saying is true, her family has a right to know. We're talking less than thirty years ago, so some of her family are probably still alive. They deserve closure. We'll have to contact the police."

"Okay. I think we should."

"I'd like to start with Detective Grierson. See what he has to say. Maybe the police should be dredging the swamp. You're saying that a ghost told you she died here, but we can't just jump to conclusions that Carmichael is involved."

I'm absolutely sure Jenny died here, and I'm pretty certain she was hit by a car. I thought the bike would prove it. But if Morris isn't sure he believes me, who will?

20

Jenny sits up on the deer stand, her legs dangling and swinging slightly a few feet above the swamp water. She's watching the huge machine as if she finds it fascinating. No one knows she's here except me. I haven't even told Morris.

He stands on the edge of the swamp with Detective Grierson, watching the dredging machine at work. It looks like a tractor inching its way through the water at the opposite end of the swamp, sifting through the slimy bottom, looking for human remains. Apparently they've been at it all day.

It was the bicycle that finally convinced the police. Same size and make as the one Jenny owned, according to the original alerts. Even a touch of the original red paint. It took some harassing by Morris, but at last Grierson made some calls and got the go-ahead for this investigation.

Morris picked me up after school and we drove straight over. He'd already checked in with Grierson, who complained that they were coming up empty. Now, as we arrive, Grierson gives me a curious look, as if maybe I can help somehow. I don't want to promise anything, but it's great to see that Jenny's here. I casually make my way through the bush along the boundary of the water, heading in her direction. The engine of the dredging machine is loud enough that no one will hear me, especially with my back to them.

As I get within twenty feet or so of where she sits, she turns and gives me a cheery wave. You never know what to expect from ghosts, that's all I can say.

"You know what they're looking for, don't you?" I have a funny feeling she doesn't, and I don't know how she's going to take it. She looks at me blankly.

"They're looking for your body." Sure enough, she seems a little surprised at that, glancing over at the dredging machine at the other end of the swamp.

"Oh," she says. Then, after a pause, "Over there?"

"Well, I guess they've been trying to cover the whole area. They don't know if your remains are even around here. And they don't know where exactly to look." I watch closely to see how she takes that. She doesn't say anything. "*Are* you in the swamp, Jenny? Your body, I mean. Did you end up in the swamp, like your bike?"

"My bike isn't in the water anymore. They took it away."

"I know. They wanted to take a closer look at it. Listen, Jenny, something bad happened to you and you died. Did it happen here? In the swamp? Is your body in the water somewhere?"

"The girls at my school hate me. They wouldn't let me hang out with them. They made me want to run away and never come back."

She suddenly has this big mood change, taking me by surprise. Her face gets all twisted like she's in pain and she starts whimpering. I feel an awful misery coming on myself. A crushing feeling of rejection and loneliness and hopelessness. It's the way she felt the day she died. I can see her crying, pedalling her bicycle along a strange road in the dark, the edge of the asphalt a wavy line through her tears.

Sitting on the deer stand now, she hangs her head so that her chin practically touches her chest. Her body begins to rock, her shoulders swaying back and forth. Her legs have stopped swinging, and I look down at them. Her jeans are drenched in bright red blood from the knees down. Her ankles are twisted and smashed. The blood drips from her feet into the dark water a few feet below. I try not to look.

"Why were they mean, Jenny?" I ask softly, afraid that she'll fade or disappear if she gets too upset.

She's still looking down, but now she sighs. "Because I can't read fast. Not like I'm supposed to. I read slow."

"So you were a little different. That's it, isn't it?"

She nods.

"I know what that's like. Being different. Lots of people get upset when other people seem different. Some people really hate it. But deep down we're all kind of the same, don't you think? When you dig down deep enough?"

She nods, then lifts her head. Her eyes come to rest on the dredging machine. Her face is wet with tears.

"Especially our feelings," she says quietly.

"Jenny, did you get hit by a car while you were riding your bike? Is that what happened to your legs?" She looks down at all the blood.

"The deer," she says, like she wants to change the subject.

"What about the deer?"

"The deer like me."

"Of course they do. Why wouldn't they? I like you too."

She looks at me with an expression of gratitude but says nothing. I try again.

"Are these men going to find you in this swamp? Eventually? If they keep looking?" She hesitates, then nods. "Okay," I say. "And do you remember where you last were? When you had a body? You know what I mean, right? You don't have a body anymore, not like you used to. Where is the old body? Where did you leave it?"

She looks into the swamp below her dangling feet. They're normal again. The blood is gone. "There," she says. "That's how far I got. And then the ice broke and I fell through. I was too tired to get out. I tried but I couldn't. I wanted to get up here. Stay here for the rest of my life. With the deer."

"The deer?"

"They were watching. Waiting for me to join them. But I was trapped. I couldn't get out from under the ice."

"Your body is right here, under the deer stand?"

She nods. "I don't need it anymore. I can run faster now."

"Still, we have to find your body. To prove you died here."

"And my backpack? With my homework?"

"Yes, all that stuff. Okay, Jenny, I'm going to tell the men to bring their machine over to this end."

"Will they give me back my bike?"

"I'm not sure. But we need to know who did this to you. That man. What did he look like?"

"I don't remember. He threw my bike in the frozen water. I watched with the deer while he did it. They saw him too."

I turn around, hoping to catch Morris's attention, and I find him and Grierson standing where I last saw them, looking straight at me, like they're waiting for instructions. I'd better go and talk to them before Grierson decides to give up searching.

"I'll be right back," I say, but when I look she isn't on the deer stand anymore.

I walk back to Morris and Grierson. "I'd focus on the area right under the deer stand," I tell them.

Grierson hesitates for a few seconds, like he's skeptical, then shrugs and walks away, whistling and waving at the dredging machine driver to get his attention. He doesn't understand how I know, but it seems he's going to play along anyway.

"Anything else?" Morris asks. "Anything new?"

"Not really. What I thought. Looks like she was hit by a car and her legs got smashed. She dragged herself into the forest, and it sounds like she made it across the frozen swamp until the ice broke and she fell in. I'm guessing she drowned, trapped under the ice. She was already dead by the time the bike got thrown into the swamp."

"Did she say anything specific about the mystery man?"

"Not yet."

We watch the dredging machine make its way along the edge of the swamp, toward the deer stand. We wait as it gets into position, moving in and locking off before starting up again. The very first deep scoop brings up something that doesn't look like it belongs at the bottom of a swamp. Something like a sack, dark with mud, straps hanging down. It's a small backpack. Grierson hurries over for a better look as the backpack is dropped onto a yellow tarp spread on the ground. Just beyond him, about twenty feet away, I see a single deer watching, mesmerized. I shout above the noise of the engine.

"Jenny?"

I edge closer. The deer turns its head from the dredging machine and looks at me, bending its ears forward.

"Jenny, this man?" The deer looks at me steadily. "Was he young? A young man?"

The deer shakes its head to the side once.

Now something else is being placed on the tarp. A jacket. A small ski jacket, black with rot.

"An old man with grey hair?" The deer shakes its head again, its eyes on the jacket.

"Did he have hair, Jenny? Do you remember?"

Another shake of the head.

Morris is listening to me but watching the deer. "Unbelievable," he mutters.

The deer takes a step backwards and I fear that at any second she'll run off into the dark trees. I look at the bright yellow tarp and the items arranged on it. One is a long bone.

"Jenny?" I say desperately. "An old bald man? Was he bald?"

The deer jerks its head, nodding toward the ground, and then bolts off into the forest, just as the metal grille of the dredger lifts a human skull, dripping with slime, to the surface of the swamp.

21

They managed to retrieve most of the skeleton of an adolescent girl from the bottom of the swamp. I didn't stay to watch. Morris ordered me to leave, not that he had to—I wanted to get out of there.

The police have already contacted the family—apparently there's a mother still alive, and a brother and a sister—to warn them that they're going to do DNA testing on human remains that may turn out to be their long-lost Jenny. It seems that's common practice, to give the family a heads-up so the shock isn't as severe.

I'm determined to find Carmichael and have it out with him this afternoon. At first Morris was all reluctant, thinking maybe we should talk to Joyce again, but I convinced him that that wasn't necessary. It's not like we're going to be there overnight. And this time I'm going to get straight to the point. Morris has a key to get in, and Clarisse gave him an open invitation to go back anytime, to see what could be done about the ghoul who's ruining her life, not to mention her business plan. It'll be hard to feel any sympathy for him now. I know too much about his life, and what he did to Jenny.

I told Joyce I was riding my bike into town to meet up with friends. Since it was a typical boring Saturday for Ethan, he wanted to come along, and I had to give him a vague reason why it was a bad idea. I had a few different people to see, I said, and I might wind up at Morgan's for a few hours, and it was just too complicated.

Joyce said she didn't want me riding my bike after dark on the highway. I told her I wouldn't. Instead, Morris picked me up ten minutes away from the house and put my bike in his trunk.

But not before I had a chance to ride south on 12th Line, past the Telford farmhouse. No sign of Matthew at the upstairs window. I haven't seen him in twelve days. There was a truck parked in the driveway, loaded with drywall sheets. I could see lights on in the living room. No sign of the owners, though, so I'm hoping they didn't come up again this weekend, and these reno guys seem to take Sundays off. Maybe the place will be empty tomorrow and I'll be able to sneak in.

On the drive over, I ask Morris about Clarisse. She finally left his place for her sister's house last week, he tells me.

"Wow, she was living with you all this time?" I'm a little shocked but I can't help laughing too. "Morris, you surprise me. You two must have really hit it off."

"Not sure that's accurate. Don't assume too much."

He squirms slightly in the driver's seat. I grin and say, "Of course not. She's a client, after all. Strictly business." That Clarisse—she's got nerve, all right.

We arrive at the Cornflower Inn and, standing on the porch, Morris reaches into the mailbox and pulls out some mail as if he lives there. He catches my expression and says, "She asked me to bring in her mail." He sounds a bit defensive.

We take our shoes off and step into the hallway. Morris flicks on some lights and dumps the mail into a basket on a hall table. The house feels kind of hollow, the way houses do when no one's been living there for a while. No one who's breathing, anyway. But even in the middle of the afternoon, you can tell something's not right with this place. Like it's waiting for something to happen.

"So, cup of tea?" Morris asks.

"Sounds good." I like the idea of sitting in the kitchen for a while, to give the ghost a chance to become aware of us on his own time.

"What's the plan?" he asks, once we're sitting at the kitchen table, the door to the back stairs open just a little.

"Well, if this guy is feeling remorse or guilt or something, and wants to be forgiven for doing a terrible thing, I think it'll be good if he realizes that we *know* what he did. Then it's not a big secret anymore, which he might find a relief."

Morris squints into his teacup, strokes his scruffy chin and thinks about that. "I suppose so," he says. "But you'd better be prepared for the worst. He may not appreciate having you shine a light on his dark past, so to speak. If he's been haunted by this since his death, he was probably haunted by it when he was alive too. He lived for eight years after Jenny died. I'm just saying, he's bound to have a lot of intense emotions around it, and we don't really know what kind of guy he was, deep down. You may be unleashing more than you bargained for. I'm wondering how we can make sure you aren't in danger."

"I'm not afraid of him. He's a little creepy with the body movements, I admit, but otherwise I don't get the feeling he's looking to hurt me."

"Well, you need to be careful anyway. Otherwise Joyce will be looking to hurt *me*. Not to mention Kip."

Kip? It jolts me to hear his name. I'm so used to hearing it only inside my head.

"How . . . how is Kip, anyway? I mean, doing well at school and all? Have you been in touch lately?" It feels like it's been so long, and I'm starving to see him again. Just to stand beside him in a crowded place, or to sit in the passenger seat as he drives a car. Anything. Anywhere. He feels so far away, he might as well be in Japan.

"He's fine. I think he's doing just fine. He doesn't say much about himself, when he calls. So. I assume he's fine." He hesitates, then adds, "He asks after you."

We sit in silence for a while, this unfamiliar feeling washing over me. *Kip asks after me.* That means he thinks about me sometimes. Maybe his new "friend" hasn't totally won him over, body and soul, yet. I'm not sure, but I think what I'm feeling is a tiny bit of hope. It makes me nervous. I'd better not let it grow too big. Finally Morris brings me back into the present.

"Well, we don't have all day. What do you say? Want to give this a shot?"

"Sure, yeah. Um, I think maybe you should stay down here, so we don't give the ghost too much to deal with, and I'll go upstairs and wander around. See if I can draw him out."

"Is there anything I should do in the meantime?"

"No, I don't think so. I'll holler if anything comes up, but I'm not expecting much. I've been thinking about what you said, though, about getting a priest to absolve him of his sins, or whatever. Maybe I'll bounce that idea off him and see how he takes it. In the end, it's all about getting him to leave this house, right? So whatever we have to do to make that happen is worth it."

I take a deep breath to focus myself and climb the back stairs, my eyes on the closed door at the top. The steps creak. On the highest step I turn around and look back down, just in case. No one there. I reach for the doorknob and turn it.

The upstairs hallway is empty too. I wander from room to room, seeing that everything looks as elegant as the last time I was here, only the air is stuffier. I check the view from all the upstairs windows, out of curiosity. I wonder what this ghost does to kill time? I think about Matthew, who is so much better off, as ghosts go. At least he's capable of interesting conversation and appreciating some things. This ghost's existence seems miserable. Maybe that's the point. Maybe this is his punishment and this house is his hell. In which case it's meant to last a while, and Clarisse is totally out of luck.

I'm near Clarisse's bedroom when a figure catches my eye, standing at the far end of the hall, near the back-stairs door. He looks even smaller and thinner and more hunched standing in full view than he did on the stairs. He's still in that washed-out robe and pyjamas that make him look like he's just wandered off a hospital ward. He's so pale I can almost see through him. His bald head is bowed and he's facing away from me, making it impossible to see his expression. But his mood I know for certain. There's such a deep feeling of sadness or regret there that I find myself feeling sorry for him again. Then I think of Jenny, and I harden.

"Mr. Carmichael?"

There's no response. You'd think I'm the phantom here.

I walk toward him, pausing with every step and watching his reaction. His bony hand reaches for the back-stairs door, fingers shaking until they settle on the metal knob. When I'm about five feet away he starts to fade, just the way Matthew does when I get too close. I stop.

"Mr. Carmichael? It's you, isn't it? I know it's you." Still no response, but then the door starts to open. "Mr. Carmichael, I need to talk to you. It's about Jenny." I can see him again but he's ignoring me. He steps down into the stairwell. "She's the girl you hit with your car," I say after him. "You said it was a deer, only you knew it wasn't." I get to the door quickly. "Deer don't ride bikes," I say as I look down. But the stairs are dark and empty.

I sit on the top step, deciding that maybe I'll just wait a while. Soon I become aware of a rocking motion at the bottom of the stairs, and gradually I make out the shape of his body, sitting with his arms wrapped around himself so that his fingers almost touch behind his back. He keeps rocking, and when I listen hard I can hear choking sounds. "I know this is hard for you. I can tell. But we need to talk about it. You need to come clean about hitting Jenny with your car, and covering up the evidence."

His head jerks up when I say that, which gives me a fright. He's stopped rocking but he's still holding onto himself tightly. Mentioning the evidence seems to have hit a nerve. He's silent, like he's holding his ghostly breath.

"I'm talking about her bike. Throwing her bike in the swamp like that. It's taken, like, twenty-five years, but we've found it, and the police have found the body. Jenny's body. She was only twelve years old." I pause, then add, "I mean, how could you?"

It's like his whole being is listening, frozen stiff.

"I'm sure you didn't hit her on purpose, Mr. Carmichael. Even if you were drunk. But it's what you did after that really sucked. I could arrange to bring a priest to the house, to help you deal with your guilty conscience. Give you absolution, maybe." I wonder if he knows what I'm talking about. "Because I know what you did is really bothering you, and you want forgiveness."

"D-d-deer."

The voice is so weird and raspy that it hardly sounds human, but I'm pretty sure that's what he said.

"No, not a deer. A twelve-year-old girl." I wait for his response.

"D-deer."

"No, a girl. On a bike."

"Deer."

"Sorry. Not a deer. And you know it." He's rocking again. "Because you went and dragged her busted bike into the forest, into the swamp. She saw you do it. You destroyed the evidence. You covered up your crime, the hit-and-run accident. Maybe drunk driving, even."

Have I gone too far? He's jerking and spasming like he's having some kind of seizure.

"P-p-pink," he sputters.

"Yes, pink!" Finally. That's practically an admission of guilt. "She was wearing pink. A pink ski jacket."

He stands up, convulsing below me on the stairs. His arms have fallen to his sides, stiff, fingers shaking. The weird gagging noises are back, getting louder and louder, like something under pressure and about to blow. A creeping chill runs up my neck and I rise and take a step back up the stairs. Before I can brace myself there's a horrific raspy wail, and the twisting body flies up toward me. A white, wasted face, eyes and mouth like deep black holes, cuts through me like a cold knife. I lose my balance and reel backwards, slippery socks sliding off the edge of the top stair. And then I'm falling, hitting every stair on the way down. *Ouch. Ouch. Ouch.* When I come to a stop at the bottom, all I feel is burning pain. Especially in my right forearm and at the back of my head.

Morris is standing over me, shouting, "Jesus Christ! What happened? Where does it hurt? Don't move!"

I'm whimpering, cursing, apologizing, all at once. He dials 911.

"An accident. She fell down a flight of stairs. . . . Teenager, female. . . . Yes, I think maybe a bone break. And possibly a head injury. . . . Yes. Hurry!" My eyes are shut because of the pain, but I hear him giving the address, his name, my name. I hear him say, "Please hurry." He hangs up, swearing.

"I'm okay, Morris. Really. I'll live." I can't move my arm.

"Can you move your neck? Can you move your legs? Did you hit your back?"

"My head and my arm. It's mostly my arm. Luckily, I went down on my ass." My arm is bent on my chest. I still can't move it. "My arm," I whimper when he touches it. I keep my eyes shut.

"You hit your head. You're bleeding."

"Yeah, my head hurts too."

I hear Morris on the phone again. He's telling Joyce that I accidentally fell down some stairs but the ambulance is on its way. We'll meet her at Grey-Bruce Regional Hospital in Emergency.

"She's going to go ballistic," I moan as he hangs up.

"What the hell happened?"

"I don't know, but this ghost doesn't need a priest. He needs a psychiatrist. He needs a team of psychiatrists."

It takes forever, but at last the wail of the ambulance siren closes in.

22

"I forbid you to go back inside the Cornflower Inn. *Ever.* Understood?"

Joyce was even angrier with Morris. No surprise.

"I just slipped and lost my balance on the stairs. I was in socks, and those old wooden staircases are worn and slippery. Really, it could have happened to anyone. Clarisse should have one of those carpet runners put in."

It was more a crack than a break, so I'm lucky. Still, it hurt like hell. My cast is blue and goes from the top of my hand around the thumb right up to my elbow. I can still write, just even messier than before. As for my head, it's fine. They had to shave a space around the cut to put some special tape on it while it heals, but it's at the back, so the hair from the top of my head pretty much covers it. It feels like a bruise.

But I had to spend two days mostly lying down. Doctor's orders, to be on the safe side, because of a mild concussion.

On my first day back at school, which was Tuesday, the kids

were all curious about what happened. Slipping on stairs in your socks is something everyone's done so it was no big deal. Just bad luck it happened near the top step and not closer to the bottom. I got another short e-mail from Kip. Three words. *Watch your step.* That's all. Not like he was inviting a big discussion, so I just wrote back, *Will do.*

It isn't until Wednesday evening that I'm able to get back on my bike. Even then, Joyce isn't happy. I tell her I'm only going for a short spin on empty roads, and it's true, that's all I can manage. No marathon trips. I can't put my weight on my right hand so I can't lean forward on the handlebars. Going up the 12th Line hill toward the Telford farm is a huge ordeal. Halfway there I begin to think I must have brain damage left over from the fall, otherwise I wouldn't be trying to do this. I'm in a sweat and I have a headache by the time I arrive.

It's after supper and I'm counting on the place being quiet, with the reno crew gone home for the night. Turns out I'm right. I park my bike around back and give the side door a little knock. There's no answer. I try the handle and it's locked. I back away to look up at the second-floor windows. It takes a while but I finally see him, a dark shadow standing off to one side of the window on the landing at the top of the stairs. The huge garbage bin they had parked below is gone. I guess that means they're finished gutting.

I wave at the shadow in the window, then go back to the side door to wait for him. It takes him ages to let me in, which is nerve-racking because I'm anxious that a car may drive by and I'll be seen standing on the porch.

The wait should have been my first clue.

"Matthew! It's so great to see you again." I try to sound cheery. "You look good. Is everything okay?"

"I'll say. Check out the new kitchen. It's pretty special, eh? Yeah. The owner's sister came for a visit. She said it was 'to die for.' I know I nearly died when I saw what they paid for that faucet."

"Matthew, you're moving really slowly. Is something wrong?"

He doesn't look that happy to see me, but I'm getting used to him being moody since the new owners took over.

"Why? Are you in a hurry?" he asks me, not really looking my way. "Do you have to be someplace else? Do you have things to do?"

I can't tell if he's being sarcastic. "It's not that. It's just that I haven't seen you in weeks. I don't know how long it feels like for you, but that's a long time. I've been thinking of you all the time and trying to get over here, but I haven't been able to."

"Is that how you broke your arm?" He says that casually, not like he's concerned about it.

"What do you mean?"

"Trying to get over here?"

"No." That kind of throws me. "My arm is a totally separate thing." I think about it. "Why would you even say that?"

"I don't know. Just trying to understand why you never come see me anymore."

All the time he's talking, he's walking slowly through the main floor—along the front hallway, into the living room, the dining room, then back into the hall. I follow him, a few strides behind, trying to walk at the same pace so I don't get too close and have him disappear on me. Finally he stops and turns to face me.

"So what happened to your arm?" As if he's trying to sound a little more normal.

"I fell down some stairs. Yeah. Another reason not to leave your 'friend' on the stairs, Matthew." He looks down, like something is suddenly bothering him. "What is it?" I ask.

He just shrugs and starts pacing again, back into the dining room.

"Matthew, tell me how you are. I'm serious. What's going on with you?"

"Did you trip over something?"

"No, not exactly. But still, falling down stairs sucks."

I tell him a little about my adventures at the Cornflower Inn. About how it's been so difficult to connect with the ghost who haunts the place.

"He barely acknowledges me, barely responds even when I call him by name. Maybe he's too ashamed. And he speaks in these one-word sentences that are this huge struggle for him to get out."

"Maybe you've got his name wrong." That's all he has to say about it.

The whole time I'm there, Matthew seems super-reluctant to talk about himself. Every time I try to get him to open up, it goes nowhere. With anybody else, that's the point where you grab them by the shoulders and give them a shake, yelling, *Talk to me* in their face. But unfortunately I can't grab his shoulders anymore. Not that I ever did. Which strikes me as kind of tragic now, given that they were definitely among my favourite parts of his body. His shoulders were unusually square and gorgeous. They still are, if I think about it.

Finally, when I realize that I'm not getting anything out of him about what's been going on, and it's getting risky to stay much longer, I just tell him how sorry I am that he seems so sad.

"Honestly, if I knew how to make life better for you, I'd try. But being a ghost is probably always going to be a rotten alternative to living. Unless you can somehow get used to it, and find some pleasure in what you have left."

"It hurts too much to remember what I've lost."

I don't know what to say. We're standing in the kitchen, him against the counter and me by the door. I look at his pale face, feeling awful for him, and realize he's getting paler by the second. Then I notice the blood on his lip. Next thing I know, it's gushing from his mouth and nose, and running down from four deep, dark holes across his abdomen, the ones from the pitchfork. I feel like I'm going to throw up.

I lean back against the door and brace myself. I don't want to pass out, with my bad arm and all. It's been a while since I've seen Matthew in this state, the way he must have looked at the moment of his death.

"Oh my God, Matthew."

"I'm sorry." He takes a slow step toward me. "I'm sorry." He whispers it this time. He takes another step.

I straighten, horrified at the sight of him covered in blood and still coming closer.

"Matthew? What is it? What are you doing?"

He takes another step toward me, and he's only a few feet away when he begins to fade.

"I'm sorry," I hear him barely whisper, and then he's gone.

A cold wave like an electrical current runs through me. I know it's him. I start to panic. Should I stay or get out? For the very first time, I'm afraid of Matthew, afraid of something I can't begin to describe. I back out the side door, slam it shut and run for my bike.

Because of my cast, I have no choice but to take my time riding home, pedalling slowly, sitting back on my bike seat to take pressure off my arm, my heart pounding all the way.

When I walk in the door, Ethan looks up from the TV and immediately asks if I'm okay. I have no idea what he's talking about.

"Did you fall off your bike or something?"

"No, not at all."

"Then what's on your face? Looks like you're bleeding."

"What?" I run upstairs and into the bathroom to look in the mirror. There's a smear of blood on my cheek.

Matthew's blood.

23

I'm standing by the side entrance to the rectory. That's the office at the back of St. Timothy's Roman Catholic Church. I've never been inside, but I think the Sunday service just ended, so I peek in through a partially opened door.

A short hallway leads to an arched opening, and I can look straight down a side aisle, along the rows and rows of benches, and see the backs of people who are shuffling out. They're the stragglers, I guess, because most have already left, and I can see a bottleneck of people at the back, squeezing outside through the big double doors. The organist is still playing.

Father Johanny, who has a Spanish accent, sounded friendly enough on the phone. He said he'd be happy to chat with me about spiritual matters, and I wouldn't be the first teenager who wanted to know there was more to life than popular culture. I hoped I wasn't giving him the wrong idea. But I had the impression I could take my chances with him and not get into too much trouble. Morris encouraged me, saying he'd interviewed him once and he was a thoughtful guy.

When the priest enters the back hall, in his black floor-length tunic, he's moving quickly, like he has a lot to do. He passes me, smiling, and says good morning, then disappears into the office. I wait a minute before following him in. The woman behind the desk gives him phone messages, notes written on pieces of yellow paper. A gold crucifix with tarnished edges hanging on the wall catches my eye. It looks like an ancient relic. Otherwise, the office is modern. They both look up at me, smiling absently the way busy people do, and I tell them my name and say I've booked an appointment with Father Johanny for one p.m. At first his face looks blank, and then he remembers and smiles warmly, inviting me to wait for him in his office. He'll just be a moment.

As I take a seat in one of two dark leather chairs across from his desk, I start feeling nervous. What will I say? How far should I go? How honest can I be? I tell myself that priests are like lawyers. They're supposed to keep your secrets, even if you're guilty of murder. You're supposed to be able to trust them not to blab and get you into trouble. But I'm not totally sure the same rules go for non-Catholics as for Catholics. I'm not sure whether I count, being a pagan and all.

"What happened to your arm?" he asks, walking into the office.

"I fell down some stairs. They were slippery and I was wearing socks."

"Ouch. Is it a break?"

"Yeah, well, a crack really."

He seems nice so I want to get to the point. "Father, I'd like your advice on how to help someone who's suffering from a guilty conscience. He did something very bad, but now, even though years and years have passed and it's too late to change anything, he's still really obsessing about it and he can't"—I try to put it carefully—"can't let it go. Can't move on."

He's listening intently. Anyway, it seems that way. After a pause he repeats my words, "Did something very bad?" looking at me steadily.

"Yes. I'd say so. I mean, he wasn't faithful to his wife, for starters. Wives, really. And he wasn't much of a father to his kids, he wasn't involved in their lives at all. And . . . well, most of all, I think he may have been guilty of a hit-and-run accident. Probably drunk at the time. So pretty bad things, really."

"Hmm." His expression is grave. "I see. Serious stuff." He looks hard at me. "And this person? Is this person your father?"

"No, no. My father is dead. I mean, this isn't my father or anybody else in my family. I don't really know him. Not personally. Not well." I shake my head. "This all happened before I was born."

"I see. How . . . how long ago, would you say?"

"Um. Well, about twenty-five years ago, I think. So it may be too late to make amends in the usual way. The people he hurt most could already be dead. But I can't help thinking he'd be more at peace if he could just receive some kind of absolution. That's what it's called, right? Confess his sins and feel like he's been forgiven. So he can forgive himself. I think that's his big problem, that he can't forgive himself."

"Hmm. Tell me, Amelia. Is this gentleman you're speaking of a Catholic?"

"Uh, I'm not sure. Does it make a difference?"

"Well, I'm just wondering if he'd be comfortable coming to the church, to talk to me in person. I could hear his confession, if he so wished. He could say an Act of Contrition—it's like a formal apology to God. That would be the usual way of dealing with transgressions." He thinks a bit, then adds, "For which one is truly sorry."

I look at Father Johanny, scrambling for my response. "Well, I don't know that he'd be able to come to the church. I mean, not in the flesh." I cringe saying that.

"Is something hindering him?" I'm trying to decide how to answer when he continues. "The truth is that a person must seek forgiveness of his own volition, and the nature of absolution granted by the priest is such that he must feel the contrite person to be fully aware of his guilt, fully desiring a reconciliation with his Maker, from whom he feels estranged. It's that estrangement from God that is the source of the pain of guilt. So whatever positive intentions you may have, you on your own wouldn't be able to mediate absolution on behalf of this person."

"Oh."

We sit there in silence for a minute, while I look around the room, thinking. I decide to give it another shot.

"So if someone's not capable of asking forgiveness but it's really obvious he wants it, you can't just say or do something to show him that he's forgiven, so that he feels forgiven anyway?"

"Not really."

"Oh."

"Maybe, if you tell me a little more about this person, I'll be able to think of a way to advise him, but it really would be best if he could come to see me himself."

"Okay. Well, that's probably not going to happen."

"I'm sorry to hear that. Is he infirm? Housebound?"

"Kind of. He's . . . well . . ." I realize that if I don't come clean, I'm totally wasting my time and his. So here goes. "I'm afraid it's worse than that. He's dead. He's a ghost. A spirit. That's what I meant by this being a 'spiritual matter.'"

Father Johanny looks down at his desk and starts moving a few files and papers around, as if he suddenly needs more space. Then he stretches his arms straight out in front and clasps his hands together and slowly lowers them, like a spacecraft hovering before touching down. Finally he just looks at me. I swallow hard, thinking how I've made a mistake with this guy, because the silence is so awkward.

"He's deceased?" He sounds calm enough, like he isn't in shock or upset or anything, but it's impossible to tell whether he thinks I'm insane. I start to talk fast.

"I'm afraid so. Father, I know this sounds strange but I have a strong feeling that there's a ghost living in a house outside of town who's haunting the place because he feels lousy about things he did when he was alive, and maybe he'd stop haunting the place and move on to wherever spirits are supposed to go after death if someone, a priest, for instance, could tell him he's forgiven. Give some kind of blessing that would absolve him of his guilt somehow. So he feels better about himself. I honestly believe that's what he wants."

"Did he tell you this?"

"No, not exactly. But . . ."

"Well, Amelia, I'm not saying that I don't believe you, or that what you say is impossible. I'm only saying that as a parish priest I have many duties and responsibilities and they keep me very busy. I have to prioritize. And I find that I keep very, very occupied just focusing on the people I can see with my own eyes. My parishioners. And when I do home visits, and I often do, it's because people are too ill to come to church. You see, it's more than enough for me to handle, just focusing on the living. I'm afraid I'm not the person you're looking for."

At least I tried. I thank him very much for his time. I say I understand, and I really didn't feel much hope but I thought it wouldn't hurt to ask. I tell him it makes sense to me that it would be hard for anybody, even a priest, to get through to this guy. I haven't had much luck myself, I say, and I've had quite a lot of experience with ghosts. His eyes widen, and I ask him not to tell anyone. Hardly anyone knows except my close family and friends, and of course the owner of the haunted house. He nods slowly, like he gets it. Only he may really be thinking how badly this psycho teenager needs help.

But when I'm leaving, he says he isn't as surprised by what I've said as he might have been just a week earlier.

"I haven't been in this parish long. Came east from Edmonton last fall. But I'm starting to realize that I've got a few things to get used to here. You're the second person this week to talk to me about problems with a ghost in the house."

"No kidding? Wow. What . . . Do you mind me asking, what did they want from you? The same kind of thing?"

"They called it an exorcism. I'm afraid their response to their ghost was a lot less charitable, but it amounted to the same thing. They wanted to know if I could make it leave their home."

"Really? Interesting. From around here?" I try to sound casual but I'm freaking out on the inside.

"No. Out of town."

I can't help it, I have to ask.

"A farmhouse on 12th Line?"

We were both heading for his office door, but that stops him in his tracks. His mouth opens. He just looks at me, not saying anything.

"It's okay," I tell him. "I know that ghost too."

His mouth closes. I think how far I've come, being able to confess my ghost vision to a stranger like this. An authority figure, even. For years, you couldn't have tortured that information out of me. "You aren't going to tell anyone what I've told you, right?"

"No. Not if you aren't a danger to yourself or others."

"So that other ghost? On 12th Line? Are you going to help them?" I can't look at him when I ask, I'm so afraid he'll guess how much I care. "Are you going to perform an exorcism or something?"

"Me? No. But I mentioned the name of a retired priest down in Kitchener they might talk to. If they were interested."

I thank Father Johanny and we shake hands. As I leave his office I feel a growing panic. I'm thinking about Matthew, worrying about what an exorcism might do to him. I mean, would it hurt him? Frighten him?

Besides, it's all wrong. He's just a ghost. He's not some kind of devil.

24

"I went and saw Father Johanny today." I'm in my bedroom, the door closed behind me. I phoned Morris in a panic as soon as I got home.

"It was fine. Not very helpful, but fine. But one big thing came out of it that you're not going to believe. The new owners of the Telford farm went to see him last week. They wanted to know if he could perform an exorcism for them. On a ghost in their house. An exorcism to get rid of *Matthew*."

"Seriously?"

"Seriously. Like he's some kind of devil."

"Father Johanny told you this?"

"Not exactly. I guessed he was talking about the Telford house and it was obvious I'd guessed right."

"I'm amazed. Well, exorcism is a ritual that can involve removing any spirit from a possessed person or a possessed place. So I guess Matthew qualifies, as a spirit possessing a place."

"But what does that mean for *him*? Could he get hurt? Is it painful or anything? And what if he refuses to obey? Will he be punished somehow? We've got to do something."

"Well, according to my research, exorcisms only work if the ghost can be reasoned with. They aren't much good against a ghost who really doesn't want to leave. I'm not sure where that leaves Matthew. I agree we've got to do something, but we'd better think first."

"It doesn't seem fair. It's not his fault, it's my fault. I'm the one who suggested he move in there in the first place." I pace around my bed, back and forth. "It's my fault he's even hanging around here." My guilt weighs me down and I collapse on the mattress.

"There's no point in panicking yet. What did Father Johanny say, exactly? Did he agree to do it?"

"No. He put them onto someone else. Another priest. An exorcist, I'm guessing. What are we going to do?" I picture Matthew suffering. Writhing in pain. I can't stand the thought. "I know he's not the easiest ghost to live with, but he's hardly evil. He's just unhappy and lonely, and who can blame him? Really, he's handling this whole being dead thing better than I would, if I were him."

There's quiet on the other end of the line. Then Morris says, "The point is, these owners must really be upset to go this far. This is a serious move."

"We've got to find a way to stop them."

Morris asks me what else Father Johanny had to say, about the other ghost problem. "Does that mean he's not keen about performing sacraments at the Cornflower Inn either?"

"He says he's busy enough forgiving the living. Or something like that. Anyway, he seemed bothered by the idea that the ghost wasn't asking for forgiveness directly, himself. Apparently you can't ask on behalf of someone else. It breaks some kind of policy."

"I understand what he's getting at. I just thought maybe he could perform some general rite of absolution. Go through the motions, at least. Maybe he's not really a believer. In ghosts, I mean."

"Then what are we going to do?"

"Amelia," he says, his voice lowered, "why don't you let me handle it? I may be able to use my standby excuse of doing research. I'll try connecting with this couple. Go over and meet them, if possible, and see what I can find out. Then we can decide whether we need to get more involved. All right? But you need to calm down."

It's true, I'm freaking out. It's because I'm thinking about the last time I saw Matthew, coming toward me, gushing blood. "All right," I say into the phone. "All right. I'm just worried about him. I admit he's changed a little since he's been hanging out in that attic. He's a little . . . stranger."

"What do you mean, 'stranger'?"

"It's hard to describe. I think he's getting frustrated. With everything."

"Okay. What are you worried about, exactly? Him getting into more trouble? Becoming dangerous, even?"

"I don't think Matthew could ever be dangerous. It's not in his nature. Ghosts may not be totally the person they used to be, but I think they're still mostly the same."

As I hang up the phone, I remember Matthew sitting beside me in the library at school, and it makes me want to cry. The last time I saw him alive, we laughed and argued and teased each other. And then I did something totally without thinking. I touched him.

I wanted to be more than friends, so I held the palm of my hand to his chest. I felt his heartbeat, I felt him take a breath. But he kind of panicked and pushed me away, like he couldn't deal with being that close. Then he grabbed my wrist and stared at my hand, like he was torn in two about whether I was his friend or his girlfriend. I guess he was afraid his strict and religious parents would disapprove of me. Anyway, he didn't live long enough to make up his mind.

I think a lot about how ghosts seem stuck inside an emotional memory, trapped in a time and place they can't leave. If that's true for Matthew, could it be that, for him, the memory is of that moment in the library? Confused, unsure, even shocked, but wanting me to stay? I think about the old doll from the attic, and how I watched him hold its tiny wrist, staring hard at its limp little hand.

Oh, Matthew. This can't go on forever.

Jack's at the front door, hollering "I'm home," as he comes inside, like in a sitcom. He's here for Sunday dinner. It's always great to have him back in the house. It seems like ages since he moved into town, into Jeremy's basement. I miss him so much.

It's a miracle how well he's doing, since there was a time when we didn't know if he'd ever walk again. He's walking a little more slowly and carefully than he used to, and he still uses a cane when he's tired, but otherwise he's practically normal. In fact, he's looking good. He's been lifting weights, bulking up again. But he used to be the best hockey player in our school, and I guess those days are over.

Jack gets an enthusiastic greeting from Joyce, who's in the kitchen fixing dinner, and from Ethan. Then we get talking and he tells me he misses Joyce's horses. That surprises me, because even though he's a good rider, he hasn't ridden much in a few years. And we were only living here with Ponyboy and Marley for a month before his fall last Halloween. But if he misses them, that's good news, because maybe he'll move back home at the end of the term. Which is only about a month away. I could use him around here again, as a secret ally in my battles with Joyce.

We walk out back toward the paddock, and the horses are already clocking us and coming over to the fence to say hello.

"You have to know what it feels like, not being able to walk. Back when I was in the hospital, the idea of moving at all, even on the back of a horse, seemed like the most amazing thing. I used to daydream all the time about riding Marley."

He puts his arms around Marley's head and gives the horse a big hug. He whispers in its ear. Then he does the same to Ponyboy. It's funny how every once in a while, when I'm up this close, I realize how much I like them too. I stop holding it against them that they belong to Joyce, that they're the reason she bought this place, making us move from our mother's house in town to the middle of nowhere. They may be getting old, but they're still her precious children. We're just the evil grandchildren. But when I watch them gently nudge Jack with their noses, big eyes on him like they know he's been gone, I know what he means.

"Later, guys," he tells them.

"Are you really going for a ride?" That sounds risky.

"Yeah, before I leave. Don't worry, I'll be careful. It'll only be a walk. A crawl."

Joyce sticks her head out the door and says not to go far. Dinner will be ready in fifteen minutes. We sit down on a bench against the paddock fence.

"So what's new, Amelia? How are you?"

I've been waiting for this moment. I decided when I heard Jack was visiting today that I'd come clean with him. Besides, I need his advice.

"I'm okay. But there's something I want to tell you. It's not new exactly, but it may come as a surprise."

"Cool. What's up?"

"Remember when you asked me if Matthew had left the barn with the other ghosts, gone off to the 'happy hunting ground,' I think you called it?"

"Sure. What about it?"

"Well, the truth is, he didn't leave. I thought he did but then, just before we left that night, after the cops said we could go home, I saw him. He'd decided to stay behind after all. He was just hanging out nearby."

"HOLY CRAP! Matthew's ghost is still here?" He's looking around and grinning, like this is amazing news. "WHERE? Where is he?"

"*Shhh!* Joyce doesn't know. Neither does Ethan. I don't think I could handle them knowing that I've been carrying around this secret for so long."

"But why? Why the secrecy? What's the point?"

"Matthew was telling me to keep quiet about it, and I figured it was his right to keep it a secret. I mean, who knows what kind of chance he's taking? Maybe he's pissing off God, or somebody, doing this. Maybe he's going to be in a heap of trouble before it's over."

"Or maybe ghosts don't have anything to do with stuff like religion. Maybe they have their own rules."

Jack clearly finds that amusing. We were raised without any religion, and I guess sometimes it shows. I used to envy Matthew his confidence in the beliefs of his parents and their church, though it hasn't been much help to him lately.

"So who *does* know about this? Kip, I'm sure. Morris?"

"Yes, but only for the last month or so. Believe me, I felt awful keeping it to myself for as long as I did. I felt I owed it to Morris especially to stay honest with him. And Kip—well, that's complicated. Too complicated. The whole Matthew thing."

"Don't tell me, I can guess. Explains a few things, though. But I still don't see the big problem. Where is he, anyway? Matthew's ghost?"

"He's still on the Telford property. Living inside the house. In the attic."

"No way!" Jack laughs out loud. "Wicked!"

"Not really. The farm has been sold, you know. And the new owners have been picking up on his presence. In fact, they've been shopping for some priest to perform an exorcism, to run him out."

"Well, why doesn't he come hang out here with you? Maybe he'd like to haunt the paddock. Or would that spook the horses?"

"It's not like that. He can't just go where he wants, do what he wants. I know it's weird but there's something about certain places, like passageways in the landscape, where ghosts can move and hang out more easily. The Telford farm is on one of those routes. This house isn't. Ghosts can get stuck in certain places that become 'haunts.' I think that's happened to Matthew. He doesn't want to leave the farm, he thinks it's his home now. But I'm not sure he could leave even if he wanted to. I'm afraid there's some freaking showdown coming. That's what I'm afraid of."

"Oh." It's finally sinking in, and Jack's brow furrows. "Jeez. I see what you mean. *The Exorcist*."

We sit a little longer, images of gross horror-movie stuff playing in our heads, until we're interrupted by Joyce yelling for us. We get to our feet and start walking back to the house.

"I don't know what I'm going to do." I feel even more deflated, realizing that Jack doesn't know what I can do either. Why would he?

"Exorcism aside, how are you holding up? You seem pretty stressed. How's the arm?"

"Like I said, I'm okay, I guess. My arm is good. I get the cast off next week. I'm worried about Matthew, that's my problem. And, I don't know, I'm just frustrated about things. About my life. What's the point of being able to see ghosts when there's so little I can do about it?"

"Why do you say that? What do you *want* to do?"

"I don't know. But it would be nice to have a positive effect, at least. Maybe make the ghosts less tormented, or make whoever they're haunting less frightened."

"Well, you seem pretty down. Kip was right to be worried."

"What?"

"I wasn't supposed to say anything, but he asked me to check up on you."

"He did?" I'm frozen on the back porch. Jack opens the door to head inside. "*He did?*" I cry.

Jack turns and gives me a quick wink, steps into the kitchen and yells, "Starving!" at no one in particular.

We're sitting down to bowls of chicken curry when Joyce says, "And when were you going to say something about *that*?" She nods toward the local paper on the kitchen counter, opened to a headline.

HUMAN REMAINS RECOVERED
IN WETLANDS NEAR BOGNOR

Ethan's head rockets from Joyce to me so sharply that it gives me the creeps. I don't need the extra drama.

"Jeez, calm down, Ethan," I say under my breath.

"What did *I* say?"

"It's your body language." He blinks hard at me, offended.

"Well?" asks Joyce. "They're saying they found the bones of an adolescent girl." She eyes me with suspicion. What? Does she think *I* did it?

"It's like I mentioned to you before. A girl who disappeared ages back, like twenty-five years ago. I asked you if you'd heard about a girl getting killed who was about twelve years old, remember? So it's no big secret. I knew she died around there, that's all."

"And you knew *how*?"

She already knows the answer to that. She just wants to hear me say it. I look over at Jack. *See what I have to put up with, still?*

"I saw her. I saw her ghost. I came across her by accident, riding my bike to the Cornflower Inn a while back. It wasn't hard to figure out she'd died somewhere around there. She's just been hanging out since, in the woods, with the deer. Off 28th Sideroad."

"With the deer?" It's like living with a prosecutor from one of those courtroom dramas. She makes me want to say, *Guilty! I plead guilty. Happy?*

"Maybe even causing a few car accidents," I add, remembering how Joyce hit a deer there.

"What do you mean, causing car accidents?" Her face changes, a shadow crossing it, as if she's recalling that painful memory.

"I don't know, but I'm pretty sure she sometimes possesses one of the deer. And I think she sometimes runs out onto the road. Ghosts tend to do that, they re-enact things. It's like a compulsion. I think it's a way of dealing with the fact that, even though they died, they're still stuck in the same old world. It makes them crazy."

She's eating slowly, her eyes on her bowl. Ethan and Jack, mouths full, keep their eyes on me, like I'm terribly entertaining. With table talk like this, who needs to eat in front of the TV?

"Was she murdered?" Ethan's eyes are popping. He's squirming in his chair, stirring his curry with his fork like it's a can of paint.

"I don't know, but I don't think so. I think she got hit by a car. She was riding her bike." Joyce looks up at me. "It was dark. Maybe it was a drunk driver. Anyway, it looks like she got confused and crawled into the forest, injured. I think she accidentally drowned in the swamp."

"Wow," says Ethan.

"You know all that? Did she tell you?" Joyce's voice sounds strange, as if she finds the whole thing totally disturbing. I don't blame her.

It's hard getting used to the new Joyce. For three years I had to watch everything I said around her, hiding everything about ghosts. Now this.

"Yeah. She told me."

Joyce seems upset but she doesn't say anything more, and it feels a little awkward, like she surrendered too soon.

"Hey!" says Ethan. "That's what you were doing research on in the archives place. When I was helping you. You were looking up missing girls. I wondered why you were doing that."

"So what happened?" asks Jack. "Was it you who told the cops she was there? Are you gonna start working with the police now, like on TV? Feeding them information from beyond the grave?"

"No, I am not. That was just a one-time thing."

His expression tells me he doesn't believe me.

Joyce seems focused on her meal now, as if she doesn't want to talk about it anymore.

After dinner I head out back with Jack again while he gets Marley ready for a short ride. As soon as we're alone, I ask him what he meant by what he said about Kip.

"Has he been in touch with you?" He doesn't answer right away. "Tell me! Did he contact you?"

"Maybe. Maybe he did. I guess he didn't want to keep asking Morris how you were. He worries about you a lot, if you ask me."

"I can't believe it. I never dreamed that he . . . thought about me much while he was in Chicago."

"Well, I guess that proves that while you may be able to see ghosts, you're not psychic. A word of advice—don't keep leading the poor guy on. It's not nice. I know what I'm talking about, remember? I've been through that whole scene with Morgan. Even you thought she was being cruel. So why would you do the same thing to him?"

I'm almost speechless. "Lead him on? Are you kidding? It's not like that. Not even remotely."

"Well, what do you call it? It's impossible for him to figure out if you're interested or not. Believe me, it sucks being in that position."

"Hey, how do you know it hasn't been him leading me on? This isn't like your situation with Morgan at all. Not at all."

"Okay, okay. If you say so. I'm just saying you should be nicer to the guy. If you still have feelings for him."

I'm in shock as Jack mounts Marley's back. "One more thing," he says, looking down at me. "I don't want to give you a hard time, but you should cut Joyce some slack. Really. Lighten up a bit. She does her best with you, and she's trying to make up for past mistakes. It's not easy for her either. Try to be a little more forgiving." Then he smiles and winks, and it's impossible to get angry with him.

I stand by the paddock fence and watch him and Marley move slowly across the field.

Forgiveness. There's that word again.

Is it possible that Kip might forgive me?

25

I check the time. I've still got almost two hours to kill before the exorcism. There's a three o'clock blast-off.

I'm glad Morris somehow got us invited but, now that it's almost here, I don't know how I'll handle it. He says it's going to be okay, and he'll pick me up at two-thirty. I guess Saturday afternoons are when this exorcist does his rounds. He's got a long drive, Morris says, and he wants to be home before dark.

"I spoke with the guy who bought the Telford place," Morris told me. "His name is Phil. He says the exorcism was his wife's idea. Apparently she's the one who's been having most of the bad experiences, hearing things and feeling some 'presence,' he says. Sounds like he's just going along with it. They got a reference from Father Johanny and contacted the priest after a particularly bad night. Phil says he's a very old guy, sounds frail but friendly on the phone. No fire and brimstone. He'll just say a few prayers and politely ask any spirits in the house if they wouldn't mind moving out. I don't think there's going to be anything harsh."

I'm dreading seeing Matthew today because of this priest visit. I'm afraid he's going to think I had something to do with it. I've felt more nervous with every passing day, on account of how things were left between us, with me running out of there that day, his blood on my face. I tried to see him a few days ago, to warn him about the exorcism, but some reno guy was there, working late. His truck was out front, the sign on the side saying something about floor tiles. There was no sign of Matthew at the upstairs window. I had to give up.

I've asked Morris to see if we can get there a little early so I can have a word with Matthew first, prepare him before the priest arrives. I don't want him to take any of this personally.

Think about it. I want the ghost haunting the Cornflower Inn to leave, but I want the ghost haunting the Telford farm to stay. I haven't figured out how I feel about the rights of ghosts versus the rights of homeowners. It depends on the ghost, obviously.

Maybe it's because I have this feeling of impending doom, but sitting alone in my room, waiting, I start feeling that I've got nothing to lose. When it comes to Kip, I mean. I read through his old e-mails. I think about Jack saying that Kip asked him to check up on me. I've been putting this off, but now's the time. I hit compose and start to write.

Your dad says your spring term is almost over, and you'll be studying for exams.

I stare at the page for a bit. What next?

I think when you've finished, you should reward yourself with an Owen Sound vacation package. I hear there's a sell-off this month, and you can get a great deal. There's been a recent vacancy.

Is that enough? Should I say something about the exorcism today?

Besides, your father misses you.

My finger hovers over the send button. Should I tell him anything at all about Matthew? I enter one more line.

Everybody misses you.

I lean back in my chair and look out my open bedroom window. It's a beautiful, sunny spring day. A strange day for the mayhem that could be waiting for us down the road this afternoon. I feel it should be overcast and stormy, with thunder and hailstones. Instead, it's perfect out there. The birds are singing back and forth among themselves. It's the kind of day I'd like to see Kip standing on the front porch, squinting in the sun, saying, "Let's go for a drive."

P.S. I miss you.

I hit send.

It's Phil who answers the door. This is my first time walking into the house through the front entrance, properly invited and not trespassing like a burglar. I know this place better than the owners do, I bet. We stand in the living room as Morris introduces himself to Phil, then me. Phil looks amused, like he's trying to keep a straight face. I recognize that attitude. A definite non-believer.

The only reason Morris got a break with him is the weekly column he writes on local history for the *Owen Sound Daily*. People figure that since Morris is a long-time regular writer for the paper, with his name and a little picture and everything, he can't be a total wacko. Over the phone, Morris told Phil that he was doing research on farmhouse hauntings in Grey County, and that I'd been helping him on some locations because I'm more sensitive to paranormal energy. More or less the truth. Morris promised them he wouldn't reveal their identities or home address or anything to anyone, for the sake of the real estate value. He says he told Phil he's just looking to "verify a pattern" he's researching, and it's nothing specific to Phil's house.

What we won't admit is that we know who's haunting their place, and why. Or that we hope this exorcism fails.

"So what's the connection between you two?" Phil asks, looking from Morris to me.

"Old family friends," Morris says.

"Ah." Phil nods.

"I used to work with Amelia's mother."

There's always that awkward moment where people are trying to figure out if Morris is a pervert. Thankfully, it never takes them long to realize he's just a harmless eccentric who's obsessed with ghosts. I'm not sure what they make of me.

Phil apologizes for the state of the house. "We've hardly been here," he says. "Heavy workloads in the city. We've barely dropped in a half-dozen times. Only slept over, camped, really, a couple of times. The place has needed so much work, no point in us hanging around through that. So as you can see"—he's taking us through to the dining room, where a small table and chairs have been set up on the rough, bare floors—"not much furniture yet. We've still got a lot of work to get done. All the floors need refinishing, for one thing." He scowls, looking down at the planks.

A woman appears at the top of the staircase and comes down,

rather reluctantly, like she's embarrassed and uncomfortable. Phil introduces her as Barb.

"I don't know what to expect," she says to Morris. "Do you? A friend recommended we take this route. With a priest. She knew about a similar situation where it made a difference." Morris nods sympathetically, then shrugs as if it's anybody's guess, but he doesn't say much. She laughs nervously. "Poor Phil. I was the one pushing for the country retreat. It can be so nice to get away on the weekends. Lots of our friends do. But I can tell you, if I could turn back time"—she shakes her head—"if I could only turn back time," she repeats, more loudly and with greater emphasis, "I'd buy that other property we were considering, the one closer to Thornbury. Less acreage but a nicer view." She sighs weakly.

"I can imagine it hasn't been easy. It never is," Morris says, as if ghosts in the house are always a pain—like a damp basement. He thanks her for letting us be observers during the exorcism. "We have to be very careful about how we gather our research. Paranormal investigation attracts a few unstable people that we aren't interested in mixing with." Then he introduces me, and she checks me out.

I look past her, back up the staircase. Matthew's sitting on a step near the top. I have to think fast.

"The noise you've been hearing, the unnatural noise, do you find that it's coming from the second floor?"

"Yes, I'd say so. Why do you ask?"

"Well, would you mind me doing a bit of a reading? Maybe taking a look at the stairs and the second-floor landing?"

Morris jumps in. "Amelia's quite helpful at picking up energy, as I've mentioned to your husband. Might be a good idea to see what she's able to pick up now, before the priest arrives and . . . maybe disturbs things. Father . . . ?"

"McGordy. Father McGordy. Well, I . . . I guess that's okay," she says, sounding like she's worried I might steal something up there.

I manage to make eye contact with Matthew and he slowly gets to his feet, turns around and heads back upstairs. As I leave the dining room, I hear Morris whisper to Phil and Barb. I can't quite catch what he says, but I think it's something about it being best to ignore me.

"Matthew?"

I find him standing just inside the front bedroom, with his back to me, facing the window. There's an inflated air mattress on the floor and a suitcase along the wall.

"Matthew?"

He seems preoccupied, staring out across 12th Line, past the far fields and into the western horizon. Finally he turns toward me.

"What's this about?" His eyes are dark and cautious.

"You haven't guessed? You've pushed them into taking action against you. They've arranged for a priest who does exorcisms to come over, this afternoon. *Exorcisms*, Matthew. Morris managed to talk them into letting us be here while it's happening."

He stares at me, his face expressionless.

"You know what I mean, right? By *exorcism*?"

"I'm a ghost, not a devil."

"I know, I know. Morris says not to worry. The guy is just going to say a prayer. Ask you politely to leave."

"Will he wave a crucifix at me?"

"I don't know. I don't think so. That's probably just in the movies. They say he's a nice guy. Matthew, we can get through this. Just stay calm. Don't take any of this personally."

"Why not? Isn't it personal? Don't they know me? I never missed Sunday church service in my life."

"Of course they don't know you! You could be some hundred-year-old, mean and nasty baby-killer, for all they know. Just remember, Morris and I are here to protect you. Any way we can."

"How are you going to do that?"

"I don't know yet. You have to trust us."

"Hello?" It's Barb, calling from the bottom of the stairs.

I mouth the words *It's going to be okay, don't worry,* and try to look reassuring as I give him a small wave and head back downstairs. I wish I'd had more time with him. I'd have reminded him not to do anything, make any noise. With Barb looking up at me from the bottom of the stairs, I stop.

"Sorry, just want to check one more thing," I say.

Her eyes narrow suspiciously, but I turn and run back upstairs.

I find Matthew in the front bedroom again. "Matthew? Pretend you aren't even here, okay? Can you do that? No matter what anyone says or does? Just don't react. Pretend you aren't here at all." I look for some response but I get none. "I'm going back down now." Nothing.

As I reluctantly return to the dining room, Morris speaks up. "Barb started telling me what she's been experiencing, Amelia. I thought maybe we should fill you in, see if you've got any impressions."

"Sure," I say, taking a seat. Trying not to look worried.

"Well," Barb begins, "it started with creaking sounds like foot-steps. In the hall upstairs and on the staircase. That was from the first day. Then sometimes even above me, on the roof or in the attic. We talked about putting a few mousetraps out, but it's never really sounded like a mouse."

Phil cuts in. "I kept telling her it's a hundred-and-fifty-year-old wood-frame house. It's going to creak."

"Yes, and I could have lived with the creaks if it had ended there," she says, sounding defensive. "But I've had feelings, too. Like . . . I don't know. Shivers. Especially in the upstairs front room. It's happened too many times. Too often to mean nothing."

I nod. "Well, those are classic signs of a presence. Ghosts can give you a creepy cold sensation when they brush by. When it's really intense, it's more like a cold electrical current passing through you." If I had planned to freak her out, I couldn't have done better. I feel guilty seeing the look of horror on her face.

"Ghosts. Dead people's ghosts," she says, more to herself than to us.

I nod again. "Afraid so."

"How . . . how many of them?"

"Hard to say. But there's at least one. At least." As I say that, I see Matthew slinking down onto the bottom step, where he can watch us in the dining room. I try not to let my eyes focus on him. I was hoping he'd stay upstairs. Thank goodness he's trying to be quiet. "Anything else?" I ask. "Any other strange experiences?"

"Well . . . there was the doll," says Phil.

"The doll?"

"Oh my God," whispers Barb.

"Do you want me to tell them about the doll?" says Phil.

"Yes," she says. She shudders.

"Well, there was this creepy old doll. Must have been at least a hundred years old. One of those ones with cloth-stuffed bodies and porcelain heads. Very Victorian-looking. Battered and yellowed, with no hair . . ."

I'm aware of Matthew leaning toward us on the step, listening more intently. His head lifts and his eyes drift up, as if he's thinking of his doll hiding all alone in the attic.

Don't even think about it, Matthew.

Barb jumps in. "It just showed up suddenly. We'd come up for the weekend and we had stepped out for something in Meaford. We got back and found it. On the stair, that first time. I nearly drove myself and Phil crazy trying to figure out how it could have gotten there. I thought the house had been broken into. But there was nothing to steal. And why leave an old doll?"

"And I agreed it was a little strange. *I agreed*," he repeats, as if this has been a sore point between them. "Anyway, Barb put it in the garbage in the kitchen, but later in the afternoon, there it was, propped up on the windowsill in the bathroom. We'd spent a bit of time outside, but no one had come by. We hadn't seen anybody except the odd car driving by. So, needless to say, Barb assumed I'd done it as a practical joke."

Matthew sits on the step, smiling to himself. When he looks over at me, his smile fades.

"I thought she'd kill me. I couldn't prove I hadn't done it, not so she'd believe me. Anyway, she put the doll back in the garbage can. Then . . . well, then it got really bad."

Barb cuts in. "Let's just say the doll came back that night. It was the night of that really severe thunderstorm, the one where half of Grey County lost power. So I think I had every right to flip out."

"We left the house," says Phil. "We drove back to the city at midnight. As we were leaving, Barb threw the doll into the contractor's bin by the side of the house. She called the contractor first thing Monday morning—he was here—and told him she'd thrown it into his bin and she wanted him to burn it. But he said he hadn't noticed any doll. She freaked and insisted he double-check. Definitely no doll in the bin, he said."

There's a sound outside and we all jump, then realize it's a car coming up the driveway.

"Father McGordy," says Phil.

"Oh God," Barb mutters.

Phil turns back to us. "Anyway, we haven't seen it since."

Matthew gets to his feet. I jump up too, one eye on Matthew. *Stay where you are,* I'm praying. *Be good!*

I can see the priest through the front window. He's got to be in his mid-eighties. He carries a briefcase and walks with a cane, taking forever to come to the door. He moves a bit strangely, and I realize he has an artificial leg. He steps inside with a friendly greeting. He's dressed all in black. Not a business suit, exactly— something different. He has thick white hair and a wrinkled face, like he's spent a century smiling. He has bushy white brows and shiny round little eyes, quite blue. He looks like a sweet old guy.

"Not selling tickets, are we?" he asks, smiling, when he sees Morris and me.

There are introductions and chit-chat about the drive, and the basics about Phil and Barb's jobs and lifestyle and renovation plans for the farmhouse. He listens, nodding with polite interest. I notice him casually looking about, and my heart starts pounding. But his eyes never seem to settle on Matthew, who's standing at the end of the hall a few steps from the bottom of the staircase. *He doesn't see him.* Excellent. Matthew looks relieved too. I catch Morris's eye, wishing he could read my mind. It's frustrating that he doesn't know what's going on.

Father McGordy moves down the hallway and Phil invites him to take a seat in the dining room. He pauses at the entrance and looks up the staircase and right through Matthew, who slowly moves backwards up the stairs, keeping his eyes on the priest the whole time. He stops on the second-floor landing and looks down. I hold my breath and watch Father McGordy look up, listen, then drop his head and focus on the floor by his feet.

"Well then," he says, in an abrupt and cheery voice, as if he just remembered where he was and why he was here. "Shall we get down to business?"

26

atthew disappeared upstairs not long after Father McGordy began his little talk. I wonder if that means he'll stay away until it's over. I hope so. I hope he's not eavesdropping.

Reassuring Phil and Barb with his gentle voice, the priest sounds like some kind of grandfatherly crisis counsellor. The way he talks, it's hard to tell if he's even very interested in ghosts. There's nothing to feel threatened about, he tells them. There's nothing evil in the house. Well, so far I like where he's going with this exorcism.

After he's talked to them for about a half-hour, he announces that he's going to go around and bless each room of the house. That makes me nervous again. He takes a crucifix out of his bag, and I wonder if this is where it gets ugly. But it doesn't. He walks into the living room, with Phil and Barb and Morris and me at his heels, and says a kind of prayer, making like he's drawing a cross in the air with the crucifix. He says some stuff that sounds like a message to a restless spirit, saying how he's praying for the spirit to find eternal peace, that kind of thing. The idea seems to be that if there's any ghost around, it just needs to know there's a better place to be, and God is waiting, *blah, blah, blah*. It sounds very positive and friendly and it makes me think of the minister's words at Matthew's funeral. The upside of death. Father McGordy repeats the same words and gestures in the dining room and kitchen, then asks if he can go upstairs.

He's got to put weight on his cane and take a step up with his good leg, then raise the fake leg behind him. It takes him a long time. We all wait and follow slowly, step by step, behind him, like a procession.

Where is Matthew?

Upstairs there are three bedrooms, a big one at the front and two smaller ones, the middle one having the closet with the entrance to the attic. Father McGordy heads for the front room first, and we follow on his heels. I'm holding my breath, looking for Matthew, since this is his favourite lookout. But he's not in sight, thank goodness. Then the priest approaches the room with the attic. *Matthew must be up there.* The closet door is open. I don't want to look up. *Please don't let there be some strange light shining up there.* Father McGordy goes through the same blessing, then pauses, like he's waiting. Does he suspect something? Morris catches my eye, looking worried. Finally the priest's eyes narrow and he kind of bites his bottom lip, then slowly moves to the back room, repeating the blessing.

On the landing the priest stops as if he needs to rest before tackling the stairs again. I wouldn't have noticed anything if I hadn't turned at that moment toward the room with the attic hatch, only to catch Matthew out of the corner of my eye—hanging upside down, halfway out of the attic, a fringe of ink-black hair, white face, red-soaked shirt, and blood running from his nose and mouth into his open eyes.

My legs buckle under me like I've been shot, and suddenly I'm down on my hands and knees, looking at Morris's feet. He pulls me up.

"I'm okay, I'm okay," I say. "Sorry. I'm okay, really."

Barb looks at me wide-eyed, her hands over her mouth as if they're keeping her from screaming.

"Can we just go downstairs?" I whisper to Morris, trying desperately to let him know I mean *now. ASAP. Let's get the hell downstairs!* We make our way down, with me leaning on Morris, Barb leaning on Phil, Father McGordy leaning on his cane. Morris grabs a dining room chair for me to sit on. Barb slumps on another. Father McGordy stays standing. He hasn't said anything, but he's looking at me like he's curious.

I'm so relieved to have everyone downstairs, away from Matthew, that I'm already feeling better. "I'm really sorry, everybody. That's what I get for skipping breakfast." I try to laugh a little. Try not to shake so much.

Barb looks absolutely white. I've given her a terrible fright, that's obvious. Phil doesn't look happy either. *Just when things were lightening up around here* is probably what he's thinking.

Finally Father McGordy speaks up. "A little too sensitive for this kind of business, perhaps?" He's talking to me. And smiling, but in a strange way, like he knows something's up.

Phil offers to make a pot of tea. Since I'm blaming my near faint on hunger, he puts some bread and cheese on a tray. Blue cheese, which I've never tried before and which doesn't smell like anything anybody should ever eat. I have to force myself to take a bite of a small piece of the bread, chewing slowly.

Father McGordy gets up to leave, apologizing and saying he's got a two-hour drive home. He turns to Phil and Barb at the door as he says goodbye.

"I think, if you've got a spirit in this house, it's not malevolent, and I think it will choose to leave of its own accord. Eventually. You may need to be patient."

I feel sad but grateful for his attitude toward Matthew, which seems kind. Phil and Barb look disappointed.

Morris and I make our move to go not long after Father McGordy's car disappears. Morris thanks Phil, wishing him the best and inviting him and Barb to get in touch if there's anything more they'd like to discuss. He gives Phil his card.

The scream comes from the kitchen, where Barb's just carried the cheese tray from the dining room. There's a crash on the new tile floor, then more screaming, and crying and cursing. We come running down the hall to the kitchen just as she bashes through the side door and out onto the driveway.

"What the hell?" Phil says.

We see her through the window, pulling on the locked car door, freaked out and yelling hysterically at Phil to get the car keys.

"Jesus Christ! Barb!" Phil stumbles over broken teacups, sending pieces flying across the tiles. He lunges for the door and runs after her. She's now racing in circles around the car like a lunatic, grabbing at the door handles, all locked.

Morris and I are left standing in the kitchen, staring at Matthew's doll. It's propped up on the kitchen counter. A fork is stuck deep into its middle, and its cloth belly is soaked with blood.

27

J'm sitting in physics, trying to make it through to the end of the class. Twenty more minutes until the bell rings. I've been struggling to keep my grades up this semester. I've worked so hard and sometimes it's taken everything I've got to focus on school. Or even care. Now, with less than a month left in grade eleven, I'm running out of strength. I feel like I'm losing my grip. *I haven't done my homework, Mrs. Pearson. Please, please don't ask me any questions today.*

Ghosts have taken over my life. Ghosts are driving me crazy. Matthew, especially. I keep reliving the scene at the farm last weekend—Barb and Phil screaming and yelling. The blood. How could he stick a fork in his doll like that? Isn't she supposed to be *me*?

For a long while, Phil and Barb sat outside on the porch while she cried. Then Phil came in, went upstairs and came back down with a suitcase and her purse. Morris and I had already swept up the broken teacups, and I'd pulled out the fork and stuffed the doll in a plastic bag.

"We'll lock up if you'd like," Morris offered, and Phil just handed him a house key.

"I don't know when we'll be back," he said. "She says the doll's head *moved*. She says the bloody thing looked right up at her."

Then they drove off without saying goodbye, and left me wondering what would happen next.

Mrs. Pearson is picking on Sarah Riddell today. It's not fair but it's a relief. Eight minutes to lunch break.

Matthew says they asked for it. Morris says Matthew's little stunt was probably the last straw for Phil and Barb, but he doesn't seem that upset with Matthew. In fact, he seems kind of fascinated by his behaviour. We stood there in the kitchen for a time after they left, trying to absorb what had happened, Morris and I. Matthew stood nearby, looking restless and a bit guilty. Morris said he'd love to be able to ask him a few questions about what he did, and why.

Matthew listened and then asked, "Well, do you own a Ouija board?"

I didn't think he was serious, so I didn't bother repeating the question to Morris. Besides, I was angry.

"Admit it," I said. "Hanging out of the attic, dripping blood? That was for my benefit. Thanks a lot, Matthew. I thought you were my friend."

He just looked down. Probably trying not to laugh. "You're going to leave her here, right?" he asked, as we were leaving. He meant the doll, now in a plastic bag on the counter. I shot him one of Joyce's looks-that-kill.

"You can keep it," I said. "I sure don't want it."

Two minutes until the bell. Hang on. It's almost over.

I hit my locker, dump off books and fish for my lunch bag. I'm not even hungry, especially for the sandwich I made this morning.

I head to the cafeteria, hovering at the entrance before getting up my nerve, as usual, to walk over to Morgan's table. At least, during lunch, no one can ask me questions I don't know the answer to.

"How about you, Amelia? Do you believe in ghosts?" Brittany's going on about how her cousin *swears* she saw a ghost last summer at a cottage her parents rented. I wonder, is this someone's idea of a joke?

"I SO believe in ghosts," Morgan says. "At camp, when I was little, the counsellors would scare the crap out of us kids with ghost stories around the campfire. Oh my God! I believed every word."

Everybody laughs hard at that. I pull open my shoulder bag and make like I'm going through it, looking for something. I'm trying to look completely distracted, as if I'm not even listening to what anyone's saying. *La-la-la*, I can't hear you.

"Amelia believes in ghosts. You can tell from how she won't admit it," says Brittany.

Kristen says, "My mom used to live in a haunted house, when she lived in Southampton."

"Really? Wow. Was it scary? What kind of ghost?"

"I don't know. I guess so. It was a teenage girl who died a tragic death, something like that."

"Wow," says Brittany. "Cool. I really like that whole undead look."

"Actually, ghosts are different from the undead." Oops—why did I say that?

Everybody looks at me like I just farted or whatever, and then they carry on like they must have heard wrong.

"Yeah, I like the undead thing better than a tan. I'd like to be an albino."

"I know what you mean. But good luck getting it in summer. You have to stay totally out of the sun."

"If you use number 60 sunblock—"

"I totally disagree, everybody looks better with a tan. My legs look ten pounds fatter with no tan. Yuck."

"There's this girl at my cousin's school who's so white she looks sick. But she looks wicked with red lipstick."

"I'm getting ten passes to a tanning salon for my birthday. My mom finally agreed. As long as I follow the tanning rules."

"What rules?"

Just when I think my head will explode, Brittany turns to me. "You should wear red lipstick, Amelia. You could pull off that look. Loads of black eye shadow—go for it!"

The table falls silent as everyone turns to see Lester walk by with Taylor Johnson. They have lunch trays with matching pizza slices, and they're looking for space at a table on the far side of the room. All eyes stay on them until they're seated, then Brittany turns back and leans in to me.

"Rebound," she says. "Taylor is Lester's rebound."

Morgan snorts. "Poor substitute for you. She's an aspiring Olympic athlete or something. A snowboarder. Look at her calf muscles! Oh well. No big loss, eh?"

I watch Morgan staring at Lester, and she looks far too irritated. Like a scheme she's been working has been trashed.

"Morgan?" I whisper. She looks at me. Definitely guilty. "Tell me the truth. Was Lester ever interested in me?"

"Of course he was," she gasps, as if she's shocked I have to ask. Then she starts talking fast under her breath. "I mean, he got dumped a while back by some girl who was a friend of his cousin, he met her skiing at Blue Mountain over the Christmas holidays, so he was kind of whining about that and, well, I thought . . ." She's stalling, trying to think.

"Go on."

"Well, I just happened to mention you to him. You seemed so down and all, I figured it couldn't hurt, and he admitted that, well, her hair was a lot like yours. Same colour and length, you know? That's all. And, well . . ."

"My hair? You're not serious. You tried to set us up on the basis of my HAIR?"

She smiles a little sheepishly. "Don't knock it. It almost worked."

It was only Morgan all along, trying to set Lester and me up together. Telling me he was interested, and probably telling him the same thing about me. "It did NOT almost work," I hiss. "Not even close! The whole thing was a figment of your imagination!" We both steal a glance at the happy couple, then face each other again. I sigh and try to smile. "Look, I know your intentions were good. But really, please, don't try that again."

She smiles back, giving me a small kick under the table. She mouths, *So cheer up then!*

My brother Jack grabs an empty chair beside me, spins it back to front and straddles it. He has to say hello to all four girls around the table, one at a time, or they'll kill him. I can't help but notice Brittany straightening, big time, as if she's trying to reach right across the table with her breasts. I've never noticed her smile at him like that before. Like she's being aggressive and shy at the same time.

"Where are you gonna spend the summer? In town or out on the farm?" Morgan asks him. She's the one he's had a crush on for ages, getting nowhere. But now something's changed. She's eager to chat him up, but it's Brittany he seems to be talking to when he answers. I don't know what game he's playing, but it just might work. He's obviously got something figured out.

They all chat back and forth, laughing and acting up, and I let my attention drift. My eye accidentally settles on Lester and I quickly look somewhere else. It's not like I care, but there's this ache gnawing way inside me and I don't even know what it is.

"You good?"

"Sorry, what?"

"Are you good?" Jack repeats, leaning in a bit so no one else can hear.

"I don't know. I'm okay. Whatever." Jack frowns at me. "I'm fine," I reassure him. I force a smile. "You?"

"Great. Yeah. I'm good."

"Well, I'm glad. I'm happy for you. So . . . will you move back home this summer? Do you know yet?"

"Not sure. Depends. On a few things." He rubs a finger along the bridge of his slightly crooked nose.

I look at his face as he scans the table of girls. He's changing, all right. He's got this future he's looking forward to. I bet he won't be spending much time at home soon, if ever. And he won't be here at school. How will I ever see him?

"What's wrong, Amelia? Why are you so down?" Is it really that obvious? He doesn't wait for an answer. "You should cheer up," he says, giving my shoulder a shake. "You never know what's waiting around the corner."

He pulls himself to his feet. "Ciao, ladies," he says, blowing them a collective kiss, but it's Brittany who gets the eye contact. Then he swaggers off like Mr. Cool. Yeah, he's been lifting weights, all right. He may never run track again, but I can see him throwing shot put. He's not even using his crutches today. I'm happy for him, but I still feel like crying.

———

I walk down the front steps of the school and stop. Funny what passes for an apparition these days. Take this vision of Kip standing on the sidewalk across the street, in a black T-shirt and blue jeans. It's not him. He's not really here.

"Hey," he calls to me with a wave.

I step straight into the street, in front of a blue van that leans loud on the horn, swerving to miss me. I ignore the swearing from the driver's window. I dodge two more cars, one with squealing tires. I walk up to him like he's the only person on the planet and I throw my arms around him. My hands lock behind his back and squeeze, holding his chest, hard and warm, against my cheek. It *is* him.

He laughs. "Wow. You know there's this old-fashioned 'look both ways' tradition in Chicago. You don't have it here?"

I reluctantly release him from my bear hug, dizzy with gratitude. I take a step back on the sidewalk, blinking back tears, embarrassed.

"I'm sorry," I say. "I'm just . . . just happy to see you."

"Well, that's a relief. From the look on your face, I wasn't sure. Bad school day?"

"Always."

"Well, life gets better. No reason to walk into traffic just yet. Hang in."

"I'm trying, honestly."

"One more year, right?"

"A lot can happen."

"You only need to survive one year. Then everything will be fine."

I try to take in his face. It's not easy without looking into his eyes, and I can't handle that yet. His mane of hair is longer, brushing his shoulders. There are the same piercing blue eyes, those cheekbones with a faint scar from his fight last year in the haunted barn, the shadow of beard. Beautiful as ever.

"I know you can do it," he says with a smile.

I have to look away. Control my feelings, my face. "It's so nice to see you," I manage to say to the sidewalk, barely whispering.

"Hey, stranger!" The voice from behind us makes me jump. It's Jack.

Kip laughs and puts out a hand. Jack grabs his arm and they give each other a half-hug hello. "How ya doing, man? How's that spinal cord?"

I can't resist staring at Kip's face as he chats with Jack. This is real, I tell myself. He came back. And then I realize that Jack knew he was coming. *Thank you, Jack. For whatever role you played. Thank you, brother of the year.*

Ten minutes later, Kip and I are walking down the street toward the mall parking lot where his car is. I'm trying to sound casual, friendly and not completely ecstatic.

"I can't believe Jack didn't tell me you were coming. Or Morris."

He asks if I'm free for a drive.

"Sure. Totally. I'll call Joyce and tell her I'll be home later."

I get into the passenger seat and he starts the car engine and backs out of his space. Sitting beside him again feels like heaven.

"Where should we go?" he asks.

"Anywhere."

"How's your swamp girl doing lately?"

"I haven't been out to see her since they dredged up her bones."

"Well . . . I always did want to check out that deer stand. See some deer. The ice will be gone, right?"

I laugh. It's the sixth of June.

"All right, then. Let's do it. But I can't guarantee she won't drop by."

"I know. I can handle it."

"Or that you'll see a deer."

"That I can't handle. I *have* to see a deer. So . . . Amelia," he says, his tone changing. He's about to get serious. I brace myself.

"I just want to say I'm sorry about the night at the inn. I'm sorry I got so angry. Truth is, I was upset before that and I was trying not to show it." He pauses and takes a deep breath. "And then you told me about Matthew. I was so pissed off—maybe, partly, because everything started making sense. Total sense. I think I finally get it, you and Matthew. What had me so confused before—the way you were acting so distant—I just wish I'd known sooner. I wish that you'd told me sooner, or that I'd somehow figured it out myself."

His words bring back all the regret I've had over how badly I've handled everything. We drive in silence along the highway, then down country roads past forests and farmers' fields. I think about the cost of keeping my secret. The damage it's done to our relationship. It seems we're back to being just friends, nothing more. Probably he's forgiving me because his love life has moved on. To some cheerleader type in Chicago.

"So . . . still friends?" he asks.

I nod, trying to smile, but my heart sinks.

He slows down on 28th Sideroad, then pulls over to the right, coming to a stop on the gravel. He asks if I've heard anything lately about Clarisse. Is she back home yet? His tone is casual again, like nothing's happened. I try to match it. I tell him I don't think so. Last I heard, she was staying with a friend out west. I tell him about my last encounter with her ghost on the stairs. How I only just got my arm cast off. He already knows about it but he says he wants to hear about it directly from me.

"I'm convinced it's Mr. Carmichael, the retired town councillor. He's guilty of a hit-and-run car accident somewhere along here. It killed the girl in the forest. Jenny. She was only twelve years old. I'm positive he knew exactly what he did, and that's why he ditched her bike in the swamp, to hide the evidence."

"So, mystery solved!"

"The problem is, I've failed. I mean, I'm glad Jenny's family knows the truth about how she died and where. But as for helping to rid the Cornflower Inn of its ghost . . ."

"Well, you did your best."

I failed is what I'm thinking. *My best is a fail.*

We get out of the car and Kip locks up. I take a minute to remind myself which approach we should take into the woods. With summer almost here, the undergrowth is much thicker and everything looks different.

"Just warn me if something bad is about to happen to me," he says. "I'd like to be able to brace myself this time."

I have to laugh.

"You have fond memories of that, I'll bet!" he accuses me. "Not funny!"

"I warned you then."

"This time, try harder."

"Right."

As we carefully push our way through the trees, I think out loud about Mr. Carmichael's ghost. "I guess I still don't get what makes ghosts tick. If he's carrying around this big ugly secret that has him feeling so guilty—*hawthorns!*" I say, pointing out the thorns. "Watch out!"

He manoeuvres around them. "Warning appreciated."

"Anyway, you'd think he'd feel better—relieved, even—if someone broke the ice about it, so to speak, and told him to get over it. It's history. Wouldn't that make him feel better?" But what do I know about guilt and forgiveness? Kip seems to have forgiven me but I'm still confused about what that means, where it leaves me.

"How did he react?"

"He freaked out. All raging."

"Angry that he was finally exposed?"

"I doubt it. Maybe. But it's not like he was pretending to be innocent before."

"Well, maybe ghosts don't behave like living people. Maybe ghosts are a whole different species."

"I don't know. I don't think so. I think they're a lot like the people they used to be. Maybe more obsessive and repetitive and . . ." I think about Matthew. "Pigheaded."

"Never dangerous?"

"Sure, but living people can be dangerous too."

"Good point."

It takes longer than it did before, batting back branches and bush now that the leaves are growing in, but I finally get us to the edge of the swamp. I check out the deer stand. There's no one in sight.

"If we come at it from behind, it's closer to the edge and the water's not as deep," I suggest. "But we'll have to go barefoot and roll up our jeans. Game?"

"Are you kidding? Let's do it!"

His enthusiasm makes me laugh. He's like a big kid.

"You won't like how it's going to feel. It's going to be disgusting and slimy. I'm just warning you."

"Anything in there that bites?"

"Well, that's the fun thing about swamps. You never know."

The bottom of the swamp feels about as gross on bare feet as I had expected, soft and full of strange textures—rotten plants and green guck and black ooze stirring up from the bottom and clouding the surface. It's like walking through a thick, mushy cold stew with your eyes shut. We reach the wooden uprights of the deer stand in only a half-dozen awkward strides, sinking knee-deep in water. A rickety ladder up the side, held on with rusty old nails, leads to the platform, about three feet above the water. We try to wash the worst of the mud off our feet before climbing up. The dry planks of the platform remind me of the colour of the old Telford barn. We sit side by side facing the swamp, legs dangling over the edge, feet above the dark water. Our legs below the knees are streaked with mud.

"Awesome!" Kip declares, leaning back on his elbows and looking out across the swamp, scanning the forest. "Totally."

I laugh. "You're such a nature freak," I say. "Guess it comes from living in cities where there isn't any. We should have brought a picnic basket," I add, getting in the mood. I look down at the rough grey planks. "And a blanket."

"And a bottle of wine."

"Hello? Do you know what would happen to me if Joyce caught me drinking with you in the woods?"

"She'd understand."

I laugh out loud. "Yeah. Right. Are you nuts?"

"Okay, you win. We won't tell her."

"She's psychic. She can't see ghosts but she picks up everything else. Pissing her off takes the fun out of being bad."

"And what do you know about being bad?"

"Not much."

"Just checking." He squints at me with a half-smile, then lies right back, flat on the platform, arms folded behind his head, eyes closed. I steal a glance at his face, his eyelashes, his lips. Rays of sun cut through the treetops and bounce off the dark gold waves of hair on his forehead. I look at his body stretched out beside me and my eyes crawl over him. His strong shoulders, his hard chest, his lean hips and legs. Oh my God.

"What else are you afraid of these days?" he suddenly asks, his eyes still shut. "Besides Joyce."

"Afraid of? Uh . . . what do you mean? I'm not afraid of anything. I'm just a little stressed." I try to peel my eyes off his body but it's impossible.

"You know what I mean." He looks up at me, squinting against the sun. I jerk my eyes away, embarrassed. "What are you afraid of?" he asks again, more softly this time.

I exhale slowly, trying to cool myself down. *What am I afraid of?* I try to think. I listen to myself, deep inside. "The truth? Well, for starters . . . the universe. I'm afraid of the universe. That's just for starters."

He sits up on one elbow and grins. "You're afraid of the universe? Come on!"

"You asked."

"Go on."

"Well, maybe not 'afraid' exactly," I say, feeling defensive. "But it makes me anxious. Doesn't it make you anxious?"

"The universe?"

"Life. Just . . . life."

"I don't know. It's not all bad, is it? Could be worse."

"I know. But at any moment things can *get* worse. That's the point."

"And what's the worst that can happen?"

I look down at him. "Losing people."

"Death?"

"Not only death, but yeah, death, for one thing. The way people can die at any time. Children, teenagers, parents who are hardly forty years old." I feel my throat getting tight.

Reaching up, he runs a finger down my arm, absent-mindedly, as if he's thinking of something else. His touch feels electric to me.

"Doesn't seeing ghosts make you feel better about all that?"

"No. No, it doesn't," I say, getting all worked up. "It makes death even *more* real. And life less real."

"That sucks. Life is just as real as death. I thought maybe the more real death feels, the more real life feels."

We both fall silent. It's a sunny spring afternoon, and we're surrounded by birds chirping and leaves rustling in the breeze and insects buzzing along the water, but inside, I'm somewhere else. I'm lost. I look at Kip lying on the platform beside me. So close I can reach out and run my hand along him, from his knees to his neck. Every single time I've felt close to him before, he's slipped away. And someday he'll be gone for good.

"Kip, I'm sorry I'm so screwed up. But the way I feel about you has made me feel guilty about Matthew. It's been a kind of nightmare. I still don't know what to do about it."

He lifts his head and looks at me. He says, "You know, I'd sit in class this semester, and when I should have been listening, I was thinking about you. And what hit me is how I'm always worrying about you, about something bad happening to you." He pauses. "I'm afraid of losing you. That's what I'm afraid of. So there." He looks out across the swamp, along the far line of trees. "Matthew aside, how do you feel about me?"

"I can't believe you have to ask."

"Call it curiosity."

I force myself to look him in the face. "I don't know why it's so hard to say it out loud. I . . . I say it to myself all the time."

"What?"

"Like, if this isn't some kind of love I'm feeling, then it's friggin' madness."

"That's how you feel?"

I look down and nod.

He's quiet for a moment. "Why madness?"

"I don't know. I just think about you and sometimes I think I'll go crazy."

"But maybe it's some kind of love?"

"Yes."

That's it. I'm done thinking. I dive on top of him, belly-flopping on his stretched-out body, full length. He's winded by the impact, and his arms fling out. I kiss his shocked face. A lot. It takes a few seconds for him to relax.

"Is this the crazy you?" he asks, his words muffled by my kisses.

"I'm sorry," I say, gasping. "I didn't hurt you, did I?"

He grins. "Yes. Several times," he says, and kisses me back.

He wraps his arms around me and holds me against him. His breathing gets heavy, his chest rising and falling under me, and then without warning he rolls me over onto my back on the hard wood, one hand cradling my head, the other around my waist. Our legs tangle together and he presses hard against me. He kisses me on the mouth until I feel so dizzy that I wonder if I'll black out. Then he stops, barely lifting his lips from mine. I'm panting as he hovers over me, his hair brushing my face. *Don't stop now.*

"Amelia, what I was trying to say is, it's more than wanting to see you, or wanting to kiss you." His rough cheek brushes gently against mine. "I want to watch your back. I want to be there for you," he says, giving me a flicker of a smile, searching my eyes for a response.

I nod. "Okay, fine. Deal."

He kisses me again, pressing against me so hard that I think he might crush me to death. A perfect way to go—

"Is that your boyfriend?"

My head shoots up and I twist around to see Jenny standing in the water below us. She's dripping wet, her pink ski jacket shiny with dirty swamp water. Her face looks bad—pasty white and puffy, with dark sunken eyes and a slack mouth. As if she's been in the water a long time.

"Oh my God!"

"What?" Kip asks, rolling onto his side as I struggle to pull myself out from under him. "What's wrong?"

"Jenny."

"What?"

"Jenny."

"Here?"

"Yes. Jenny, hi. Uh . . . yes. This is my friend Kip. He's a . . . good, good friend."

He slowly sits up, looking stunned. "Picnic's over," he mutters.

Jenny studies him. "He looks cute."

"I know. But you . . ." I'm wondering how to put this. "You've looked better."

She ignores me. She's looking in awe at Kip, her mouth hanging open, her tongue thick and black.

"Is he your boyfriend?" she asks again. I hesitate to answer.

"What?" Kip asks. "What's she saying?"

"She wants to know if you're my boyfriend."

His eyes widen. He's looking in Jenny's general direction but seeing nothing. "Well, tell her *yes*. As a matter of fact, I am."

I shoot him a surprised look and he smiles.

"Why not?" He leans in, his lips touching my ear, and whispers, "*Why not?*"

"He really likes you," Jenny says, sounding sad with envy.

Poor little girl. She never got a chance to feel liked by a boyfriend. She never got any chance at all. And now she looks like some kind of swamp monster. I have to look away.

"Do you want me to go? So you can kiss some more?"

I sigh and shake my head. "No, Jenny, it's okay. We have to go soon anyway."

"What? What's she saying?" Kip asks.

"You're right. The picnic is over," I tell him. I turn back to Jenny. "But I have a favour to ask. My friend doesn't get to see many deer where he lives. Do you think a deer could come by here? Before we leave?"

Her face has gone soft and gross, like rotting fruit. I can't make out her expression. She slowly sinks into the water, eyes and mouth still open, until her whole head goes under. I close my eyes and press my fingers against them, trying to squeeze out the awful image.

"Are you okay?"

"She's gone. She was . . . really horrible-looking today. The worst I've seen her."

"Her looks change?"

"Yeah. It's like she appears at different stages after death. Today was . . . gross."

"Do we really have to go?"

"I think so. But look!" I point to the clearing on the far side of the swamp. Deer are coming out of the forest, stepping into the high grass at the edge of the water. Four deer, standing together, looking directly at us. Light beige-brown coats with white brows and necks and black noses. They hold their heads high, eyeing us calmly.

"Wow! That's amazing. That's totally awesome." His face lights up; he's grinning like a child. "Did *she* make them come out like that?"

"I think she's one of them right now. I think she sometimes possesses one of the deer, and when she's in a more troubled mood she takes it out onto the road. And she either pretends she's been hit by a car, or gets hit by a car for real."

"No kidding! So a ghost can possess an animal? I thought they could only possess people."

"Well, she can. But mostly she just does it to hang out with them. They're her friends." We watch the deer watching us until they turn back into the forest. They leave a lump in my throat.

In silence we make our way back through the swamp water to dry ground. I feel overwhelmed. The trauma of seeing Jenny in that gruesome state is starting to fade, and the flood of feeling I had kissing Kip is coming back. I'm amazed and embarrassed that I could go crazy on him like that. Now I feel completely brain-dead. Drugged. Like a zombie in love. I can barely think straight, but something is weighing on my mind. When we get back to the car, I come out with it.

"Kip, there's something I've got to do. I've been putting it off. I didn't have the courage before now."

"Uh-oh. Sounds serious."

"I've got to level with Matthew, about you and me. I've got to stop pretending there's nothing going on. That I don't have feelings for you. Trying to protect him from the truth. It makes me feel dishonest—which I am—and he doesn't buy it anyway."

Kip stops by the car and leans against the driver's door. Then he takes my hand. "Are you sure?"

I nod quickly.

"But what if he can't handle it? What happens if he goes psycho on you?"

"He won't. Matthew is still Matthew. He's not some stranger, he's my oldest, closest friend. It's just that there's no . . . no chance of romance between us anymore. There can't be. And it's not only because he's dead. I've fallen in love with someone else. I've got to tell him the truth."

"You've fallen in love with someone else?" He smiles like he's suspicious.

"Kind of." I shrug, like it's no big deal.

He leans in and pretends he's going to head-butt me, then smiles, and knocks his forehead lightly against mine. "Well, okay," he says. "But if you're going to tell him something he doesn't want to hear, I want to be there. Just in case. I'm going with you. That's the deal."

Instead of answering, I take his face in my hands and kiss him again. His hands drop to my hips. We kiss some more, leaning against the car door, till I've forgotten where I am. I've forgotten everyone and everything but him. His grip on my hips is the only thing keeping me on the ground. Otherwise I'd be floating like a helium balloon, high above the trees.

28

"My dad wants to talk to you. Hold on."

Just like old times. A phone call from Kip when it's Morris who needs to talk. I guess Morris is still trying to keep a low profile with Joyce, in case she's the one who answers.

"I hear you want to take Kip over to see Matthew? What's that about?"

"It wasn't my idea. Matthew asked me to bring him over next time I come."

"When was the last time you were at the farm?"

"Yesterday. After school."

"Oh." He sounds tense.

"Matthew seemed pretty calm, Morris. He's settled down a lot since the whole exorcism disaster."

"But why does he want to see Kip? I'm not sure we can trust him with Kip."

"He just wants to make peace, that's all."

"When were they ever at war?"

"Well. . . ." This is awkward. Morris still doesn't want to know that Kip and I are more than just friends. "Believe it or not, Matthew has been noticing that I get along well with Kip, and he's been . . . a little jealous. And he wants to get over that. He wants to be friends with Kip too."

"I see. I'm just saying, Matthew's found his footing in the ghost world. He's stronger than he was before. He could be trouble, if he wanted to be."

With two close calls in the barn last fall, I don't blame Morris for being protective of Kip. But I'm protective of him too. I don't want anything bad to happen to him. Hell, I've hardly been able to think of anything but Kip since he got back.

"Morris, I'll be there. I can't imagine Matthew doing anything to upset me. It's one thing tormenting Toronto lawyers, but Kip's different. He's your son. And I think Matthew respects you. He likes you."

"Really? Well, that's nice if it's true. I mean, if you're sure nothing can go wrong. If you're sure Matthew is being sincere . . ."

"I don't think he's ever been insincere in his whole life."

"He's not in his life anymore."

"He's still Matthew. More or less. One of the nicest human beings I ever knew. One of the best."

"Okay, okay. You win."

It was so hard, visiting Matthew yesterday to tell him the truth about Kip. Standing outside on the porch, I had to force myself to go inside. My mouth was dry. My heart was pounding. The first thing I did when I got into the kitchen was pour myself a glass of water at the sink. He just stood against the opposite wall and watched me. It took time, but I finally got up the nerve to say what I'd been rehearsing over and over in my mind.

"Matthew, our friendship saved my life. It really did. After my mother died, and I knew for sure I was seeing ghosts, I didn't want to keep living. Remember what I was like? I thought about ending it *every day. Every single day.* I don't know if you even understand how you saved me. You changed the way I felt about life. Last summer when you went away I missed you so much, and, well, I realized how much you meant to me." I had to stop and take a deep breath. Gather more courage. "But we know what happened when you came back. You died, and it felt like the end. That's what I thought, at first. But then I realized that I was a changed person. You'd had such an impact on me that, even though you were gone, I still wanted to go on living. That was entirely because of you."

Matthew listened quietly, looking not quite at me but just off to the side. Like something sitting on the kitchen counter had caught his eye. He finally spoke up.

"Why do I get the feeling I'm not going to like where you're going with this?"

I took another deep breath. I couldn't back out now.

"Here's the thing. I've developed feelings for Kip Dyson. Romantic feelings. It happened gradually, but it probably started the first time I ever met him, at the Halloween party, before I even knew who he was. Before I knew you were still hanging around, one of the ghosts trapped in the barn. And those feelings . . . they've been growing."

Matthew stepped away from the wall and walked out of the kitchen, crossing the hallway into the dining room. Then he turned around and walked back, stopping at the kitchen door. He stood there, eyes down, waiting for me to continue. I felt I was going to freak. I felt stuck, like the words wouldn't come.

"Go on," he said, stepping back and sitting down on the stairs.

"It's just that you two are so different, in so many ways," I said. "It's like apples and oranges. . . ." I cringed, hearing myself sound so crass. "Look—if it's possible to love two people at once, then I do."

He sat quietly, looking down the whole time. His face was tired and sad but not angry.

"It's so hard to explain, Matthew. But I'm tired of pretending I don't have feelings for Kip. Strong feelings. I'm sorry. It's not only because you're dead and he's alive. I really believe that. I think, if you were both alive, I'd still be torn in two."

"Or if we were both dead?"

"Yes," I say, suddenly uncomfortable. "Then too."

He was quiet for a while longer, then he lifted his head. "I guess I knew it would end like this." His voice sounded distant. He straightened a bit. "You know, I understand more than you might think. No matter how close you and I are, or have ever been, there's this big divide between us now. It's funny how much being dead tells you about life. All the stuff I never thought about before, because I didn't have to. I can see now why people like the idea of reincarnation. It would give them a second chance at life, knowing so much more about what it means to be alive."

"So there's no such thing as reincarnation?"

He looked up at me, seeming annoyed. "How should I know?"

"Oh." For a second I felt distracted, and then I focused again. "But is being a ghost nothing but a drag?"

He sighed. "For a while," he said, "I thought being a ghost might be okay. But I don't know anything anymore. Maybe that exorcist priest was right, and it's time for me to go. I don't belong here."

Now that I'd gotten the worst of what I had to say out in the open, I felt awful and depressed. And worried. "I wish there was another way," I said. "Maybe there is." *But maybe not.* I hated admitting that, even to myself. It made me feel sick.

"The trouble is . . . ," he said, "the *real* trouble is that I can't stop thinking about being with you in the library on that last day we were together, before I got possessed in the barn. How you tried to tell me you wanted more from me. How you touched me like I'd never been touched before, your hand on my chest, right over my heart. It was like your blood was rushing through me. I thought my chest was going to burst."

I stood in the hallway facing him, my hands pressed against my mouth. *You're not making this any easier, Matthew.*

"And all I did was freeze like a scared rabbit, when what I wanted to do was touch you back. That's all I wanted. That's all I still want."

"I'm sorry, Matthew. I'm so sorry. We thought our lives would be so different from how they turned out. But thinking about how things might have been is *torture.* You've got to try not to dwell on it. You've got to make an effort. Don't let the past ruin everything."

"What *everything*? The past is all I have. Can't you understand that?"

"But you must have something! This existence—this presence—it's got to have some kind of value. Otherwise what's the point? Why hang around?"

His head dropped. "Good question," he said.

After apologizing again and again for any hurt I'd piled on him, I said I had to go. I thanked him with all my heart for understanding and forgiving me. That's when he said that the next time I came, I should bring Kip. "I have to get used to him being in your life. Being close to you. Your boyfriend, even." He paused as if he was swallowing hard. "Might as well get started."

Wouldn't that be painful for him? The most pain yet? He looked at me with steady eyes and I told him I'd try, but what I was thinking was, *How much more can he take?*

Confessing to Kip that I'd gone to see Matthew without him was a whole other pain. Morris had told him, and the moment he showed up on the front porch, I could see that he was upset.

"Why didn't you tell me you were going yesterday? You *knew* I wanted to come along."

"I never agreed to that. I knew I had to break the news to him first, alone. No matter how much you might worry."

He's at the wheel as we back out of my driveway, on our way to the farm.

"It was fine, Kip. He handled it well. He wasn't surprised. He already knew, deep down. And he knows I still care for him and always will."

Kip's brow furrows and he looks stern. "I'm not crazy about the fact that you don't care whether I'm concerned or not."

"That's not true. I care about *everything* to do with you. But I felt I had to face him alone. I thought that was best for both of you."

"And what about what's best for *you?*"

"I'm the reason we're in this mess. I've got to be the one who tries to fix it." I grab his free hand, raise it to my lips and kiss him on the knuckles. "How come you look even cuter when you're mad?"

He scowls. "Even if you'd let me wait outside in the car, that would have been better."

We're just about there. The car slows down as Kip turns into the farm driveway. As usual, as we approach the house, my eyes drift up to the bedroom window. Is that his shadow against the curtains? I'm not sure.

Ever since the exorcism, when Phil gave Morris a house key, I've been feeling less guilty about coming here, less like a cat burglar breaking into someone's home. At the door, Kip pulls out the key and struggles with the lock. It finally opens and we step into the kitchen.

"Matthew?" I say quietly. "Matthew? Are you around?" The house seems unusually still.

I walk to the staircase and look up. "I thought maybe I saw him in the front room. I'll just run up to see if he's still there." I whisper, "This probably isn't easy on him. Maybe he's having second thoughts about seeing you up close."

"At least he can see me," Kip whispers back. "He could be anywhere, for all I know."

"He's not down here, I'm pretty sure. Stay in the kitchen while I check upstairs."

I run up the stairs two at a time, then walk cautiously toward the front bedroom. I don't want to startle him. "Matthew?" I whisper. Not here. I walk into the other bedrooms, stopping in the one with the attic hatch. The hatch is open. I take a deep breath. *Okay, Matthew. Don't play games.*

"Matthew?"

No answer.

I look around, find the stool and carry it to the closet, positioning it under the opening.

"Matthew, if you're there, I'm coming up."

Maybe this is harder on Matthew than I realized. Maybe, after I left him yesterday, he had some kind of meltdown. Then I remember what he said about the exorcist—that maybe the priest was right about it being time for him to leave.

"Matthew? Are you there?"

I take a deep breath and climb up on the stool, my legs wobbly. Up on my toes, I can just about see inside the attic. It's too friggin' dark. All I can make out are the shapes and shadows of the old chair, the sewing machine, the lamp. I wait for my eyes to get used to the dimness. As they do, I make out something on the chair. It's the doll, propped up in a sitting position, head flopped forward, chin on chest. The bald little head reminds me of the Cornflower Inn ghost.

"Matthew?" He's not here.

I make my way downstairs, not sure what I'm going to say to Kip. When I get to the bottom of the stairs I find Kip alone in the kitchen, his back to me. He's got his hand on the door, and now he opens it and steps out onto the porch.

"Matthew's not anywhere. I can't find him," I say. "I don't know what to think."

I follow Kip outside and down the few steps to the driveway. "I'm sorry, but I think we should forget about seeing Matthew today," I say. "I'm afraid . . . maybe he just didn't feel up to it." I'm worried. Was it stupid to come here? Selfish? Has Matthew up and left the house? Has he actually gone?

Kip spins around to face me, grinning ear to ear. His blue eyes are shiny with tears.

"What? What is it?" I'm confused. "What's wrong?"

"Nothing. Everything's fine. It's just such a beautiful day." He almost doesn't get the last words out, he's so choked with emotion. Even as he smiles, his lips are trembling.

"Are you okay? You're upset. What is it?" First Matthew, now Kip—this is a disaster.

"No. I'm happy. I'm happy!" He takes a step toward me. "Amelia, you shouldn't worry so much. You should be happy too." He reaches out and takes my hands in his. He holds them, squeezing tight. He's looking at me so intensely, so passionately, that I hardly know what to do.

"Maybe we should go?" I say. Something's wrong, I can feel it. I begin to move toward the car but he stops me. He grabs hold of my wrist and pulls me closer to him. He raises my hand and places my palm on his chest, against his heart.

"Kip? What's wrong?" I try to pull back but he holds my hand tight. "You're acting weird." His eyes are locked on mine, brimming with tears. My whole body goes tense. The chill of fear rises in me, running up my back and head.

"Kip?"

"Don't go."

Matthew?

He raises his left hand, fingers trembling, palm facing me. I'm shaking hard and starting to cry. Then his hand is on my chest, against my breast, over my pounding heart, while his other hand still holds mine tight against him. In panic I try to yank my hand back, but he's strong. I scream, fists flying, arms flailing. I land one punch on his mouth as I twist and turn to break free of his grip.

"No, Matthew!" I shriek. "Let me go!"

Suddenly he releases me, and I double over and fall to my knees. I'm going to be sick. He stands over me for a moment, then walks to the door and into the house while I heave and sob, hands over my face. *Oh my God!* I stagger to my feet. I've got to get Kip out of there.

I bash my way in through the kitchen door and find Kip, his back to me again, leaning against the kitchen counter, head down and breathing heavily. Matthew is a shadow at the far end of the kitchen, with a fear in his face that I've never seen before.

Kip spins toward me, gasping. "What the hell happened?" His mouth is bleeding. "What the hell *happened*?"

I stare at him, at Matthew, and back at Kip.

"Kip? Are you . . . okay?" I rush over to him and he grabs me by the arms.

He shakes me, shouting, "WHAT DID HE DO?" He looks around the kitchen wildly, red-faced with rage. "WHERE IS HE? WHERE IS THAT GODDAMN BASTARD?" He starts throwing things, trying to hit something he can't see. He grabs a coffee maker off the counter and hurls it across the kitchen, smashing it against the wall.

"My God, Kip, stop!" I scream.

"WHERE IS HE?"

Matthew is backing into the hallway, a look of guilt and horror on his darkened face.

"Where is the son of a bitch? I'll kill him. I'LL KILL HIM!"

I've got to calm Kip down. I throw my arms around him in a bear hug. "It's okay," I tell him. "Nothing happened. He stopped right away. I'm so sorry I hit you. I can't *believe* I hit you."

It's as if he can't hear me. He searches my face in panic, his body shuddering with rage—blood on his lips, eyes wild. I fight to hold him close to me but he won't stay still. He pulls away from me and his fist slams the kitchen counter so hard that everything jumps. I grab his shoulders, trying to steady him, then hold the sides of his head with my hands, pulling his face close to mine.

"Look at me, Kip," I urge him, desperate to get through to him. "Nothing happened! Please, let's just go!" I push him toward the door. His whole body is stiff but he doesn't fight me. I struggle to get the door open and shove him outside.

When I take one last look behind me, I see Matthew hunched over on the stairs, head in hands, shoulders shaking.

29

It took ages before Kip was calm enough to drive home. Then we sat behind the house by the paddock for another hour, as I tried to reassure him that Matthew hadn't used him to hurt me. I told him how devastated Matthew had looked afterwards, totally guilt-ridden—not that Kip cared, but I said I couldn't believe he would ever try something like that again.

"You don't know Matthew," I said. "He's got a conscience. He knew he'd done something terrible. It was a moment of weakness but it's never going to happen again." I really believe that, but it wasn't easy convincing Kip.

"You don't know what it's like to be ripped off, until someone's stolen your *body*."

"It was, like, two minutes. And I knew something was wrong, I knew straightaway. It took me ninety seconds to get my head around it, that's all. Then it was game over. He didn't come close to pulling it off."

"Well, suppose he gets better with practice? Don't you understand? Don't you see what he wants?"

"It won't happen again. Honestly, you should have seen how mortified he looked when we left."

I think Kip was mostly angry at himself, for letting it happen. As if he was even more to blame than Matthew. Not that he had any clue how he could have prevented it. But before he left last night, he finally admitted that he does feel sorry for Matthew.

"He's already lost his life. And now he thinks he's lost you."

Since we'd left the farm, he'd been keeping some distance from me. It was almost as if he was too ashamed to touch me. But later, when he said good night, he put his arms around me and held me tight, which was a huge relief.

"The worst part is how I thought I could protect you from him, and instead he just used me like I was his puppet. Like his stupid doll."

"Are you going to tell your dad?"

"I have to. But not tonight. One of these days." Then he added, "But just so you know, if he ever tries that again, I *will* kill him. I'll find out whatever it takes to kill a ghost, and I'll do it."

At night, in the dark of my bedroom, I cried for a long time. I don't think you can kill ghosts. But sooner or later they decide to go away. Forever.

Joyce has gone off to work at the stables for the day, and she asked if I'd get some vacuuming done while she's gone. I do the living room, working around Ethan, who's watching TV sprawled on the floor, ignoring me. He turns up the volume on the TV to drown out the vacuum. When I yell at him to move, he gets to his feet and steps back and just watches me work. Then, when I hit the off switch, the TV is blaring and I have to yell at him to turn it down. I start dragging the vacuum into the hallway, and he follows me.

"Did you and Kip have a big fight last night?"

I realize he's worried. He doesn't know anything about what's really going on, but he doesn't want our little ghost club to break up.

"It's okay," I tell him. "Just a misunderstanding. We made up."

He seems relieved.

"Well, you look sick this morning. Like you have a cold or something."

"Thanks for letting me know."

"What about that ghost? At the inn? What happened? Did you get rid of him?"

"No, afraid not. Not that I know of, anyway. Last time I saw him, he really freaked out. I think we lost that battle."

"But what are you going to do about it? Give up? Just because he broke your arm?"

I scoff at that. "The ghost didn't break my arm! That was an accident. To tell you the truth, I don't know. I haven't been thinking about it. I'm kind of stuck for ideas."

"But did you visit that lady? The one I found for you? His last wife? Didn't she give you some clues?"

"Not really." Then I remember. "Well, yes, kind of. Thanks to her I learned quite a bit."

"Well, I don't think you should give up so easily. Use it or lose it. That's what they say."

"Where did you hear that?"

"I don't know. But you're so lucky, seeing ghosts and all. It's boring being normal, you know. If I could see ghosts, I'd want to do it all the time."

"Well, ghosts can get boring too. Maybe not boring, but frustrating. Which is almost as bad."

I start up the vacuum cleaner again, concentrating on the hall and front entrance. Ethan stands there watching me, hovering and fidgeting. Finally he flops onto the living room floor again, yelling something that I can't hear. Irritated, I turn off the vacuum. "*What?*"

"I said I could help, maybe. If you gave me a chance. If you took me with you next time."

"Yeah, *that* will happen! Joyce won't even let *me* go back there. How much trouble do you think I want to get into? Do I look nuts to you? Anyway, you've already been a big help. Seriously. Thanks to you, I've totally got this guy's number. He just doesn't want to talk. He's not what you'd call talkative."

"But he was a politician, right? I thought all politicians were bigmouths. So they can talk people into dumb stuff."

"Good point. There's the mystery. I have to admit it, Ethan, you've hit the nail on the head."

"Well, if you ask me, you're being a quitter." Then he turns up the TV volume again, shutting me out. Annoying little brat.

I finish the vacuuming, then head up to my room to get dressed. I don't hate Matthew for what he did, or tried to do. I could never hate him. But I've got to go back, to talk to him about it. As upset as I am with him, I can't get that last image out of my head—him crying on the stairs. I want to yell at him, but I also want to make sure he's all right. Now is the time to sneak out. Joyce won't be home for hours.

I tell Ethan I'm going for a bike ride. He looks like he might say something, but he doesn't.

———

I was worried whether Matthew would talk to me. Whether he'd hide from me. This time, though, I do find him in the attic. Sitting in the rocking chair, the doll on his lap. I'm relieved to see him, though he doesn't look good. He doesn't look at me.

I don't say anything at first, and neither does he. I struggle with my usual difficulty getting up through the hatch, and find a place to sit on the joists. His lamp light is on, just barely. It lights up half of his face, his straight black hair, one narrow dark eye, his tight jaw. He's still looking off to the side of me but he's aware of me, I can tell. The doll is leaning over on her side, face down as if she's dead. We both sit there in silence, like we're at a funeral.

"How did you get the blood off her?" I finally ask.

"I don't know."

I think about that, looking at her. It's the first time in ages she's looked like a normal doll, a lifeless object, and not some spooky little person.

"Is she . . . okay?" I can't believe I asked that.

He looks up at me, his eyes flat and lifeless. "No, she's not okay. She's a doll."

"I know that, but . . ." I realize I don't know what I'm saying, and I stop myself before something truly stupid comes out. I stare at her bald head, trying to think of where to go from here. I need to make some small talk.

"Actually, she reminds me of one of those kids who get cancer and lose all their hair."

He looks down at her, saying nothing.

"From chemotherapy," I add. Some small talk!

"My aunt lost all her hair that way," he says.

We both fall silent again. Five minutes or more go by while I try to figure out what I came here to say. It's Matthew who breaks the silence.

"Amelia, I've reached a decision. There's only one way I can show you how much I regret what I did yesterday. Only one way to convince you it will never happen again."

"I *know* you regret it, Matthew. I know you won't do it again."

"No you don't. Not the way I want you to. Not the way I need you to."

"What are you talking about? I'll take your word for it. That's enough."

"It's not enough. There's only one way to prove it. I have to leave. Like the priest said—time for me to go."

"Why . . . why are you saying that?"

"I'm giving you a guarantee. The only one I can. Words are never enough."

"But time will prove . . ."

"You don't *have* time. Don't you get it? Life is short. Like a walk around the block and then, *bang.*" His voice is starting to shake.

"Matthew . . ."

"I don't want to use up any more of your time. I want you to be . . . happy, in the short bit of life you have left. I really do."

"But I don't want you to cross over to some . . . mystery place, who knows where, who knows what . . ."

"Yes you do. You want this to be over. You just feel bad admitting it."

"That's not true. It's not that simple."

"You're *making* it complicated." The last words I barely make out, they're so faint.

I don't know what more to say. Is it right to try to talk him out of it? I don't know what's best for him. For his soul, I mean. I'm afraid that my selfishness is the reason he's still here. Maybe if I loved him more, I'd make it *easier* for him to go, not harder.

"I regret not getting to know Morris better," he says. "Tell him that, okay? Tell him I'm sorry it didn't work out, me helping him with his ghost research and all."

I realize he means it. I nod, my throat getting tight.

"And Kip. I know he's a decent guy. He's Morris's son, so how bad can he be? And I know you're in love with him. I'm not asking him to forgive me. He doesn't even have to try. It's okay. Because it'll never happen again. I'm taking myself out of the picture. Permanently."

I blink hard, fighting to keep my eyes clear, focusing on the lifeless doll. "Matthew . . . I don't want to say goodbye again."

"Then don't."

"What do you mean?"

"I'll be gone before you know it."

"But would you ever come back? If you could?"

He looks away, then turns back toward me. "Something tells me it doesn't work that way."

I know what he means. I remember how I felt the last time I saw my mother's ghost. Somehow, I just knew it was the last time.

"I did love you so much. I still do, in some crazy way I don't understand. You're in my heart."

"I know," he says softly. He closes his eyes. "Thank you for giving me a reason to hang around this long. I don't regret that." He starts to fade, and when I lean closer I can't see him anymore.

I walk my bike back up 12th Line feeling like I'm walking against a wall of water, the surface somewhere above my head. I can't see much and the pain in my chest makes it hard to move. His last words to me were "Don't worry about me. I'm not afraid."

I'm trying to imagine not having a reason to go down this road anymore. No one waiting, watching. No Matthew in my life.

I think about Kip's hand on my chest. Matthew's. I honestly don't know whose hand that was. Everything's getting muddled in my head, all blurry, like this road.

I start imagining my own death. Will it be sudden, like in a car accident? Or torture, like in a fire? Will I drown, the way I feel right now? Or die slowly, from cancer? And when I die, will I become a ghost, lost between worlds like Matthew, with feelings and desires but no body? Distant from everybody and everything? And then I think about the time I have left before I die. It could be decades, or it could be days. How much would Matthew have given to postpone his death, by no matter how little? Sixteen years—that's how much he got. Half of that he spent being a little kid, playing with action figures on the carpet. That sucks. No wonder he got attached to that doll.

I don't know when it hits me. I can see my house just up the road. I can see the paddock out back, Marley and Ponyboy out in the field, their long manes moving in the breeze. I think about Matthew's doll, and my idea of it losing its hair because of chemo-therapy. Because a girl can definitely lose all her hair that way. Why else would she go bald?

I stop, paralyzed, on the road in front of my house. *Which is why a bald ghost could be a woman!*

30

"Morris? Oh my God, I've been blind. Completely blind. I can't believe I never thought of it before. It could make all the difference."

"Slow down, slow down. Breathe. Now, what are you talking about?"

I squeeze the phone receiver with both hands. "Something crossed my mind when I was looking at Matthew's bald-headed doll. The way people with cancer sometimes lose their hair. Then it hit me—it doesn't only happen to men, right? It can happen to women getting chemotherapy. What if the Cornflower Inn ghost is a *woman*?"

"You're talking about Rose? The third wife? The one who died of cancer?"

"Yes, Rose! Can you phone Edith Bartlett back? Ask her about Rose? What kind of cancer did she have, anyway? Did she get chemotherapy? Did she lose her hair? Because if I'm right, I *have* to go back to the inn. I have to talk to her. I have to call her by the right name, at least. I have to apologize."

I sit in my room, rocking, pacing, waiting for Morris to call back. I research chemotherapy on the Internet. Side effects. Baldness. I walk out back to see the horses, and put my arms around Marley. *Don't ever leave us, Marley. Don't ever die.*

I'm losing it.

Ethan throws open the kitchen door. "Phone!" he yells. "It's Morris."

I run back to the house.

"Cancer of the larynx. She gradually lost her voice, almost completely. She wasted away, Edith says. By the end, she was just skin and bones. She was only forty-six. And two rounds of chemo, the second completed just before she died. All of her hair fell out." He takes a deep breath and exhales. "Amelia, when she died, she was bald."

Morris is fretting. "I'd feel better if we could have waited long enough to get hold of Joyce. I left a message on her cellphone, but I promised I'd let her know in advance next time. Give her a chance to say no. She's still your guardian."

Morris is lecturing me from the driver's seat but I'm not listening. I don't care. Kip is up front beside Morris and I'm in the back. We're driving onto 28th Sideroad.

We're coming, Rose. We're almost there.

"Look out for Jenny," I remember to say. We drive along the forest-lined road, alert for movement on either side.

Kip looks okay, thank God. No sign of a fat lip. But he's quiet. Why is it that when he spends a bit of time with me he loses his sense of humour? He turns to me in the back seat like he's reading my mind, and gives me a half-smile.

"Lighten up," he whispers. "We're going on an adventure."

Thank you, Kip. You are absolutely right. This is an adventure. It's the first time in a long while that I feel I can have a positive effect on a situation. He hasn't told Morris about what happened yesterday at the farm. Just as well.

Morris parks in front of the inn and we get out, looking up at the windows. It's a habit now. But this isn't a ghost who looks out of windows anyway. She's stuck wandering halls and a dark, narrow staircase. Like a prisoner.

Inside, Morris starts flipping on lights. Suggests we open a few windows, as it's stuffy and dusty in here. The house feels so sad and abandoned. Nothing poor Clarisse ever imagined.

"I'm going to make a suggestion," adds Morris. "Let's stay in the kitchen like we did the first time, during the seance, keeping the back-stairs door open wide. And let's see if she shows up. I'd like to keep you off the stairs, if you don't mind. Just to be on the safe side. And I'd like to keep you close by. No splitting up today. We stay together."

Morris and Kip carry the small round table closer to the stair door. They pull over three chairs.

"No theatrics," Morris says. "Let's just relax and wait a bit. See what happens." He unlocks the door with the key hanging from the hook nearby, and pushes it open all the way, so that we can see the bottom of the staircase. We all sit down. I take a deep breath. *Concentrate.*

"No holding hands? No candles?" asks Kip, being a tease. "How's this ever going to work?" We ignore him. "Later, then," he says, winking.

I smile but then I start to feel something weighing on me. It's the feeling I've had here before. A heavy sadness, a horrible regret. I try to stay calm, looking at the lower steps of the stairs. I wait and keep my eyes open.

She's standing just inside the kitchen, in the corner near the door. Thin, frail, white, wearing the same pale pyjamas and robe. How did I ever mistake her for a man? Her head is bowed and her hands are at her sides. I can't see her face until she slowly begins to lift her chin, and for the first time I see her delicate features, her small mouth, lips slightly parted. I see that, even bald and gaunt, she is a pretty woman.

"Rose?"

She's trembling slightly but her eyes seem steady. I can tell that she knows I've finally figured it out—her identity. Her eyes lift and she focuses on me, and I can feel that she sees me.

"Rose?"

Her head nods, just a little, and her features relax, as if she's relieved. I can feel Kip's knee against mine under the table. He's biting his lip, sitting on the edge of his seat, watching my face for a sign. I nod slightly and look over at Morris. "It's her," I whisper.

Morris nods too, as if urging me to continue. I take a deep breath.

"Rose. I'm so, so sorry I didn't recognize you before. And you couldn't tell me the truth. Please forgive me. I can't imagine what that was like, having me practically accuse you of your husband's crimes."

Her eyes drop when I mention her husband, and she seems to sway a little. *Can a ghost faint? Please don't faint.*

"I know you've been ill. I know the cancer took away your voice, along with your hair. But can you talk at all? Can you try to talk to me now?"

Her eyes lift again and she nods. After a moment she starts to speak.

"He . . . he said I'd been seeing things . . . all night."

I can't believe it—she's talking! As if she's turned back the clock on her cancer. Her voice is raspy but so much better than before.

"He said . . . it was my imagination again. B-b-because I was sick. I was so sick that night."

I have to be sure she's talking about the night of the accident. "You had just begun cancer treatment the week or so before. You went to the bingo, your husband's fundraiser. And you drove home alone."

"I was crying as I drove, and the road was so dark." Her eyes are unfocused now, from too much remembering. "Eric and Edith—Edith, his assistant—that's all I could see. I never saw what I hit." Her hands are shaking, and she raises them to hide her face, as she did before. Her voice is muffled but I can still make out the words.

"I nearly lost control. But I didn't stop. I . . . I thought it was a deer. What else would be on this deserted strip of road? They roam around here and sometimes they run out onto the road. When I got home I was shaking so badly I could barely walk. He . . . he found me here . . . in the kitchen." She's beginning to sob and choke between the words. "And I told him I hit a deer. Only . . ." She sinks onto a lower step of the staircase. Wrapping her arms around herself, she rocks. "Only I told him I saw something strange in the headlights. Something p-pink." She's crying. "And maybe . . . m-maybe it wasn't a deer after all."

I feel Morris and Kip react, and I realize that they too are hearing something from the stairs. Not words, but the creaking as she rocks. I can tell from their expression.

"Rose? He went back out, didn't he?"

"He said he found the deer dead in the woods. He told me to forget about it. It happens to everybody, he said. And I said something was pink, and he said I'd been imagining things all evening, because I was sick." She stands up, swaying as if she's dizzy. She shuffles back to the doorway and into the kitchen, to stand only six feet from our table, pale and thin, with sunken eyes. For the first time, I notice a ghastly scar on her neck. She's losing her voice again.

"I . . . didn't . . . stop." The words come in pieces. She spits them out as if each one cuts her throat.

"That night I tried to sneak out . . . down the back stairs . . . back to the forest . . . but he locked me in the house. I spent the night on the stairs." She shuffles over to the counter and pulls open a large drawer of cutlery. I feel the tension rise at the table as Morris and Kip watch the drawer open by itself.

"He thought I'd never . . . find out."

A knife whips out of the drawer and flies over our heads, bouncing off the wall behind us, making my ears ring. We all jump. Then a spoon flies by. Then another knife, this one hitting the table between Morris and me. Then a fork flies past really close to my head. She's seizing pieces of cutlery with both hands and hurling them backwards at us, arms bending unnaturally from the sockets, as they did before, on the stairs. I can barely see her now—only these flying pieces of Clarisse's good silverware, shooting across the kitchen like arrows.

Before I know what's happening, the table has been tipped over and I've been yanked down behind it. I crouch there with Morris and Kip, the tabletop shielding us from the barrage of forks and knives and spoons clattering against it and ricocheting around the room.

Morris curses and yells that we've got to get out. He grabs hold of the table by its edges and tries to drag it to the hall door, as we crouch and crawl behind it. But suddenly he yelps and pulls his hands in. He's been cut, and the fingers on his right hand are bleeding. We huddle together behind the table, trapped in this war zone, trying to think of an escape. What happens when she runs out of cutlery? There's a whole block of knives sitting on the counter. We'll be cut to ribbons before we can get out of here.

"Why do bad things keep happening in kitchens?" asks Kip.

"We've got to try to lift the table and make a run for the door!" Morris says.

We each take hold of a table leg. I realize that my hand is bleeding too. A knife must have nicked me.

Morris starts to count to three, but then the bombardment stops dead, like some sudden battlefield truce. We peek around the edges of the table, cautiously. I can't see Rose, but the drawer she's just emptied is starting to rattle and shake, pulling farther and farther out of the cupboard until it crashes to the floor.

We wait, wondering what the hell she's up to now. A few minutes go by. Huddled behind the table, cradling his injured hand, Morris says it's time to get out. Make a run for the front door. On the count of three.

"Wait a minute," I whisper, my ears still ringing. "Something's odd."

"You think?" Kip whispers back. "What could be odd?" He grabs hold of my bleeding hand, takes a closer look at the cut.

"I'm okay. Are you okay, Morris?"

"It's not my hand I'm worried about. It's my blood pressure."

"I don't think she's here anymore." I stand up slowly and look around the room, through the door, up the back stairs. "Yeah, I think maybe she's backed off." I see the drawer that came out, and about a hundred pieces of cutlery littering the floor around us. "You know, I don't think she was intending to hurt us."

"No?" Kip grabs my arm to hold me back. "That's not the way most people set the table."

"I don't know if this is about cutlery at all. Give me a second." I slip out from the shelter of the tabletop and pick up the drawer, then bring it back to Kip and Morris. I look at the drawer. There's a loose tray inside, and I pull it out. Behind that there's some vinyl lining paper, the kind that comes on a roll with a sticky backside. It looks pretty old-fashioned, with an ugly pattern—it definitely predates Clarisse. I pick at it. Whatever it's stuck to, it isn't the bottom of the drawer. It's a piece of cardboard cut to fit the bottom. Picking at the corners, I manage to lift it out.

I immediately recognize the thin, faded newspaper clipping hidden underneath. I saw it in the archives the day Ethan helped me with my research. I show Morris and Kip the picture of Jenny, in an article from the local paper on the anniversary of her disappearance. An unsolved mystery on its way to becoming a cold case, with no leads after a year of investigation. Was she a runaway? A victim of abduction? Is she still in the province? Is she still alive? Last seen travelling north on Highway 6 on her bike, on March 25, 1986, wearing a pink ski jacket.

I look up and there is Rose, curled up in the far corner of the kitchen, her stark white face frozen like a tragedy mask, her eyes fixed on the newspaper article in my hand.

"She could have been my daughter," she says in a weak, raspy voice, "and I didn't stop."

"Rose? I don't know if you realize this"—I break the news as gently as I can—"but she's still out there."

31

hen we leave the Cornflower Inn, Kip is at the wheel and Morris is in the back seat, his bruised and cut hand wrapped in bandages he found in Clarisse's bathroom. I'm beside Kip, up front. Our nerves are still on edge but we're high with excitement. We've made the big breakthrough we were looking for. We did it, and we got out alive. The last sight I had of Rose, she was back to sitting on the stairs, but now she was sitting up, not hunched over, with her hands in her lap. She had a look of resolve on her pale face.

Morris says he's sure we'll get her to leave now. "All she's got to do is step outside and follow the trail heading west. And who knows how long ghosts have been doing that? This route is a super-highway to the spiritual world. Think of the centuries of souls that probably passed this way."

"And think how happy Clarisse will be with you, for getting her house back, eh Dad?" Kip turns and gives me a wink.

And that's when the deer jumps in front of the car, from out of nowhere.

Kip pulls the steering wheel hard to the right, screeching the tires and throwing us sideways in our seats. Trees are closing in on us fast and gravel is flying everywhere. A violent swerve to the left and the car spins out of control, off the road and into the forest.

We're going to hit a tree and die.

My arm flies out to grab Kip's shoulder as his hands grip the wheel, and I hang on as I feel myself rising above him. My side of the car is leaving the ground. The whole world spins as we float through space lost and falling. *Don't let go.* There's the terrible noise of smashing metal and shattering glass, and we grind to a halt. I feel the seatbelt straps cutting into my hips and chest.

I'm dangling upside down from my seatbelt, blood rushing to my face, my hair brushing the car ceiling. I pull back on the straps cutting into my stomach and chest and shoulder, trying to relieve the pressure. I feel dizzy, like an astronaut in outer space. I think of Kip. Morris. I struggle to look at Kip hanging upside down beside me in the driver's seat, and his hand reaches out to touch me. We catch each other's eye, reading fear and then relief. Morris groans from the back seat.

The car has landed on its roof, facing back in the direction of the Cornflower Inn. I catch sight of a deer jumping up from the side of the road and bounding back into the forest.

"Dad?"

"I'm okay," Morris says, his voice shaking. "It's just the car. What the hell happened?"

Everyone's okay. Thank goodness.

Kip starts cursing and apologizing like crazy. "It was a deer. A deer jumped right in front of the car. I swear." He apologizes again.

"It did, I saw it too. Ouch. The seatbelt," I say.

"A deer?" Morris is skeptical.

I look sideways at Kip, who's working at his seatbelt buckle. "It was a real deer," I say. "But a deer possessed."

"Just what we needed," Kip grumbles. He's got his buckle released and manages to untangle himself from the straps. I'm still struggling with mine.

Morris tries his car door but it's jammed shut. He manages to get his cellphone out of his pocket, and dials 911. "We've had a car accident. . . . Yes. Afraid so. Three of us. . . . Only my car. Everybody seems okay, as far as we can tell. The car rolled over. Landed on the roof. . . . About a minute ago. We're still upside down in our seatbelts. 28th Sideroad, just east of the Cornflower Country Inn. . . . Subaru Outback, 2008. Silver. Please." He hangs up. "Jesus Christ. . . ." he mutters.

Now his cellphone rings. "Oh God, it's Joyce," he says to us. "Hello? Joyce, glad you called. We're a little tied up." He admits that we've had a car accident, flipped the car. "Emergency crew on the way. No one seems injured. I guess we'll know for sure when we get the hell out of this thing."

Kip crawls on his knees along the roof and gets under me, working at my seatbelt buckle. He releases it, and as I start to fall awkwardly out of the straps his arms catch me, letting me down gently. Morris says Joyce is on her way.

Kip crawls into the back seat and struggles to get Morris out of his seatbelt. "Let's get out through Morris's window," he says. That one window is half open. My side window is shut and miraculously unbroken, but there's no way it will open now. The right side of the windshield is intact but on the driver's side, Kip's side, the window and windshield are shattered. I feel such fear and gratitude that he seems unhurt.

Crouching on what used to be the ceiling, I peer out the

windshield on my side, facing back the way we came. There's something on the road, moving toward the edge. Jenny, lying on her stomach, lower legs smashed, drags herself slowly off the road and onto the gravel. I watch her, unable to speak. Then I see something else—a vision moving this way, coming from the direction of the Cornflower Inn. From this distance it looks like a thin white line. As it gets closer, it looks like Rose.

I can barely find my voice. "Guys." They're busy getting Morris out through his side window. "*Guys?*" I'm hoarse with emotion. Morris is now on his hands and knees outside the car, slowly getting up on unsteady legs.

"You next, Amelia," Kip says. "Do you think you can make it into the back seat?" He waits for my answer. "Is something wrong?"

"No," I whisper, keeping my eyes on the scene. "Not wrong. Just . . . it's Jenny. Jenny's lying at the side of the road." I take a deep breath. "And Rose is coming down the road toward her. Rose is *running* toward her. Oh my God!" I can't take my eyes off them.

"Amelia, get out of the car!" Morris yells. "Soon is good."

"If you can get back here," Kip says, "I can help you through the window. Let's go."

Pale and gaunt, eyes wide and mouth gaping, Rose is running to Jenny. Her thin robe is flying open at her sides like angel wings.

I feel Kip grab my shoulder and shake me. He takes my arm and starts to pull. "Do you need help? Can you move?"

No. I can't move.

Jenny is face-down in the gravel. Rose drops to her knees beside her, leans over Jenny's body. She pulls Jenny up into her arms, cradling her shoulders and head. Stroking her face. She rocks, head bent, forehead against forehead. And then Rose gets to her feet, bends down and, as if Jenny were light as air, lifts her in her arms.

The bloodied legs hang below Jenny's cradled knees, and her arms are looped loosely around Rose's neck.

Carrying Jenny, Rose turns and begins to walk away.

"Amelia! Kip! Get the hell out of there! What's keeping you?"

"She's in a trance or something. *Amelia?*" Kip leans over and grabs me from behind, arms tight around my chest, and drags me into the back seat.

When I'm on my stomach on the ceiling, he shoves my head and arms through the window. Morris grabs and pulls from the outside while, behind me, Kip pushes me through. The edge of the half-open window scrapes my back. Once my hips are through, I twist myself and sit on the road, pulling my legs out the rest of the way. Then Kip struggles to get through the window behind me, Morris helping him.

Behind us, coming from the other way, we hear sirens. Police cars, an ambulance and a fire truck.

I sit in the road, transfixed.

"What do you see?" Morris asks.

"Rose and Jenny."

Rose is no longer carrying Jenny. They're walking together, side by side, holding hands. Rose has shoulder-length blonde hair. Jenny is wearing her pink ski jacket.

"Rose and Jenny—they're making the journey together." I'm so happy I'm crying. "They have each other now."

I stand up, legs shaking, between Morris and Kip. They hold me up. *Goodbye, you two. Goodbye.* And then I can't see them anymore.

"What are you lookin' at?" asks the first cop who comes to our side.

"It was a deer," Morris says. "Jumped out at the car."

"You hit it?"

"No, thank God. It ran back into the forest."

The cop nods. "Lucky deer." He turns and sizes up the flipped-over car. "You guys, not so much."

"You don't know the half of it," Morris says under his breath in his cowboy drawl, as he catches sight of Joyce running toward us.

I need to deal with Joyce. But how can I do that with tears streaming down my face?

32

One of the paramedics has taken Morris into the back of the ambulance. He's strapping on a blood pressure cuff and asking a load of questions, and looking at his bandaged hand. Kip's been taken into one of the cruisers for a statement.

I'm waiting for Joyce by the side of the road, bracing myself for a blast. A police car has blocked off the road a long way down so she had to come the rest of the way by foot. But she's moving fast, taking giant strides, with Ethan alongside, running to keep up.

She walks up to me and puts her arms around me, giving me a hug. "Are you all right?"

That nearly knocks me over. I was expecting her to yell. She finally lets me go and sizes me up. "Are you okay?" she asks again, more urgently.

"Yes . . . yes. I'm fine," I say. I'm still shaking, and she can see that I've been crying. "It was upsetting at the time, thinking we were hitting a deer, but we survived okay. Nobody got hurt. Poor Morris's car, though."

"A deer?"

"Yeah. Kip was driving, and he swerved to miss a deer."

"You cut your hand," Ethan points out.

I look down, remembering Rose's flying knives. "Oh, yeah. It's nothing."

"Did you hit the deer? Did you kill it?" he asks.

"No. Missed it."

"This stretch of road is cursed," Joyce says. Through the open ambulance back we watch the paramedics take Morris's pulse, listen to his chest, flash light in his eyes. Finally, they seem satisfied that he's okay. He saunters toward us, rolling his eyes, shaking his head, embarrassed. As he does, a tow truck rolls up and stops in front of his car. We watch as the driver and three of the cops all get on one side of the car, lift it and roll it back onto its tires. Morris cringes as it lands with a thud, like he feels its pain.

"Anything you need in there, now's the time to clear it out," one of them says, and manages to tug one of the passenger doors open.

Morris gets inside and empties out the glove compartment and console. He shoves everything into his black canvas bag, the one that usually holds his ghost-tracking supplies. Kip leaves the cruiser where the police have been taking down his statement, and he's nabbed by a paramedic. He gestures to show that he's perfectly fine.

"Just taking the vitals," I hear the woman say. "It's routine. Gotta do it." She points Kip to the back of the ambulance, then crosses the road, heading for me.

"I'm fine," I say.

"Just need to be sure, miss. Can you join your friend?"

I stand outside the ambulance watching Kip get his blood pressure checked. He looks pale and shaken, his dishevelled hair half hiding his features. What a couple of days he's had. He looks up at me with a dazed smile. I guess we're all still in shock. Next, the paramedic listens to his heart. After a few minutes it's my turn.

Kip climbs out as I'm getting in, puts an arm around my neck as we pass and pulls me close. He kisses me on the cheek, and holds on for a moment. He feels hot.

"Are you really okay?" I whisper.

"Yeah," he says. "But I'm not doing a great job of looking out for you."

"Not your fault." I put my arms around him and squeeze.

"Careful." He pulls back, glancing around to make sure Morris isn't watching. "My dad's had enough shocks today. Besides, you'll screw up your pulse rate."

As soon as I get the okay from the paramedic, I cross the road to join the others, who are watching the car get hitched up to the tow truck. Engine running, the driver leans out of his truck window to tell Morris where in town he'll be taking the wreck, so he can arrange for his insurance to send an adjuster to appraise it.

"This baby won't be back on the road again," he says, smiling as he slowly pulls into the road and drives off, towing the car behind him. Morris watches him leave, muttering under his breath.

"Sorry, Dad." Kip puts a hand on Morris's shoulder. "I'm so sorry."

"Nobody got hurt. That's all I care about." He gives Kip a hug.

There's another car coming up the road, manoeuvring around the cruisers as if they don't mean a thing. Detective Grierson gets out and walks up to Morris.

"I heard there was an accident on this road and I looked up the call, just out of curiosity. I don't know why, but I wasn't surprised. Flipped your car, I hear. A deer? Nobody hurt?" He looks at Kip and me, giving us the once-over.

"We were lucky," Morris says. Grierson glances down at his bandaged hand. "Believe it or not, I did that earlier today, before the accident. Yeah, cut up my hand a bit." Grierson stares at him like he has Morris all figured out. "But, it looks like you may not be getting any more middle-of-the-night calls from the Cornflower Inn," Morris adds. "We may have solved that little problem."

"You don't say?" Grierson breaks out in a grin. "Well, good news. Damn, you know, I might have a few other strange cases kicking around. Unsolved mysteries. You might be hearing from me again."

Morris is intrigued and raises a eyebrow at Kip and me, as Grierson waves and nods in Joyce's direction, looking serious now. He walks over to her and they exchange words I can't hear. An odd guy, that Grierson.

"I can give you people a lift home," he says after a few minutes. "Where do you want to—?"

"That won't be necessary," Joyce interrupts. "We can all squeeze into my car. I'll see that everyone gets home."

We say goodbye to the detective, then start walking away from the Cornflower Inn, this time for good. Morris, Joyce and Ethan walk in front. Kip and I fall behind. The feeling I have is one I've had before, like we're on hallowed ground. I remember my last vision of Rose and Jenny, and I feel a rush of happiness.

"Well, it wasn't a totally disastrous day," I say to Kip. "Those two ghosts found each other, and now they can cross over together."

"All was forgiven?"

"Absolution!" I say. I watch Morris walk ahead of us, moving stiffly, limping slightly, carrying his big black bag. "Someone looks pretty sore, though."

"Yeah. He's going to feel this in the morning. We all will."

He's right. Everything still seems unreal. Nothing's sunk in yet.

Not even the aches and pains. Kip kicks at the stones along the side of the road.

"Dad's going to need a new ghost mystery to solve," he says. He gives me a half-smile, and we lock fingers, just for a second, then release.

Leaving the last two cruisers at the scene of the crash, Detective Grierson drives past us and on down the road, waving. I watch the car for so long, as it disappears into the distance, that my eyes blur. I give them a rub and look again.

There's someone on the road up ahead, walking this way. I don't say anything at first, fear blocking my thoughts. But as we get closer to Joyce's car, I can't deny it any longer. Lanky strides, black hair, pale face. I stop. The wind has been sucked out of me; my chest feels crushed flat.

"Morris?" I call weakly.

He turns to look back at me, and in a second he's at my side. "What is it? What's wrong?"

"Matthew's on the road. He's coming this way." My knees feel weak and I lean on Kip, who looks from me to Morris and back.

"You're sure?" Kip asks. "Is this about yesterday?"

"What about yesterday?" Morris looks confused.

"I . . . hate to break this to you now. I mean, I was going to tell you eventually. But here goes." Kip takes a deep breath, like it's hard for him to admit. "Matthew took possession of me yesterday."

"Oh my God," Morris says.

"Yeah. It didn't last long, apparently. Amelia says only a couple of minutes. I was standing in the kitchen minding my own business, and the next thing I knew, I felt like I'd been in some kind of scuffle and my lip was bleeding. I had no idea what happened in between."

"It wasn't as bad as it sounds." I'm fixed on Matthew. He's getting closer.

"It *wasn't?*" Kip looks at me, surprised.

"I saw him this morning," I say quietly.

"You *did?*" Now he's turning red.

"It's okay, Kip. He was full of regret. He actually said he was going to leave, cross over, to prove to us it will never happen again. He said it wasn't enough to give his word. He had to give us a guarantee. That's what he called it. A *guarantee* it would never happen again. Kip, he said he's finally prepared to let go of this world altogether. Because of what he did to you."

"You thought he was serious?" Morris asks.

Kip turns to me. "Yeah, how do we know he wasn't just saying that to impress you?"

I shake my head. "It wasn't like that. Why do you think he left your body after only two minutes? It wasn't because I punched him. It's because he has a conscience. He *knew* he'd done a bad thing. He didn't mean to hurt Kip." *I know you didn't mean to hurt me, Matthew.*

"If that's true," Morris says, "that's very impressive." He shakes his head and sighs. "Very impressive."

"So what does this mean?" Kip asks, gesturing vaguely up the road.

"It means he wasn't bluffing," says Morris. "It means he's on his way. Crossing over."

"*Oh my God.* What do we do?" I feel a rising panic. There must be another way. There has to be.

Kip turns to me. "Nothing, Amelia. We do *nothing.*"

Joyce and Ethan stand at the car, staring back at the three of us stopped in the road. They know something is up.

Matthew has almost reached us. He's looking straight ahead and far away, as if he's already in another world. He doesn't seem to notice that we're here. My heart pounds as he passes only feet away. Surely he can hear it. But he walks right by without even a glance.

"*Matthew?*" It slips out.

He doesn't look over. Doesn't speak. Doesn't stop. My voice breaks. "Matthew? Is . . . this *it?*"

"What did he say?" Morris whispers.

I'm starting to shake, watching him walk away, on down the road.

"Nothing."

Then I blurt out, "If you hurry, Matthew, you can catch up to Jenny and Rose."

I don't want you to go alone. I don't want you to be lonely.

He keeps walking with a steady stride away from us.

Morris is squinting down the road, a pained look on his face. Then he turns to me with anxious eyes. "Do you think he heard you?"

"I don't know."

Take care of yourself, Matthew. Somebody please take care of him.

"What's happening now?"

"Nothing," I say. "But . . ."

I look harder. Are his strides getting shorter? My eyes zoom in like a telescope on his back. *Yes.*

"He's slowing down." My hands are pressed against my heart. "He's stopped."

Breathless, I watch and wait. Matthew is standing still in the road. He turns around to face me. His eyes are locked on mine. I raise my shaking hand to wave.

Goodbye, Matthew. Goodbye.

His hand begins to rise too. Slowly, slowly, his fingers reach up and touch his lips.

"What's happening?" Kip whispers. "What's he doing?"

Matthew blows me a kiss. I blink back tears, bite my lips hard to keep a sob from pushing through.

"He's just waving goodbye," I say, and force myself to turn away.

ACKNOWLEDGMENTS

I am full of gratitude for the enthusiastic support and unabashedly biased promotion that my family has given to my writing. Thanks to the whole clan—my six brothers and sisters, my wonderful nieces (you know who you are!), nephews and first, second, and third cousins.

I am extremely fortunate to work with Amy Black at Doubleday Canada. I am grateful for her wisdom and empathy, and for making me inexplicably happy one day by telling me that she had a crush on Kip. I want to thank Susan Millican for her very personal response to the first draft of *Absolution*. Sincere thanks to Jackie Kaiser and Chris Casuccio at Westwood Creative and to Allyson Latta, freelance editor of the first draft. Thanks, too, for the 'tough love' copy edit of Gena Gorrell.

Finally, I want to express my undying gratitude to my husband Michael Allder, and to Ben Kotchie, my son and close advisor.